BOOKS BY OLIVIA MANNING

THE DANGER TREE

Olivia Manning

THE

DANGER

TREE

Atheneum

NEW YORK

1977

Library of Congress cataloging in publication data

Manning, Olivia.
  The danger tree.

  I. Title.
PZ3. M3213Dan 1977 [PR6063.A384]   823'.9'14
ISBN 0-689-10802-8   77-2435

TO REGGIE, WITH LOVE

THE DANGER TREE

1

Simon Boulderstone, aged twenty, came to Egypt with the draft. For nearly two months, as the convoy slid down one side of Africa and up the other, he had been crowded about by other men. When he reached Cairo, he was alone.

He had two friends on board, Trent and Codley, who had been his family, his intimates, the people nearest to him in the world. The sense of belonging together had been deeper than love – then, at Suez, a terrible thing happened. He lost them.

As the three were disembarking, Simon had been ordered out of the lighter and put in charge of a detachment of men whose officer had gone down with jaundice. He shouted to Trent and Codley 'See you on shore' before joining the men who had been holed up in the corridor all morning. They were weary of waiting, and they had to wait longer. It was mid-afternoon before Simon reached the quay and discovered that his friends had gone. No one could tell him where. There was an emergency on and each truck, as it arrived, filled up with waiting men and went. Simon was not only alone, he had missed his transport. It seemed, too, that he had reached the most desolate and arid place on earth.

The sergeant to whom he spoke said Trent and Codley might have gone to Infantry Base Depot or they might have gone to one of several transit camps that were in and around Cairo.

'Wherever they are,' said the sergeant, 'they won't be there long. Things are in a bloody mess. Just heard Tobruk's fallen. What bloody next, I'd like to know?' He gave Simon a travel warrant and directed him to take the afternoon train to Cairo and report to Abbasia barracks.

'Anyone in particular?' Simon hoped for the reassurance of a name.

'See Major Perry in Movement Control. I'll phone through to him. Good bloke, he'll fit you up.'

Simon, waiting at the station, was numb with solitude. Everything about him – the small houses packed between dry, enclosing hills, the sparking glare of the oil tanks, the white dockside buildings that reflected the sky's heat, the dusty earth on which he stood – increased his anguish of loss. He had never before seen such a wilderness or known such loneliness.

The train came in, a string of old carriages fetid with heat and human smells, and set out slowly through the Suez slums and came into desert. Simon saw a lake, astonishingly blue, with sand all around it, then there was only sand. The sand glowed when the sun set. The glow died, the darkness came down – not that it mattered for there was nothing to see. Simon tried to open the window but the two Egyptians in the carriage said 'No'. One, holding up his finger in an admonitory way, explained that sand would be blown into the carriage. As the journey dragged on, the heat grew and Simon felt that he was melting inside his clothes. He longed to leave the train, imagining the night air would be cool but when he reached Cairo, the outer air was as hot and heavy as the air of the carriage.

Waiting for a taxi, he breathed in the spicy, flaccid atmosphere of the city and felt the strangeness of things about him. The street lamps were painted blue. Figures in white robes, like night-shirts, flickered through the blue gloom, slippers flapping from heels. The women, bundled in black, were scarcely visible. The district looked seedy and was probably dirty but the barracks, he thought, would be familiar territory. He hoped Major Perry would be there to welcome him. When he was dropped at the main gate, he found he was just another young officer, another problem, adding to the overcrowded confusion of the place. He pronounced the name of Perry, to which he had clung as to a lifeline, and found there was no magic in it. He was told by the clerk in the Transit Office that the reporting point for his unit was Helwan. The barracks had been turned into a transit camp. And where was Major Perry? The clerk did not know. The major could be at Helwan or he could be at Heliopolis.

'All sixes and sevens these days,' the clerk pushed his handkerchief impatiently across his sweaty brow and Simon appealed to him:

'But can you put me up?'

'I'll try,' the man gave Simon a second glance and as an afterthought added 'Sir.'

Simon expected no better treatment. He had been picked for an early commission on the strength of his OTC training but to the clerk, a corporal in his late thirties, he must have looked like a schoolboy.

He waited in the half-lit hall while men walked about him, knowing their way around. Fifteen minutes passed before a squaddie came to carry his kit to a room on an upper floor. The stark gloom of the passages reminded him of school and soon, he thought, he, too, would know his way around.

He was led to a room, furnished with a hanging-cupboard and three camp-beds, at the top of the barracks where the ceilings were low. A single lightbulb, grimy and yellow, hung over naked floorboards.

The squaddie said, 'If you're lucky, sir, you'll get it to yourself.'

'Not bad,' said Simon, still with school in his mind, 'but it smells strange.' The smell was like some essential oil, almost a scent, but too strong to be pleasant, carrying in it a harshness that suggested evil and death.

As Simon sniffed enquiringly, the squaddie said, 'They've been fumigating.'

'Really? Why?'

'Look, sir,' the man went over to a wall that may have been white in the days of Cromer and Wolseley but was now cracked and grimy grey: 'Take a shufti.'

Simon bent towards one of the cracks and saw, packed inside, objects the size of lentils, blood dark and motionless.

'What on earth are they?'

'Bugs. Live for centuries, they say. Can't get rid of them. You ought to see the new chaps when they come here – they swell up, red, like jellies. And itch, cor! But you'll be all right. This stuff keeps them down for a couple of months.'

Feeling the fumigant rough in his throat, Simon went to the open window and looked out on a parade ground surrounded by the flat-fronted barracks building. A long wooden balcony, an outlet of the lower floor, ran immediately under the window and he could see blankets folded at intervals, indicating an overflow from the dormitories.

'There seems to be a lot of chaps on leave here.'

'Not exactly leave, sir. Ex-leave you might call it. They're stuck, waiting for transport 'cos trains've stopped running into the blue.'

'Why's that?'

'It's the emergency. The trains have wog drivers a'corse, and they're scared. The war's come too close and they think they'll run into the fighting and get shot at. If you're wanting a bite, I'd get down if I were you, sir. The mess shuts about nine.'

Simon was lucky – he had the room to himself, but when he woke in the middle of the night, he would have been glad of company. The murderous smell of the place reminded him why he had been brought here. He had fought mock battles on Salisbury Plain but now the battles would be real. The shot would be real and the bullets could kill a man. The desert itself was not so strange to him because his brother had been out here for nearly eighteen months. Hugo had sent home letters about brew-ups, desert chicken, bully splog and flies. He was very funny about it all. He said as soon as you got your food, you slapped a tin lid over it but even so you found that inside there were more flies than food.

Hugo had survived well enough and Simon did not expect to die. Yet men were dying out there: young men like Simon and Hugo.

Rising at daybreak, Simon was fortunate enough to find an army truck going to Helwan. While the civilian world was still asleep, he was driven out of Cairo into the desert again. In this country it seemed the desert was everywhere. The sun lifted itself above the houses and lit the streets with a pale, dry light. The truck driver, dropping him at the camp outside Helwan, told him if he did not get a lift back, he could take the train. He made his way among huts, over trampled, dirty sand, till he came on a large brown building like a misshapen mud pie. Here, in a small room, in front of a small table, he found Major Perry.

The major, with fat bronzed face and white moustache, was overalert in manner and looked as though he belonged to an earlier war. Half rising, thrusting out his hand, he said at the top of his voice, 'Got notice of your posting – got it here somewhere. The corporal'll dig it out,' and then began apologising for being old and overweight. 'Wish I had your chance. I'd like to be out there givin' the hun a bloody nose. You'll have to do it for me. Poor show – this latest! You heard? Tobruk's fallen.'

'Yes, sir. I suppose things are pretty bad, sir?'

'You're damn right, they're pretty bad. We've lost the whole garrison and we'll be lucky if we don't lose the whole Middle East. Still, we're not beaten yet. It's up to you, Boulderstone. Fresh blood and fresh equipment: that's what we need. Give us both and we'll manage somehow. They've got Hitler's intuition and we've got Churchill's interference: 'bout evens things up, wouldn't you say?'

Simon said nothing. He was baffled by this equating Hitler and Churchill and he could only suppose the major was slightly mad. To divert him, Simon said he was out of touch. He had spent the last two months on the *Queen Mary*, dependent for news on the radio bulletins. The last one he remembered spoke of 'strategic withdrawals'.

'Strategic, my arse!' Perry snuffled so forcefully that he gave out a strong smell of drink so Simon realised he was not mad but drunk. He had probably gone to bed drunk and got out of bed still drunk, and the drinking was carrying him through a state of near panic. 'This isn't the old Sollum Handicap, y'know – it's a bloody rout. Bloody jerries coming at us in our own bloody tanks. The stuff those bastards have picked up would have driven Rommel back to Benghazi.'

'I heard there was a shortage of transport, sir.'

'Shortage of transport! There's a shortage of every bloody thing the army's ever heard of. You name it: we haven't got it. Except men. Plenty of men but no equipment for them. No rifles, no tanks, no field guns. And the men are exhausted. Damn well had it.' Perry paused, blew out his lips so Simon saw the nicotine brown underedge of his moustache, and deciding he had said too much, his tone dropped. 'New blood, that's what we want. Too many chaps have been out there too long, fart-arsing this way and that, till they don't know if they're back or tits forward. Now you, Boulderstone – in ordinary times, you'd have a month in camp, but these aren't ordinary times. We need you out there. We've been refitting a lot of old trucks and there'll be a convoy starting soon. I think we can get you out there at the double.'

'That's what I'd like, sir.'

'Keen, eh? Good man. Might get you away by Tuesday.'

'Till then, sir – am I on leave?'

'On leave? Why not. Forty-eight hours. Give me a tinkle mid-way and I'll let you know what's doing. You can draw your pay and have a couple of nights on the town. How's that, eh? Know anyone in Cairo?'

'My brother has a friend, a girl. I could look her up.' Simon had not thought of looking up Hugo's girl but now, thinking of her, he blushed and grinned in spite of himself.

'Ah-ha!' Perry's wet, blue eyes that had been sliding about in wet sockets, now fixed themselves on Simon's young, pink face. 'Good show. And if you get a bit of . . . I mean, if anyone offers you a shake-down, that's all right so long as you ring Transit and release your billet. I know you chaps think Cairo's the flesh-pots, but two things are in short supply here. One of 'em's *lebensraum*.'

'What's the other, sir?'

'Ah-ha, ah-ha, ah-ha!' Perry snuffled wildly then held his hand out again. 'You don't have to worry. Not with your looks, you don't. So good luck. Enjoy yourself while you've still got the chance.'

Hugo's girl lived in Garden City. Simon, leaving the shabby purlieus of the Cairo station for the shabby splendours of the city's centre, thought he could find it for himself. He would probably see it written up somewhere.

The main streets impressed and unnerved him. The pavements were crowded and cars hooted for any reason, or no reason at all. Here the Egyptians wore European dress, the women as well as the men, but among them there were those other Egyptians whom he had seen flapping their slippers round the station. The men came here to sell, the women to beg. And everywhere there were British troops, the marooned men who had nothing to do but wander the streets, shuffling and grumbling, with no money and nowhere to go.

It was Sunday. Some of the shops were open but there was a lethargic, holiday atmosphere about the streets. Simon had once gone on a school trip to Paris and here, it seemed to him, was another Paris, not quite real, put up too quickly and left to moulder and gather dust. There was nothing that looked like a garden or a Garden City. He would have to ask his way but was nervous of approaching people who might not know his language, and he was shy of the soldiers who never knew more than they needed to know. He looked out for an officer to whom he could speak with ease. He saw officers of every allied country – Poles, Free French, Indians, New Zealanders – but the sort he wanted, English, young, of low rank like himself, did not come along.

14

Something about Simon, his air of newness, perhaps, or his uncertainty, attracted the beggars and street vendors. The women plucked at him, holding up babies whose eyes were ringed in black that he mistook for make-up, but, looking closer, he saw were flies. Swagger sticks, fly-whisks, fountain pens were thrust at him as if he had a duty to buy. 'Stolen', whispered the fountain-pen man, '*Stolen!*' The sherbet seller clashed his brass discs in Simon's face. Boys with nothing to sell shouted at him, 'Hey, George, you want, I get. I get all.'

At first he was amused by these attentions then, as the sun rose in the sky, he grew weary of them. A hot and gritty wind blew through the streets and sweat ran down his face. A man pushed a basket of apricots under his nose and he dodged away, shaking his head. Abandoning Simon, the man swept the basket round and pressed it upon a squaddie who spat at it. It was a pretty gilt basket full of amber fruit and the seller was proud of it. He persisted, 'Abbicots, George, mush quies. Today very cheap', and the squaddie, putting his hand under the basket, knocked it into the air. The apricots rolled under the feet of the passers-by and the seller scrambled after them, lamenting, almost sobbing as he gathered them up from the filthy pavement. The squaddie gave Simon an oblique stare, aggressive yet guilty, and hurried into the crowd. Simon wondered if he should go after him, remonstrate, take his name and number, but how to recognise one British private among so many? They looked alike, as though they had all come from the same English village: not tall, skin red and moist, hair, shorts and shirts bleached to a yellow-buff, slouching despondently, 'browned off'.

Simon's self-reliance weakening as the heat grew, he stopped a taxi and asked to be driven to Garden City.

The girl was called Edwina Little and Hugo, writing to Simon, described her as 'the most gorgeous popsie in Cairo'. The phrase had stirred Simon even though he was about to marry his own girl, Anne. Hugo had instructed him to draw five pounds from his bank account and buy a bottle of scent from a shop in the West End. The scent, monstrously expensive it seemed to him, was called *Gardenia* and it was to travel to Egypt in the diplo-matic bag. Simon scarcely knew how to explain his intrusion into the

Foreign Office but the man in charge of the bag took his request lightly.

'Another votive offering for Miss Little?'

'You don't mind, do you? I mean – is it really all right?'

'Perfectly. Perfectly. We'll slip it in somewhere.'

Because of this romantic mission, Edwina had remained in his mind as a sublime creature, luxurious and desirable, but more suited to an older brother than to a minor like himself. Letters between England and Egypt were so slow on the way that Hugo knew nothing of Simon's posting and had had no chance to offer him an introduction to Edwina. In going un-introduced, Simon felt a sense of daring that added to his excitement.

The road sloped down to the river and on the embankment the driver shouted: 'Where you go now?'

'Garden City.'

'This *am* Garden City.' The driver, a big, black fellow, had a Sudanese belligerence: 'What number he wanting?'

The taxi slowed and they spent a long time driving round curving roads, looking for one house among a great many others, all giving the sense of a rich past and present disrepair. The driver stopped from boredom and Simon protested, 'This isn't the right number.'

The Sudanese swung round, his face working with rage, 'This *am* right number. You pay or he clock you.'

Simon laughed, 'Oh, all right.' Walking noiselessly down the sandy road in the comatose air of mid-day, beneath the heavy foliage of palms and trees, he was startled by a banging of car doors and a forceful English voice giving orders. Making towards this uproar, he turned a corner and saw a tall man in khaki shorts and shirt, with a wide-brimmed khaki hat, directing passengers into two cars. His commanding shouts of, 'Move up. Now you get in there. That'll do for that one,' led Simon to suppose he was approaching a military operation. Instead, he found the first car held two women and an old man with a toy dog on his knee. The tall man was now intent on filling the second car. Both cars, Simon saw, stood in front of the house he was seeking. Hoping to avoid the man's eye, Simon edged in through the garden gate but was detected.

'You looking for someone?'

'Miss Edwina Little.'

The man frowned and though not more than thirty years of age, spoke like an angry father. 'Friend of yours?'

Simon would have resented the tone had he not heard in it a plea for reassurance. He answered mildly, 'Friend of my brother.'

From the balcony above him, someone whispered, 'Hello.' Jerking his head up, he saw a girl who had placed her arm along the balcony rail and her cheek on her arm. Looking down, smiling, she begged of him, '*Do* tell me who you are.'

Her hair, brown in its depths, golden where it had caught the sun, hid most of her face and her bath robe, of white towelling that enhanced the warm shade of her skin, hid her body except for the arm and the rising curve of her breast, yet the impression she gave was one of extraordinary beauty. He could scarcely find breath to say, 'My name's Simon Boulder-stone. I'm Hugo's brother.'

'Are you?' She spoke with wonder, bending closer to him, while he, lifting himself on his toes, could smell, or thought he could smell, the rich gardenia scent which had come to her in the diplomatic bag. He started to tell her that he had arrived only the day before but the tall man, his voice now pained and querulous, broke in on him.

'Really, Edwina, you said you were ill.'

'Oh, I *am* ill,' she pushed her hair back to smile at Simon. 'You see, I have a headache and can't go on Clifford's trip but I'll be better when I've had a rest. So *do* come back later. Promise me you'll come back later.'

'Of course, I will.'

Gathering her wrap close to her neck, Edwina stood upright, calling to Clifford, 'Take him with you, darling.'

'We're pretty crowded . . .'

'And bring him back safely.' Edwina waved to everyone in sight, gave a special smile to Simon, and went into the darkened room behind the balcony.

Clifford grumbled, 'If she wants you to come, I suppose we'll have to manage it somehow.' Returning to the command, he ordered the man with the dog to get in beside the women. Seeing the old fellow meekly giving up the front seat, Simon said, 'Oh, no . . .' but Clifford, placing himself behind the wheel, ordered him sharply, 'Get in. Get in. We're late in starting as it is.'

Feeling at fault, Simon was silent as the cars set out but he looked covertly at Clifford, wondering who and what he was. With his wide khaki hat, he appeared, at first glance, to be an officer in one of the colonial forces but Simon now noticed that he had no insignia. He was a civilian. His looks, too, deteriorated on examination. His thin, regular features sank towards a mouth that was small, hard and narrow as the edge of a coin.

Feeling Simon's regard, Clifford said, 'Always happy to have you chaps along. No point in coming out here and not seeing the sights.'

Simon, with no idea where he was being taken, agreed, though the main object of the trip for him was the return to Garden City.

'Interested in Egyptology?'

Simon, thinking of his local cinema with its Tutankhamün décor, said, 'I think so.'

'That's right. Learn what you can, while you can. This is the Nile.'

Simon looked out on the wide, grey-silver river moving with the slow lurch and swell of a snake between banks of grey and yellow mud.

Pointing with his thumb at some small boats that were going by as indolently as driftwood, Clifford said, 'Feluccas.' Simon watched the white triangular sails of the feluccas tilting in the wind. The same wind blew through the car like the breath off a molten ingot.

'Over there, at sunset, you can see the pyramids.'

Simon looked but saw only the bleary haze of the heat. They had crossed the river into suburbs where life was coming to a standstill. It was an area of large modern houses and avenues where trees held out, like inviting hands, patellas of flame-red flowers. A few cars were still making their way homewards but the homeless – vagrants, beggars and dogs – had thrown themselves down under the trees to sleep the afternoon away.

Clifford gave Simon a sharp, accusing glance. 'What's happening out there?'

'Where?'

'The desert, of course. Where else? What the hell are you chaps up to? Not long ago we were at Benghazi – now, where are we? There's a rumour we've even lost Mersa. That right?'

Simon said he knew nothing, he had just arrived with the draft, a fact that seemed to cheer Clifford who relaxed in his seat and laughed, 'Thought you looked a young 'un.'

The passengers in the back seat had not spoken during the drive out of Cairo. Looking round at them, Simon noticed that one of the women – a pale, dark-haired girl – was not much older than he was. Too thin, he thought, but he was attracted by the glowing darkness of her eyes and smiled at her.

'I'm Simon Boulderstone.'

'Hugo's brother?'

'You know Hugo?'

Simon turned in his seat, expecting to hear more from someone who knew Hugo, but the point of contact seemed merely to disconcert her and she spoke as though avoiding it, 'I'm Harriet Pringle. This is Mr Clifford's secretary, Miss Brownall.'

Miss Brownall, a wan-faced, elderly virgin, bent forward as her name was mentioned and watched him eagerly, waiting for him to speak but he could think of nothing to say, and giving her a smile, he turned away again.

Clifford waved at the windscreen and said, 'There you are!' and Simon, seeing the blunt, battered face of the Sphinx, gasped in amazement. Then came the pyramids. He had been told he would see them at sunset but not that he would see them that very afternoon. And there they were, taking shape like shadows out of the haze – or, rather, one was taking shape, then another, smaller, pyramid sifted out from behind its neighbour and there were two, growing substantial and standing four-square on the sandy rock. To see them better, Simon put his head out of the window then, blinded by the dazzle of the outside air, drew it in again.

The sun was overhead now and, with every inch it rose, the heat increased. The car, Simon felt, was a baking-tin, baked by the furnace outside. The roof pressed like a weight on its occupants and Simon envied Edwina who could sleep off her headache in bed. If he had stayed in Cairo he, too, might have been sleeping – but where could he sleep? Not in that barracks room with its smell of death. His head nodded and hit the side of the car. He sat up and heard Clifford speaking to the other three.

'They say Wavell's made plans for the evacuation of Cairo but, plans or no plans, it'll be plain, ruddy murder. It's already started. Every foreigner in Cairo's piling into the trains, going while the going's good. I don't mean the British, of course. The real foreigners. The crowd that came here from Europe.'

Harriet Pringle said, 'We came here from Europe.'

'I mean the foreign foreigners. Dagos. The gyppo porters are having a high old time at the station. I was there yesterday, saw them chucking the luggage about, roaring with laughter, bawling, "Hitler come". It's all fun now but wait till the hun really gets here.'

The old man with the dog said, 'I don't know. Not a bad fellow, your gyppo. He may laugh at us but there's no taking advantage. No insults, no rude words. I don't think they will harm us.'

Clifford let this pass but said after some minutes, 'You're not taking yourself off then, Liversage? Some of us, with jobs and homes here, will have to stay put, but you're free to go any time.'

Liversage cheerfully agreed, 'Yes, I'm free to go, but I won't unless they make me. I was pushed out of Sofia and pushed out of Greece, but now I'll stay where I am. I don't think they'll bother about an old codger like me,' and dismissing the matter, he leant into his corner of the car and closed his eyes.

Simon, surprised by this talk of flight, said, 'I heard there was an emergency but I didn't know things were so bad. I mean, if it's like that, it's a bit odd, isn't it, going on a sight-seeing trip?'

'Not really. No point in moping about in town. The trouble is, they're keeping us in ignorance of the true situation. Bad policy, that, in my opinion. Ignorance breeds fear. I'd say, "Tell people the truth. Trust them to keep their heads." By people, of course, I mean us. Not the wog. I wouldn't tell the wog the time o'day.'

Liversage mumbled through his sleep, 'Merry fellow, your wog. Can't help liking him.'

Ignoring this, Clifford said, 'First, we'll take a look at the Saccara pyramids. That over there's the step pyramid. Dangerous. No one's allowed inside. But there's another one . . .'

Miss Brownall squeaked her alarm, 'Not the one with the bats?'

Clifford with his air of authority, in his uniform that was not a uniform, asked sternly, 'And why not the one with the bats?'

'Oh dear!'

The car turned left on to a track in the sand and shapes could be seen through the limitless fog of the distance. Approached, they were revealed as heaps of unbaked bricks that had once been pyramids. Now they stood like patient, waiting animals as Clifford made a dashing swerve in front of them and braked to a stop. The following car, trying to imitate the swerve, skidded and nearly rammed Clifford's car. His expression fierce, he threw open his door but finding all well, he contented himself with the voice of leadership, 'All out. All out.' His followers, struggling from beneath the heat of each other's elbows, emerged to a more spacious area of heat.

Fly-whisk in one hand, torch in the other, Clifford pointed both objects at the largest and best preserved of the pyramids, 'We're going in this one,' then realised that Mr Liversage was still in the car. Going smartly to it, he looked at the old man, saw he was asleep and let him remain. The rest he led to a hole in the pyramid's flank.

Harriet Pringle, loitering, last in the queue, seemed reluctant to enter. Simon paused so she could precede him into the dark, ragged opening in the bricks, but she shook her head, 'I don't like the look of it.' The pyramid's outer casing of stone had been looted away and the inner structure had sunk on itself like a ruined plum-pudding. 'I don't think it's safe and I'm afraid of bats.'

Simon laughed, 'I'll go ahead and scare them.'

For a few yards they were able to walk upright, then the roof sagged and they had to bend to get under it. Ahead of them Miss Brownall was giggling and from the scuffling, scraping and grunting, it was clear that the others had been forced down on to hands and knees. Harriet stopped, then something caught in her hair and she turned and ran back to the daylight.

Simon went on until he could feel space about him and heard people breathing. The air was cold. Clifford had switched off his torch to heighten the drama of arrival in the central chamber and the party stood in darkness until the stragglers arrived. As Simon joined them, Clifford relit the torch and shone it upon him: 'All here?' Then he saw that Harriet was not there and said with displeasure, 'Where's *she* gone?'

'Mrs Pringle turned back.'

'Oh, did she!'

Wisely, too, Simon thought as he looked about him. The chamber was empty except for a stone sarcophagus of immense size. Everything else had been looted, even the sarcophagus lid. Not only was there nothing to see but Simon realised that to enter the place was foolhardy. The apex of the pyramid was breaking through the roof plaster and poised over their heads were several tons of bricks that could be brought down by the slightest earth tremor. Clifford, moving imperturbably beneath this peril, flashed his torch on to the decayed walls, saying, 'Wonderfully fresh, these colours. Book of the Dead, y'know!'

The others stood as though not daring to move and their murmurs sounded to Simon more apprehensive than admiring. Miss Brownall was slapping her bare arms and one of the men from the second car, feeling the chill, had wrapped a scarf under his chin and up over his trilby hat.

'Well, Miss Brownall,' Clifford humorously asked, 'Who do you think was buried here?'

Miss Brownall said she could not say but the man with the scarf answered for her, 'I would presume, yes . . . yes, I would presume it was Ozymandias, King of Kings.' His precise enunciation did not suggest a joke but Clifford looked suspiciously at him.

'Didn't know there was an Ozymandias.' To prevent further discussion Clifford made a quick move to an entrance in the further wall. 'Now, this is interesting. Another passage. Let's see where this leads.'

As the others filed after him, Simon made his escape and came thankfully out to where Harriet was sitting on the ground, her back to the pyramid, sifting sand through her fingers. She had collected a small pile of blue beads and scraps of mummy cloth. 'Look what I've found.'

Simon sat down beside her and took the opportunity to ask, 'Who is Mr Clifford? Is he very important?'

'In a way, I suppose he is. He's an agent for an oil company but he's not as grand as he'd like to be. He doesn't belong to the set that plays polo and gives gambling parties so, to show his superiority, he's taken to Ancient Egypt in a big way.'

'I suppose he is English? Which part does he come from?'

'You mean his accent? It's a Clifford accent. He's English but doesn't come from England. The Cliffords have lived here for generations. The men go home to find English wives so the family maintains its Englishness. Their traditions are English, but their money is not. I wonder, if the gyppos turned on us, which side he'd be on?'

'Turned on us? You don't really think they'd turn on us after all we've done for them?'

Harriet laughed at him, 'What have we done for them?'

'We've brought them justice and prosperity, haven't we? We've shown them how people ought to live.'

With his face close to her, seeing his clear skin, the clear whites of his eyes, the defined dark blue of the iris, she thought, 'How young he is!' Until now she had taken it for granted that her generation was the youngest of the adults but she realised that in the two years of her marriage, a yet younger generation had come into the war. They arrived in Egypt, fresh and innocent, imbued with the creed in which they had been brought up. They believed that the British empire was the greatest force for good the world had ever known. They expected gratitude from the Egyptians and were pained to find themselves barely tolerated.

'What have we done here, except make money? I suppose a few rich Egyptians have got richer by supporting us, but the real people of the country, the peasants and the backstreet poor, are just as diseased, underfed and wretched as they ever were.'

Aware of his own ignorance, Simon did not argue but changed course. 'Surely they're glad to have us here to protect them?'

'They don't think we're protecting them. They think we're making a use of them. And so we are. We're protecting the Suez Canal and the route to India and Clifford's oil company.' Disturbed by Simon's troubled eyes, Harriet stood up asking 'And where is Clifford? What are they doing in there?'

'Exploring another passage. I must say, he's pretty brave. The roof's so shaky, it could come down any minute.'

'He's showing off. He's challenged by you.'

'Me? Why me?'

'Because you're a fighting man and he ought to be, but isn't.'

'Oh, he needn't worry about me. If he wants to keep out of it all I can say is good luck to him.'

They could hear Clifford's voice as the party returned. Harriet opened her hand, full of tiny blue beads, and scattered the beads over the sand: 'They've been here for two thousand years. Now they can stay for another two thousand.'

Clifford, coming out frowning and blinking in the brilliant light, looked sardonically at her. 'So, young lady, you were afraid to come with us?'

'Yes.'

Nonplussed by this admission, Clifford turned on the others. 'Right. Back to the cars. I'll show you a very remarkable tomb.'

'The funny one?' asked Miss Brownall.

'Yes, the funny one.'

Clifford spoke sternly and he looked stern as he swung the car away from the dark mounds that had once been pyramids and headed them into the dazzling, swimming nothingness of the desert horizon. Silver mirage now hid the sand and, from it, oddly elongated rocks and stones stood up like wading birds. Everyone except Clifford was silent, stupefied by the atmosphere inside the car. Simon imagined them cooking, their flesh softening and melting into fat, while Clifford talked away. Apparently unaffected by the heat, he described the tomb he said he had discovered. It was – and here Miss Brownall gave eager agreement – unlike any other tomb anyone had discovered before. Absorbed by his own discovery, he ran the car off the track and Harriet, clutching at a metal handhold, cried out that her fingers were burnt.

'Is it always as hot as this?' Simon asked.

'This is only the beginning. Next month will be worse. They used to think Englishwomen and children could not endure such heat but now we have to stay here, we find we endure it quite well.'

An outcrop of rock was appearing in the distance and Clifford said 'This is it. *Now* you'll see something.'

The cars stopped and the passengers struggled out again. They were immediately assailed by flies that settled with sticky feet on to sticky hands and faces. Clifford, flapping his whisk about, said, 'Don't know what God was thinking about when he created flies.'

Miss Brownall, modest in her knowledge, asked 'Weren't they created to plague the Egyptians?'

Harriet agreed. 'The plagues came and never went away again.'

Simon began to describe the millions of flies he had seen, a black blanket of flies, all heaving together on the banks of the Red Sea, but Clifford, having no interest in this talk, ordered the party to follow him into the rock tomb.

Simon remained a moment to observe a fly motionless on the back of his hand, its mottled grey and black body covered by transparent wings that gave it a greasy look. It seemed too large, like a fly seen through a magnifying glass. He tried to shake it off but it remained, heat-struck, and having no heart to kill it, he brushed it away.

'Don't lag behind, chaps,' Clifford shouted. 'Come on. Stick together –'

They passed through an opening into the semidarkness of a large cave. The masons had squared it up and plastered the walls, then the artists had marked in the areas to be decorated but they had done no more. Some of the spaces had been roughly brushed in with red or white. Clifford, pointing to them, said, 'Have you ever seen anything like this? Isn't it extraordinary?'

There was a questioning silence then Harriet said, 'Not really. It's merely unfinished. They started to decorate it then, for some reason, the work came to a stop.'

Miss Brownall drew in her breath as though she feared for Harriet's safety and Clifford did indeed look angry. 'Why should they stop?'

'The usual reasons. Demand falling off. New religions taking over. New ideas. Or prices going up and the tomb-makers going out of business. It's interesting to see that in ancient Egypt things ended just as they have always done.'

'Perhaps. Perhaps not.' Clifford was discouraging but one of the men from the second car said, 'I think Mrs Pringle is right. It's just an unfinished tomb.'

Clifford grunted, 'That's merely supposition. Anyway, there's more to see.' He led the way down some rough steps into a small, lower cave where shelves had been cut in the rock. Here the walls were unplastered and there were no painted guidelines or panels. Looking about the empty tomb where no soul had sought instruction and no instructions were given, Harriet felt sorry for the builders who had been forced to abandon their work. While Clifford flashed his torch about, trying to whip up interest in a place that had ceased to be interesting, Harriet looked up and saw they were all crowded together beneath a gigantic stone that was poised, ready to be lowered on to the hole when all the shelves had been filled. She murmured in horror and sped up the steps and into the safety of the open air.

Simon, hurrying after her, asked, 'What's the matter? Are you all right?'

'Yes. It was that stone. If it had suddenly slipped, we would have been buried alive down there.' At the thought of their death in the darkness and heat of that underground hole, she was convulsed with fear. 'No one would ever have known what had happened to us.'

Clifford, his followers behind him, approached Harriet with a satisfied smile. 'You're very jittery, aren't you? That stone's been propped up there for over a thousand years. Did you think it was waiting to come down on you?'

She knew she was jittery. She had come jittery out of Rumania and then out of Greece, and now she lived in expectation of being driven out of Egypt. She said, 'I'm sorry. I was silly. I'm inclined to be claustrophobic.'

Appeased by her admission of weakness, Clifford smiled benignly and said they would go to the Fayoum and have their picnic under the trees. The promise of picnic and trees pleased everyone and the oasis, when they came to it, gave them an illusion of relief. There was shade from the massed foliage of palms, sycamores, banyans and mangoes, but it was heavy rather than cool. The sunlight, falling in shafts through the branches, lit dust motes in the air. Dust veiled everything, the dust of the road silenced their feet. Women, walking bare footed with pots on their heads, moved with a dream-like quiet, their black draperies grey with dust. Small houses stood by the road, simple cubes of whitewashed clay, with unglazed windows from which came the smoke of burning cow-cake. The warm, dry smell of the cow-cake smoke hung everywhere on the air.

Where the road opened into a Midan there was a sphinx, its nose rubbed off by time, and here the cars stopped under the trees. Car rugs were spread out on the sand, packets of cakes and sandwiches were taken from the boot of Clifford's car and everyone sat down, waiting for Miss Brownall to make tea on a spirit-stove. Sitting in the steamy shade, they watched camels plash by, grunting morosely, heads held high in contempt of the creatures they were forced to serve.

No one was hungry except Simon who had had nothing since his canteen breakfast, but he was reluctant to eat food to which he had not contributed.

'Tuck in. Tuck in,' Clifford shouted at him, and everyone who had brought food urged it upon him. Simon tucked in.

The heat now had a leaden weight so even the flies were stilled. The sun had passed its meridian and the light was taking on an ochre tinge that gave to the trees and the sandy air an antique richness. They all sat bowed, drowsy, and Harriet felt they had lost the present and were in some era of the remote past. Then Miss Brownall came round with cups of tea. They roused themselves and began to talk. The man who had spoken of Ozyman-dias, unwound his scarf from his hat and, sipping his tea, watched Harriet from the corners of his eyes. After some moments, he began fidgeting across the rug towards her, making an introductory mumbling and creaking in his throat that at last became words.

'This . . . yes, this is the young person who knows things. She can tell us what's going on. She's in the American information office.'

The man to whom he spoke was the one who had backed Harriet's opinion of the cave. He was thin and elderly and his raw, pink hands, tightly clenched, were nervously pressed into the ground at his sides. He smiled on Harriet, saying, 'Oh, I know. I know she's in information.'

The two of them gazed expectantly at her and she introduced them to Simon. The man with the scarf was Professor Lord Pinkrose; the other was called Major Cookson. The major was so absurdly unlike a professional soldier that Harriet laughed slightly as she spoke his name. As for information, she had no more than anyone else.

Pinkrose's face went glum. A pear-shaped, elderly man, he was wearing an old-fashioned tussore suit that buttoned up to his chin. His nose, that rested on top of his scarf, was blunt and grey like the snout of a lizard. His eyes, too, were grey – grey as rainwater, Simon thought – and looked coldly on Harriet when he realised she had nothing to tell. He was about to turn from her when he remembered he had another question to ask. 'Have you any news of Gracey? . . . any news? Every time I ring the office, I get a girl saying, "Mr Gracey is not available" and that's all she says. It's exasperating. Most exasperating. Over and over. "Mr Gracey is not available." It's like a machine.'

Gracey was the head of the organisation which employed Harriet's husband, Guy Pringle. She said, 'It is a machine: an answering machine. There's no one in the office. The place is locked up. I've tried to contact them, too. Guy's in Alexandria in an out-of-the-way place and if the advance goes on, he could be cut off there.' Harriet, her anxiety renewing itself, spoke with feeling. 'It's Gracey's job to order him to leave but Gracey's not here. He's taken himself to a safe place as he always does when things look bad. I went to the office and found the porter. He told me Gracey's gone to Palestine.'

'Gone to Palestine! Gone to Palestine!' Pinkrose seemed baffled by the news and then became agitated. 'You hear that, Cookson? You hear that? Gracey's gone to Palestine.'

'So have a lot of other people.'

'But he said nothing to me. *Nothing*. Not a word. This is disgraceful, Cookson. To go off without a word to me. Did you know he had gone?'

Cookson shook his head. 'I never see Gracey these days. Now I'm on my uppers, most of my old friends have faded away.'

Pinkrose, caring nothing for Cookson's lost friends, interrupted him. 'I'd no idea the situation was so serious. No idea. No idea. No idea at all.'

Harriet watched Pinkrose with a smile, quizzical and mildly scornful, while Pinkrose's small, stony eyes quivered with self-concern. She had known him first in Bucharest where, sent out to give a lecture, he had arrived as the Germans were infiltrating the country and had been abandoned then just as he was abandoned now. He was, she thought, like some heavy object, a suitcase or parcel, an impediment that his friends put down when they wanted to cut and run. Looking beyond him to Cookson, she mischievously asked, 'And what are your get-away plans this time, Major Cookson?'

Cookson gave a wry, sheepish smile, not resenting the question. In Greece, where he had had money invested in property, his house had been a centre of hospitality. When the Germans came down on Athens, he had chartered two freighters, intending to take his friends to safety. Pinkrose had been among those invited. They had kept their plans secret but had been discovered and Cookson was ordered by the military to include anyone who chose to leave.

Now, having spent the money he had in Egypt, he existed on a dole from the British Embassy. He had been brought by Clifford merely as a driver of the second car. His clothes were becoming shabby, he looked underfed and Pinkrose, who had been his guest in the past, treated him as an inferior. For a time those who knew Cookson's story had no wish to speak to him but now, seeing him so reduced in the world, Harriet looked on him with pitying amusement. He answered humbly, 'I have no plans, and if I had any, I've no money to carry them out. Those freighters cost me a fortune and I didn't get a penny of compensation from the army.'

'Still, you got away with all your possessions while we were allowed only a small suitcase. You even had your car on board.'

'My poor old car,' Cookson sighed and smiled. 'The Egyptian customs've still got hold of it. They refuse to release it – not that it matters. I couldn't afford to run it.'

Harriet, having decided the past was past, smiled with him, realising that now they were almost old friends, while Pinkrose went on with his fretful mumblings, the more angry because he had been left in the lurch for a second time.

A crowd of children had gathered to watch the strangers. Mr Liversage, enlivened by his tea, went over to them and trailed his dog backwards and forwards in front of them, his manner gleeful, expectant of applause. The children stared, confounded by the laughing old man and the old, bald toy dog which was a money-box in which he collected for charity. At first they were silent then one of them opened his mouth to jeer and the others took up his contempt with derisive yells and shouts of 'Majnoon'. Stones were thrown at man and dog and Clifford rushed in, wielding his fly-whisk like a flail, and scattered the miscreants. That done he ordered his party to rise. 'Wakey, wakey. We've a long drive back.'

As they moved and dusted themselves down, a passenger from the second car, a university professor called Bowen, said, 'Isn't this where that chap Hooper lives? He took over a Turkish fortress and spent a mint of money on it.'

'Hooper?' The name brought Clifford to a stop. 'Sir Desmond Hooper? Now he's the one who could tell us what's happening out there. He's always wining and dining the army big shots.'

Bowen, a small, gentle fellow, nodded. 'Well, yes. He might know more than most people.'

'Then why don't we look him up? Call in for an early sundowner?'

'Oh, no,' Bowen, aghast at the idea, had the support of Cookson and Mr Liversage, when he realised what was being argued, said firmly, 'Can't do that, my dear fellow. Too many of us. Can't march an army into a chap's house, don't you know! Simply not done.' Pinkrose, however, eager for news and concerned for his own safety, felt differently. 'Why not call in? Why not? These aren't ordinary times, no need to stand on ceremony these days. It's disgraceful the way we're kept in ignorance. If Sir Desmond Hooper knows what's going on, it's his duty to tell us. Yes, yes, his duty . . . it's his duty, I say.' Pinkrose spoke indignantly, carrying his anger with Gracey over on to the innocent Hooper.

The others – Simon, Harriet, Miss Brownall and a girl from the second car who was also one of Clifford's employees – took no part in the discussion but waited for Clifford's decision. Harriet, entertained by it, was not un-willing to see the Hooper fortress in the anonymity of so much company.

Pinkrose's agreement settled the matter for Clifford. 'We'll go,' he said. Bowen begged, 'At least ring him up first.'

'Ring him up? Where from? We'll get more out of him if we take him unawares.'

Clifford spoke to one of the camel drivers and was directed towards the river. The fortress was soon evident. Larger and more complex than most desert fortresses, it stood up above the trees, a white-painted, crenellated square of stone behind a crenellated white wall. The wall enclosed a row of palms from which hung massive bunches of red dates. A boab, looking out through the wrought-iron gates, seemed doubtful of the party but Clifford's masterful manner impressed him and he let them in. They drove between extensive, sandy lawns to an iron-studded main door where three safragis lolled half-asleep. One of them, rousing himself with an air of long-suffering, came to the first car and enquired, 'Who do you want?'

'Lady Hooper.'

'Not here. Layey Hooper.' The safragi made to walk away but Clifford shouted, 'Sir Desmond, then.' The safragi had to admit that Sir Desmond was at home.

Mr Liversage refused to leave the car but the others – even Bowen's curiosity was stronger than his discretion – followed the servant into a vast hall where the parquet was as deep and dark as the waters of a well. The house was air-conditioned. Enlivened by the drop in temperature, they seemed all to realise suddenly the enormity of their intrusion into the Hooper household. Harriet had an impulse to run back to the car but the safragi had opened the door of a living-room and, feeling it was too late to retreat, she went in with the rest. The room was as large as a ballroom and made larger by its prevailing whiteness. Walls, carpets, curtains and furniture were white. The white leather and the white-painted surfaces had been toned down with some sort of 'antiquing' mixture which Harriet noted with interest. The only colour in the room came from half a dozen paintings so startling in quality that she took it for granted that they were reproductions. Moving to them she saw they were originals.

She said to Clifford in wonder, 'They're real.'

'I don't like that modern stuff.'

'They were painted before you were born.'

'I don't like them any the better for that.'

Clifford, disconcerted by his surroundings, was in a bad temper.

Sir Desmond entered and looked at his uninvited guests with bewildered diffidence. Deciding they were friends of his wife, he said, 'I'm afraid Angela's not here. She's out on a painting expedition.' Then he noticed Bowen, 'Ah, Bowen, I did not know you were here.'

Bowen, identified, blushed and tried to excuse himself, 'I'm sorry. So wrong of us to interrupt your Sunday peace. It's just . . . we . . .' Struggling to find an excuse, he twisted about in anguish.

'Not at all. Sit down, do. Won't the ladies sit here!'

Harriet, Miss Brownall and the other girl were put into the seat of honour, a vast ottoman so deep they almost sank out of sight. The men found themselves chairs and Sir Desmond, placing himself among them, asked if they would take tea.

Clifford said they had had tea and his manner left the occasion open for a more stimulating offer, but Sir Desmond merely said, 'Ah!' He was a tall, narrow man with a regular, narrow face, dressed in a suit of silver-grey silk. His hair was the same silver as the silk and his appearance, elegant, desiccated yet authoritative, was that of an upper class Englishman prepared to deal with any situation. He looked over the visitors who, dusty, sweaty, depleted by their travels, were all uneasy, except Clifford. Clifford's assurance was such that Sir Desmond dropped Bowen and addressed the younger man: 'Well, major, what brings you into the Fayoum?'

Clifford blinked at the title but did not repudiate it. 'We're just exploring a bit. Voyage of discovery, you might call it.'

'Is there anything left to discover in this much-pillaged country?' As he spoke Sir Desmond noticed that Clifford had on his shoulder not a crown but a plain gold button and his voice sharpened as he enquired, 'What are you? Press? Radio? Something like that?'

'Certainly not. I'm in oil. The name's Clifford. The fact is, Sir Desmond, rumours are going round Cairo and we don't like the look of things. And we don't like being kept in ignorance. The station's in an uproar with foreigners trying to get away and I heard even GHQ's packing up. What we want to know is: what the hell's happening in the desert?'

'I don't think I can answer that question, Mr Clifford.'

Rancour came into Clifford's voice. 'If you can't, who can?'

The telephone rang at Sir Desmond's elbow. He answered it, said urgently, 'Yes, yes, hold on,' and, excusing himself, went to take the call in another room. A scratch of voices came from the receiver on the table. Clifford tiptoed to it, bent to listen but before he could hear anything, a safragi entered to replace it on its stand.

Bowen was indignant. 'Really, Clifford, what a thing to do! And I think we've stayed long enough. Let's slip away.'

'No, no.' Pinkrose was impressively impatient, 'This may be the very news we're waiting for.'

'It may indeed,' said Clifford.

The light was deepening towards sunset. The safragi who had attended to the telephone, opened the windows and the long chiffon curtains blew like ghosts into the room.

Bowen complained, 'It's getting late . . .' but Clifford silenced him with a lift of the hand. Before anyone else could speak, a car, driven at reckless speed, came up the drive and braked with a shriek outside the house. They heard the heavy front door crash open and from the hall came the sound of a stumbling entry that conveyed a sense of catastrophe. A woman entered the room shouting, 'Desmond. Desmond,' and seeing the company, stopped and shook her head.

The men got to their feet. Bowen said, 'Lady Hooper, is anything the matter?' She shook her head again, standing in the middle of the room, her distracted appearance made more wild by her disarranged black hair and the torn, paint-covered overall that protected her dress. Lady Hooper was younger than her husband. She was some age between thirty and forty, a delicately built woman with a delicate, regular face. She looked at each of the strangers in turn and when she came to Simon, she smiled and said, 'I think he'll be all right.'

Two safragis carried in the inert body of a boy. The three women hastily struggled out of the ottoman and the boy was put down. He lay prone and motionless, a thin, small boy of eight or nine with the same delicate features as his mother: only something had happened to them. One eye was missing. There was a hole in the left cheek that extended into the torn wound which had been his mouth. Blood had poured down his chin and was caked on the collar of his open-necked shirt. The other eye, which was open, was lacklustre and blind like the eye of a dead rabbit.

Sir Desmond entered and anxiously asked, 'My dear, what has happened?'

'We were in the desert. I was sketching and didn't see . . . He picked up something. It exploded – but he'll be all right.'

Harriet could scarcely bear to look at Sir Desmond but he answered calmly enough, 'My dear, of course. I expect he's suffering from shock.'

'Do you think we should rouse him? Perhaps if we gave him something to eat . . .'

'Yes, a little nourishment, light and easy to swallow.'

'Gruel, or an egg beaten up. What do you think?'

Sir Desmond spoke to the safragis who glanced at each other with the expression of those who have long accepted the fact that all foreigners are mad.

There was an interval in which Sir Desmond telephoned a doctor in Cairo and Lady Hooper, sitting on the sofa edge, held the boy's hand. Sir Desmond, finishing his call, spoke reassuringly to her, 'He's coming out straight away. He says Richard must have an anti⁄tetanus injection.'

'There was Dettol in the car. I bathed his face.'

One of the safragis returned, bringing a bowl of gruel and the visitors watched with awe and amazement as Sir Desmond, bending tenderly over the boy, attempted to feed him. The mouth was too clogged with congealed blood to permit entry so the father poured a spoonful of gruel into the hole in the cheek. The gruel poured out again. This happened three times before Sir Desmond gave up and, gathering the child into his arms, said, 'He wants to sleep. I'll take him to his room.' Lady Hooper followed her husband and Clifford, knowing he was defeated, was willing to depart.

Outside, beneath the palms and the roseate sky, he gave a long whistle. 'Now I've seen everything.'

'They couldn't face the truth,' Bowen sighed in pity. 'They couldn't accept it.'

'They'll be forced to accept it pretty soon. And we never heard what that phone call was all about.'

Mr Liversage lay asleep in the car. Bowen elected to move him over and sat beside him while Miss Brownall joined her friend in the second car. Remembering the boy, no one spoke as they drove through the Fayoum. The trees merged, dark in the misty evening. Lights were flickering inside the box⁄shaped houses. It would soon be night. As the oasis was left behind, the boy's death lost its immediacy and Harriet thought of all the other boys who were dying in the desert before they had had a chance to live. And yet, though there was so much death at hand, she felt the boy's death was a death apart.

Bowen murmured, 'A tragedy. An only child.'

'And the last shot in the old locker,' said Clifford. 'They're not likely to have another.'

The sun had almost set when they approached Mena and the last, long rays enriched the sand. It glowed saffron and orange then, in a moment, the colour was gone and a violet twilight came down. The passengers were sunk together with weariness but Clifford had still not had enough. A few hundred yards before the road turned towards Mena, he drew up and said, 'There's an ancient village about here. Let's take a shufti.'

33

'Is it really worth the effort?' Bowen asked.

'Oh, come on!' Clifford rallied the party, insisting that if there was anything to see, it must be seen. They wandered about on the stony mardam and found the village which was sunk like an intaglio in the sand. Jumping down, they walked through narrow streets between small, roofless houses. The dig must have been a students' exercise for the dwellings were too poor to yield more than a few broken pots and it was hard to understand why anyone had chosen to live in this waterless spot. In the deepening twilight, it was so forlorn that even Clifford was glad to move on to the Mena House bar.

While Bowen and Simon were buying the drinks, Clifford moved eagerly round the officers in the bar until he found a group known to him. Putting his head among them, he said, 'Just come from the Hooper house. Their kid's been killed by a hand grenade he picked up. You won't believe this, but old Hooper tried to spoonfeed the boy through a hole in his face.' Tomorrow the story would be all over Cairo.

When their drinks were finished, Harriet said to Simon, 'Shall we climb the great pyramid?'

'Is it possible? Goodness, I'd love to, but can you manage it?'

'I've done it twice before. The last time, I was wearing a black velvet evening dress which hasn't been the same since.'

They went out to the road that was lit only by the lights of the hotel. The pyramids were no more than a greater darkness in an area of darkness. Harriet led Simon to the noted corner from which the ascent was easiest and as they climbed on to the first ledge, the local Bedu sighted them and came running and shouting, 'Not allowed. No one go up without guide. Law says you have guide.'

Simon paused but Harriet waved him on. As they scrambled upwards the Bedu shook their fists and wailed, 'Come back. Come back,' and Harriet laughed and waved down at them. Standing on one ledge, she jumped her backside on to the one above then swung her legs up after her. She was very light and moved at such speed, she passed Simon and was first at the top. There she waved again to the guides who were still making half-hearted complaints before they drifted away.

The apex of the pryamid was missing, purloined to provide stone for other buildings, and now there was a plateau some twelve yards square. Harriet, seeing it as a dancing-ground, held out her arms to Simon as he reached it and they circled together for a few minutes, singing 'Run rabbit' until they were overcome by laughter. They went to the edge of the square and sat, looking into the darkness of the desert. The sky was fogged and there was nothing visible but the blue quilt of lights that was Cairo. Speaking as a soldier, Simon said sternly, 'There ought to be a proper black-out.'

'You could never enforce it. It would take the whole British army to get the Cairenes to black their windows. Besides, it would be no use. A pilot told me that the Nile is always visible. They'd just have to follow it. The lights frightened me when we first came here but nothing happened and I got used to them.'

'You mentioned my brother. You didn't say much about him. Didn't you like him?'

'Hugo? Of course I liked him. I liked him very much. We met him in Alex. He was in the Cecil bar and he looked so young and alone that we went over and spoke to him. He talked about the desert. He said he was sick of it but he had to go back next day. He asked us to have dinner with him because it was his twenty-first birthday.'

'Really!' Simon was entranced by this information. 'You were with him on his twenty-first?'

'Yes, we went to Pastroudi's and had a great time.'

'How splendid!' Simon waited, expecting to hear more about this momentous dinner-party but Harriet had said all she meant to say. The numinous sequel to that dinner was not for Simon. It had been the night of full moon. Passing through the black-out curtains at the door, they had entered the startling brilliance of the night and stood together to say goodbye. Hugo, his handsome, smiling, gentle face white in the moonlight, thanked them for giving him their company on his birthday. Guy wrote down a telephone number saying, 'When you come back on leave, let's meet again,' and a voice inside Harriet's head said, 'But he won't come back. He is going to die.' She felt neither surprise nor shock at this foreknowledge, only the certainty that it was true.

Simon broke into her memory, saying, 'I must try to find him but I'm not sure if I can. I don't know what it's like out there.'

'I don't know either. It's strange, living here on the edge of a battlefield. It's like living beside Pluto's underworld.'

Simon, knowing nothing about Pluto's underworld, moved to a more desirable subject. 'You know Edwina's Hugo's girl. She's really something, isn't she. She's very beautiful.'

Harriet laughed saying only, 'I hardly know her. She's an archivist at the Embassy.'

'I say, is she?' Simon could not have said what an archivist did but the word impressed him. He wanted to hear more about Edwina but felt the need to curb his interest. 'Actually, I'm married. My wife's called Anne. We were only together for a week and then I had to go to Liverpool and join the draft. She came to the station to see me off and she couldn't speak. She just stood there, crying and crying. I said, "Cheer up, the war can't go on for ever", but she only cried. Poor little thing!'

Simon's voice faltered so Harriet feared that he, too, would cry. She wanted to agree that the war could not go on for ever but she had no certainty. She stood up and said, 'The others will wonder where we are. Having come up at top speed, there's nothing to do but go down again.'

The cars no longer stood outside Mena House. Harriet sent Simon to the hotel desk, expecting a message had been left, but there was no message. Clifford's party had gone and she and Simon were left behind.

Abashed, Simon said, 'But Edwina told Clifford to take me back to her. She made me promise to return.'

'I see.' Harriet could imagine Clifford seizing the chance to decant a rival, even such a young and temporary rival as Simon. If Edwina asked where Simon was Clifford could say, 'He went off with a girl', and that would be the end of Simon.

'It was my fault. I shouldn't have taken you away like that.'

'It was an experience. I've been hearing about the pyramids since I was a kid but I never expected to go up one.' Simon smiled to show he did not blame her but it was a dejected smile. Harriet, thinking how few experiences might be left for him in this world, felt enraged that Clifford, so much concerned for his own safety, could abandon Simon who would soon be risking his life. She said, 'Don't worry. We'll find a taxi and I'll drop you off in Garden City.'

'But can I just barge in like that?'

'Of course. If Edwina invited you . . .'

'Yes, she did invite me.'

They waited outside the hotel until a taxi, coming from Cairo, was willing to take them back. Harriet was relieved to see a light in the living-room of the flat where Edwina lodged. Simon, too, looked up, delighted, never doubting that Edwina was there.

He said, 'I say, I'm terribly grateful. We'll meet again, won't we?'

'I expect we will.'

The safragi who opened the door of the flat seemed to confirm Simon's expectations. Inviting him in, the man grinned in an intimate, insolent manner as though conniving at some act of indecency. He said, 'Mis' Likkle here,' but Simon found the person in the living-room was not Edwina. It was a man in late middle age who rose and gazed on him in courteous enquiry.

'Miss Little invited me here.'

'Did she? I'm sorry, but she has gone out to dinner. She's usually out at this time.'

Apologising, Simon began to back from the room but the man said, 'Do stay. I'm Paul Beaker, one of the inmates. If Edwina's expecting you, I'm sure she'll be back quite early. Why not have supper with me!'

Supper with Paul Beaker offered a bleak alternative to Edwina and Simon hesitated, considering refusal, reflecting on the possibility of her return. There was a snuffle behind him and he realised the safragi had waited to observe his reception. He said, 'Your man thinks I'm some sort of joke.'

Beaker, looking over Simon's shoulder, ordered the safragi away and explained to Simon, 'This is an Embassy flat and we live here in a sort of family freedom that is incomprehensible to the Moslem mind. Hassan can no more understand the innocence of our proximity than you can understand his grins and giggles.'

Beaker, a fat man with a broad red face, raised the glass he was holding and said, 'Have a drink. *Do* have one. It will give me an excuse to have another.'

Simon was handed a tumbler of whisky. Pouring in a little water, Beaker asked, 'That all right?'

Simon, who had never before drunk anything stronger than beer, supposed it was all right as Beaker was drinking the same thing. Beaker, before he had even reseated himself, started to drink with avid satisfaction.

The room was sparsely furnished with sofa, two armchairs, a table and not much else. 'Rather a makeshift place,' Beaker said as Simon placed himself on the edge of an armchair, intending to leave when his drink was finished. 'The chap who holds the lease, one Dobbie Dobson, does not want to lash out on furniture. It's expensive and hard to get and who knows how long we'll all be here! I, myself, am leaving in a few weeks. I've been appointed to the university of Baghdad. I'm not a diplomat. I'm a professor of romance languages.' Doing his best to keep Simon entertained, the professor ruminated about the flat. 'Not a bad flat, really. It's designed for a Moslem family. This would be the audience room, then there's another room behind here, the hall's there and you see that baize door? It leads to the gynaeceum, the women's quarters. It's all arranged so the women of the house could pass from one end of the flat to the other without being seen by the visitors in here.'

Simon, uncertain whether Beaker was speaking of past or present, thought of the women moving secretly in the hidden rooms, then thought of Edwina and his cheeks grew pink. 'Do you mean Edwina is kept behind the baize door?'

Beaker laughed. 'Oh no, no indeed. Would one dare? No, I mean that it was in accordance with Moslem custom. Edwina *does* have her sleeping-quarters behind the baize door but no restrictions are placed upon her. She comes and goes as she likes.'

At the mention of Edwina's sleeping-quarters, Simon's blush deepened. He lowered his head to hide it while Beaker refilled the glasses and asked, 'You been out of England before?'

'Oh, yes. I once had a week in Paris.'

'Paris, eh?' Beaker laughed as though the name had some peculiar connotation for him. 'And now you're going into the desert, is that it?'

Simon, who was listening for Edwina's return, realised he must explain himself. He told of his journey round the Cape then asked if the professor had ever met his brother, Hugo.

'Yes, I seem to remember a young fellow called Hugo, one of Edwina's swains. So he's your brother! And you're joining him at the front. Bit worrying for your people to have two sons out there, isn't it? Are you their only children?'

'Yes, just the two of us,' Simon was suffused by the memory of his home and said, 'We live in Putney – not really Putney, more Roehampton.' He saw the street of small Edwardian terrace houses, all alike except that the Boulderstone home had a conservatory leading from the living-room. Mr Boulderstone had built it himself and said it added to the value of the house. Warmed and activitated by the whisky, he told Professor Beaker about the conservatory that was filled with his mother's geraniums and a very old sofa. In the summer she would sit among her plants, mending clothes and knitting and listening to talks on the radio. The clouded glass, the scents, the summer warmth of the conservatory came back to him so vividly that he described them to Beaker as though they were important in the scheme of things. There was one remarkable thing in the conservatory. When the local mansion was being demolished to make way for a housing estate, Mr Boulderstone had acquired an old vine which he planted against the wall outside, bringing the main stem in to spread under the glass roof. He told his family that the vine was a Black Hamburg, like the vine at Hampton Court that produced great bunches of purple grapes, but, whatever Mr Boulderstone did, his vine had nothing but small green grapes like bunches of peas. He bought the vine buckets of blood from the abattoir. He puffed sulphur over the bunches but they never got bigger. Sometimes a sour flush of mauve would come over the grapes but they tasted as bitter as aloes.

Beaker, gazing intently at Simon's glowing face, seemed deeply interested in all this, encouraging Simon to talk so by the third whisky he was as far back in memory as his infants' school. When Beaker made to refill his glass Simon said, 'Oh no, I'd better not. I've got to find my way back to Abbasia barracks somehow.'

'Why not stay here,' said Beaker. 'We often put you chaps up. There's a small spare room.'

Thinking of Edwina, thinking of the abominable, death-smelling room at the barracks, Simon said, 'Oh, I say, thanks. But I've got to ring Transit.' When he rang Transit, he found a message had come for him from Major Perry. He was to be at Kasr el Nil barracks at six the next morning.

He said to Beaker, 'I'm afraid, sir, I've got to make an early start.'

'Don't worry. I'll give you the alarm clock. We're used to chaps making early starts.'

Simon settled thankfully back into the armchair and let Beaker give him another drink. But that, he knew, was enough. Hassan came in to set the table and Simon now was happy to accept Beaker's invitation to supper. Four places were laid but only Beaker and Simon sat down. Beaker asked him about the long voyage out to Egypt and Simon tried to describe the wonderful communion that had existed between him and his two friends, but already the deathless friendship, the understanding, the intense sympathy, the very smell of the ship itself, were fading from his mind like illusions that could not survive on dry land.

While he was talking, the front door opened and shut and Simon's voice dried in his throat. Paused in expectation, he realised that Beaker, too, was listening for Edwina's return. Then a male voice shouted, 'Hassan', and Beaker twitched nervously. 'Dear me, that's Percy Gibbon. I didn't know he would be in. He *will* be cross that we started without him.'

Percy Gibbon could be heard talking in Arabic to the safragi while Beaker, awaiting him, made an effort to appear sober. When Gibbon entered, Beaker began in a confused and fussy manner, 'So sorry, I really thought . . . I really did . . .' Gibbon held up an imperious hand and Beaker's apology limped to a halt.

Gibbon said, 'There are more important things to worry about.'

'Oh, really, are there? You've heard something?'

'Nothing that I'm free to impart.'

A very subdued Hassan put down Gibbon's soup and Gibbon bent to it, his nose just above the plate. It was a very large nose, the cheeks falling back so sharply that, from the front, Gibbon's face looked all nose. His mouth was small and his weak, pinkish eyes seemed colourless behind brass-rimmed glasses. Having downed his soup, he blinked at Simon. 'One of Edwina's, I suppose?'

Simon said, 'Not really. I only arrived yesterday. I came out on the *Queen Mary* with the draft.'

Gibbon frowned down in disapproval. 'That's something you should keep to yourself.'

Beaker, having incited information from Simon, now sided with Gibbon. 'Dear me, yes. Quite right. People are on edge. Rumours and so on. Unwise, I agree, to tell anyone anything.'

Gibbon said nothing. A dish of sliced lamb with carrots and sweet potatoes had been put on the table and he shovelled nearly half of the lamb on to his plate. He ate briskly, repeatedly sniffing as though he had a cold in the head. He took no more notice of Simon and as soon as the meal was over, he jumped up and took himself out through the baize door.

Simon asked in a low voice, 'What does he do?'

Beaker, too, spoke quietly as though fearing a reprimand. 'Don't know. Whatever it is, it's very hush-hush. I've been told he breaks codes.'

'He must be very clever.'

Beaker laughed and let his voice rise. 'He certainly thinks he is. My theory is that he's modelled himself on one of those Byron heroes. You know: "Vital scorn of all", "Chilling mystery of mien", "Haughty and reserved manner" – that sort of thing.'

Simon nodded, too sleepy to speak, and Beaker suggested that having to make such an early start, Simon might be wise to go to bed. He was put in a room behind the baize door. It was as bare as the barracks' room but for Simon, it was another thing. It was a room in a household and what was more, it was near Edwina's room. The whole corridor behind the baize door had been redolent of flowers.

He was roused some time after midnight by the noise in the living-room. Several people were talking and laughing, then came the plink-plink of a guitar and a voice rose high, pure and dulcet, singing in a language Simon did not know. From the long, melancholy notes, he guessed it was a sad song of love and he murmured to himself, 'Poor little thing'. Then the voice warmed into impetuous emotion and he knew the singer was Edwina. The song tantalised him with the memories of young women he had known in England and the women he had met that day. He saw in his mind not only Edwina, but the dark girl called Harriet and the woman with the dead boy in the Fayoum House. Even Miss Brownall entered his thoughts with a certain seductive pathos because she was a woman and tomorrow he must go where there were no women.

While he lay listening, in a state of ardent anguish, a door was flung open in the corridor and Gibbon bawled out, 'Shut up. I do an important job, not like you bastards.'

The guitar stopped. The song devolved into giggles and Simon returned to sleep. Professor Beaker's alarm clock wakened him to darkness and silence. He had no idea how he was to find his way through the unknown, sleeping city but down by the river a taxi was parked with the driver curled up on the back seat. He reached Kasr el Nil barracks as the first red of dawn broke across the sky, and saw the convoy strung out along the embankment.

There was no sign of movement. He had had to go first to Abbasia for his kit and was relieved to find himself in time. He wondered if he looked a fool, turning up in a taxi but, reaching the lorries, he realised no one knew or cared how he had got there.

The lorries were a mixed lot, made up from one unit or another, but on most of them the jerboa, the desert rat, could be discerned through the grime. They had arrived sand-choked from the desert and were returning sand-choked, but here and there a glint of new metal showed where a make-do-and-mend job had been done. Among the men packed on board them, he recognised faces he had seen on the *Queen Mary* and he felt less dejected. Finding the sergeant in charge, he said, to show he was not a complete novice, 'I suppose a lot of your chaps were on leave when the trains stopped?'

'That's right . . .' there was the usual pause before the 'sir' was added.

It was up to Simon to take over now. He counted the lorries and said, 'Thirty. That's the lot then, sergeant?'

'That's the koulou . . . sir.'

The sergeant strolled off with the blank remoteness of a man to whom war was an everyday affair. Simon, with no idea of what lay ahead, looked about him as though seeing everything for the last time. There was an island in mid-river, one end of it directly opposite the barracks. In the uncertain light it looked like a great schooner decked out with greenery. The light was growing. The island, touched by the pink of the sky, was taking shape, its buildings quivering as though forming themselves out of liquid pearl. Palms and tall, tenuous trees grew from the shadows at the water's edge. Nothing moved. The island hung on the air like a mirage or an uninhabited place.

A wind, cool enough to be pleasurable, blew into Simon's face and he said to himself, 'Why, it's beautiful!' The whole city was beautiful and for a few minutes the beauty remained, then the pearl hardened and lost its lustre. The sun had topped the horizon. The air was already warm. The terrible crescendo of the day had begun.

Major Hardy, arriving at the barracks square, chose to place his staff car half-way down the column. Simon, given no order to join him, climbed in beside the driver of the leading lorry. Trying to sound knowledgeable, he asked, 'How are we going out, corporal?'

The corporal, whose round, sunburnt face was even younger than his own, replied, 'Oh, the usual way, sir', and Simon waited to see what way that was. It proved to be familiar. They went, as Clifford's party had done, past Mena House and the pyramids. The corporal did not give the pyramids a look and Simon, seeing for the second time the small one sliding out from behind the greater, felt less wonder and said nothing. When they passed the excavated village, only Simon noticed it. They were travelling slowly so the lorries would keep together. At first the pace – it seldom exceeded ten miles an hour – was tolerable but when they faced the open desert, with the sun rising and shining into the cab window, tedium came down on them. Until then, Simon had still been attached to the known world but now it was disappearing behind him. He felt apprehensive, disconnected and rootless, and asked himself what on earth he was doing, going off like this into the unknown? Then, it came to him that, though he was vulnerable, he was not alone. He was a man among other men who, if they had to act, would act together. Yet the apprehension, fixed in his stomach, could not be moved. To reassure himself, he asked the driver, 'What's it like out there?'

'Oh,' the driver, called Vincent, ducked his head in a deprecating way, 'not bad, sir. You get browned off, a'course, but it's got its moments.'

Vincent had been one of those stranded in Cairo and had to find his battalion. He had no certainty he would do so. 'Never know what's happened when you're away. Don't want to start with a fresh mob, not when you're used to your own lot.'

This statement conveyed a sense of confusion ahead and Simon asked, 'How do you find your way around in the desert?'

The corporal laughed. 'You get a feel for it, sir.'

The sun rose above the cab roof and mirage hid the sand. The sky, if anyone could bear to look at it, had the molten whiteness of mid-day. They touched on the edge of a town. It was like a holiday scene with small, white villas, date palms and walls hung with purple bougainvilia, then came the white dazzle of sand and a sea, in bands of green, blue and violet, that seemed more light than water. They passed abandoned camping sites where regimental flags hung over emptiness, then drove between two shallow lakes, one of them green, the other raspberry pink, both dotted with floating chunks of soda. Simon could not hide his astonishment.

'What a weird place!'

'It's only Alex, sir.' Outside the town, Vincent tentatively asked, 'Time to brew up, sir?'

'Good heavens, yes. I should have thought of it, shouldn't I?'

'That's all right, sir.'

The red flag was hoisted and the convoy drew into the side of the road.

Numbers of army trucks and cars were going east. It seemed that that day only the convoy was going west. Looking down its length, Simon saw Major Hardy getting out of his car. The major was merely a passenger to the front but Simon, with no great confidence in his own power to command, felt it would be politic to treat him as if he were in charge. As Simon strolled down to the car, the major, spreading a large-scale map out over the bonnet, lifted a dark, lined face with a bar of black hair on the upper lip and gave him a stare of acute irritation. Simon started to introduce himself but Hardy interrupted him. 'Your section's brewing up. Better get back to see fair play.'

The sergeant, whose glum, folded face was kippered by the sun, was demonstrating, with an air of long-suffering, how to make a fire and boil water for the brew. The new men looked on as two large stones were set up to form a hob for the brew can which was a cut-down petrol can. The water came from the convoy's reserves but the sergeant said sternly, 'You don't use it, see, if you can get it from anywhere else.' He packed scrubwood between the stones and set it alight. Down the convoy, other fires were being started for other sections. At intervals, at the roadside, groups of men stood and watched for water to boil.

'Now,' said the sergeant, 'y'puts in yer tea, see.' He broke open a case of tea and threw two large handfuls on to the boiling water. 'Right. Now y'lifts it off, see.' He lifted the can as though his dry, brown hands were insulated against heat. 'Right. And now – where's yer mugs?'

The mugs stood together on the sand, a concourse of mugs, one for each man in the section and a couple over. Vincent trailed condensed milk from mug to mug, giving an inch or more of milk, and then the sergeant splashed the brew can over them. The men, picking up their tea mugs, moved into groups as though each had sorted out the companions natural to his kind. Already, Simon thought, they had ceased to be a collection of strangers and soon they would be wedded into twos and threes of which each member belonged to the others as he had belonged to Trent and Codley. Feeling himself solitary and apart, he looked for Vincent but Vincent had his own friends, men who had been with him, stranded, in Cairo. The sergeant brought over one of the spare mugs and two bully beef sandwiches. 'Spot of char, sir?', then remained beside Simon who, deeply gratified, asked him where he had been before he went on leave.

'Mersa. The jerries were just outside.'

'Where do you think they are now?'

The sergeant snorted. 'A few yards up the road, I reckon.'

Simon saw that he was not, as he had thought, sullen or remote. He was dejected by defeat. 'We had Gazala. We had Tobruk. It was hunkey-dorey. Looked like in no time we'd be back in Benghazi, then this happened.'

'What *did* happen?'

'Came down on us like a bat out'a hell.'

Vincent called, 'Blue flag, sir?'

'Oh, yes. Yes. Blue flag.'

Looking towards the horizon where the heat was thickening into a pall, Simon could imagine the German tanks appearing like monstrous bats, advancing with such speed and fury, the convoy could be wiped out before it had time to turn round. But the horizon was empty and even the eastbound traffic had stopped.

'Quiet, isn't it!'

Vincent said, 'Jerry's too busy to bother us,' and as he spoke, a Heinkel, returning from a reconnaissance flight, dived over the convoy. He braked sharply. The Heinkel, returning, sprayed the sand like a gesture of contempt. The bullets winged harmlessly into the sand. The plane flew off.

As the sun began to sink, Simon was concerned about the routine for the night. At some place and point in time he should give the order to make camp but before the need became an anxiety Vincent said, 'Think we should leaguer here, sir?'

There was a glimmer of white on the coast. The glimmer grew into a village of pleasant holiday homes with a bay, like a long white bone, that curved into the desert's cinderous buffs and browns.

'Who lives out here?' Simon asked.

'No one, now. They all moved away long ago.'

The lorries were positioned into a close-rank formation that served as camp and defence. Vincent, smiling as though he had begun to feel a protective affection for Simon, asked him, 'Permission to bathe, sir.'

Simon followed as the men, running between the dunes, shouting at each other, pulling off their shirts and shorts, went naked into a sea as warm and clinging as milk. Lying on the sea, in the haze of evening, he looked back at the village and was surprised to find it was still there. Had he been asked as they covered mile after mile of sand, 'Where would you choose to be?' he might well have chosen this oasis beside the white shore, with its villas under a shelter of palm trees. He raised his head to look westwards into the foggy distance of the desert coast and seeing nothing, he had an illusion of safety. The enemy must be further away than the sergeant imagined. Content filled him and he smiled at the man nearest to him. 'We didn't expect this, did we?'

The man laughed and twisted his head in a movement of appreciation. 'Dead cushy,' he said.

That night, startled out of sleep by the rising moon, Simon felt the earth vibrating beneath him. He sat up, uncertain where he was, and saw the brilliant whiteness of the houses patterned over by the palm fronds. There was a booming in the air, distant but heavy, and he knew it must be artillery. Pulling himself down into his sleeping-bag, he put his hands over his ears and sank back into sleep.

For most of the next day the convoy seemed alone in the desert. Occasion-ally a dispatch rider passed on a motorcycle and once a staff car came up behind them and went by with the speed of a police car. Then, in mid-morning, a pinkish smudge appeared on the horizon. Simon asked Vincent what he thought it was.

'Could be a sandstorm.'

The smudge, pale and indefinite at first, deepened in colour and expanded, swelling towards the convoy until, less than a mile away, it revealed itself as a sand cloud, rising so thickly into the heat fuzz of the upper air that the sun was almost occluded. Inside the cloud, the dark shapes of vehicles were visible. The first of them was a supply truck, lurching, top-heavy with mess equipment. The procession that followed stretched away to the horizon. Like the convoy, it moved slowly, creaking and clanking amid the stench of its own exhausts and petrol fumes. As they reached and passed it, Simon felt the heat from the vehicles that followed one after the other on the other side of the road.

Transports carried tanks that had lost their treads. Trucks towed broken-down aircraft or other trucks. Troop carriers were piled with men who slept, one on top of the other, a sleep of exhaustion. Guns, RAF wagons, recovery vehicles, armoured cars, loads of Naafi stores and equipment, went past, mile after mile of them, their yellow paint coated with sand, all unsteady, all, it seemed, on the point of collapse. As they moved nose to tail, they gave an impression of scrapyard confusion yet somehow maintained a semblance of order.

A staff car, that had pulled on to the wrong side of the road, brought the convoy to a halt. Major Hardy, striding towards it, shouted, 'What's going on? Is the whole damned army in retreat?'

Another major looked out of the disabled car, his face creased with weariness, and shouted back, 'No, it damn well isn't. The line's holding a few miles up the road. The Aussie 9th Division is rumoured to be on its way – and it better be. They're a mixed bunch back there: 8th Army, Kiwis, South Africans, a few Indians. How long they can hold out is anybody's guess.'

'But where's this lot going?'

'Ordered to prepare defences further east.'

'Where? The back gardens of Abou Kir?'

'Likely enough,' the major wiped the sweat from his face and gave a grin. 'We'll fight on the beaches.'

'This convoy's to report to 7th Motor Brigade. Any idea where that is?'

'Search me. Could be anywhere. It's hell and plain bloody murder where we came from.'

The obstructing car was pushed off the road to await a mechanic and the convoy went on, moving westward when it seemed that everything else in the world was going east. The breakdowns became more frequent. Every few hundred yards there was a halt and men were sent to push some vehicle away while Major Hardy questioned anyone he could find to question. He became more flustered, finding no one who knew or cared where the convoy might find its divisional headquarters. He shouted at Simon, 'Don't dog my heels, Boulderstone. Get a move on or we'll have another night on the road.'

They made what progress they could. Structures appeared beside the road, temporary and flimsy but suggesting that at last, among the muddle of wire and piled up stones, the tired newcomers might find their destination. Some sappers were at work on a crack in the tarmac and Simon, seeing them before Hardy had a chance to get to them, ran to make the usual enquiries. From their manner, he was uncertain whether they were telling him the truth or not. One sapper said, 'The Auk's down the road. Been standing there all day without his hat, just watching this ruddy circus go by. He'll tell you where to go.'

Simon doubted that but asked, 'What does he look like?'

'The Auk? Great man, ruddy hero. Big. Big chap. You can't miss 'im.'

The sappers, still laughing, stood back to let the convoy bump its way across the broken surface and drive on towards a red blur where the sun was beginning to set. The booming that had disturbed Simon the night before, now started again; a much more ponderous sound. Stars of red and green were rising into the sunset and Simon asked Vincent: 'Is that the front line?'

'No, the front's a good ten miles on.' They drove another mile. 'Think we'd better get down, sir?'

It was time to leaguer. The men sprang from the trucks, shaking the cramp from their legs, cheerfully congratulating each other as though they had reached home. The westbound traffic had been stopped by its own congestion and the dust had begun to settle. The air cleared but there was not much to see: only a vast plain, crimsoned by sunset, from which two columns of smoke, black as soot, rose into the blood-red brilliance of the sky.

2

At eight a.m., the hour when the Egyptian sun exploded in at the edges of shutters and curtains, Harriet Pringle heard an uproar outside her bedroom door. The noise was only one woman's voice – the voice of Madame Wilk, the proprietor of the pension – but so heightened was it by panic and outrage that Harriet jumped out of bed, certain that calamity was upon them.

Madame Wilk was shouting into the telephone, 'They were seen. How do I know who saw them? It is known everywhere. I am telling you – thousands of them, all broken and useless, the men dead to the world. I have friends in Heliopolis and they rang me. They said, "They're still coming. A terrible sight, a whole army in retreat".' Madame Wilk, her indignation growing, began to thump the door beside her, Harriet's door. 'Get up. Get up. You're finished, you British. The Germans are here already. Oh, oh, oh, what shall I do?' The voice rose into a funereal wail of such agony that Harriet opened the door.

Outside, Madame Wilk stood with the receiver still in her hand, a shrunken little monkey of a woman with large brown eyes, faded and swimming with tears. She was a Copt, married during the first war to a British officer who had gone home leaving her with nothing but a British passport. Now she realised that if the British were finished, she, too, was finished, and the tears overflowed from her wrinkled eyelids and trickled down her withered cheeks. 'All my shares is gone. What have I? What is to happen to me?'

'What will happen to any of us?' Harriet asked.

'You? – you will run away, but me! What can I live on? Here I have worked, I have saved for my old age. I bought my pension, I bought shares because of my good sense, and now what are they worth? Nothing. They're worth nothing.'

Major Perry, putting his head out of the room opposite, said 'They'll recover. The exchange goes up and down like a bally yo-yo.'

'What good my shares recover and me not here where my shares are?'

Major Perry's laughter distracted Madame Wilk so Harriet was able to close her door. She hurried to take her shower and dress so she could find the truth of this latest, frightful, rumour of retreat, then went out to the long hallway that was the heart and centre of the Pension Wilk. The hall served as dining-room and sitting-room (not that anyone would sit there for long), and the tables and chairs, lined along one wall, almost blocked the passage. Guest-rooms opened off on either side. They were small but each had a shower-room attached and this enabled Madame Wilk to claim for the pension 'luxury' status.

Windows were shuttered during the daylight hours and meals had to be taken by artificial light. Harriet found this oppressive but had to accept that in Egypt the sun was an enemy. If it were not excluded, the indoor heat would be intolerable. Still, she felt a sense almost of triumph when she found that a door in the hall had been left open and daylight shone on the breakfast tables. The door, propped open at dawn for the sake of ventilation, had to be closed, locked and bolted before the guests were up. Harriet had often heard Madame Wilk's voice raised when a safragi had forgotten to shut it, but this morning, with other things to scream about, Madame herself had forgotten the door. Walking through it for the first time, Harriet could see why she was so concerned to keep it shut. It led on to a flat roof. The Pension Wilk was at the top of a tall block of flats and Harriet, going to the edge of the roof, found that only a single rail ran between her and the drop down to the street. Conscious of daring, she stood by the rail and looked towards Giza, half expecting to see the defeated army wandering in past Mena House. But there was no army. She saw nothing but the pyramids, that were visible only in early morning and at sunset, looking as small as the little metal pyramids that were used as pencil sharpeners.

The morning was so still, it did not relate to war. The traffic had not started up and she could hear, from a hundred yards below her, the bell of a camel and the slap of the camel-driver's bare feet.

She moved round the roof, astonished by the extent and clarity of the view in this early sunlight. Soon the town would be hidden under heat but now she could see the small houses washing, like a sea of curdled foam, up to the cliff-face of the Mokattam Hills. Above them Mohammad Ali's alabaster mosque, uniquely white in this sand-coloured city, sat with minarets pricked, like a fat, white, watchful cat.

Once, before history began, a real sea had filled the basin and beaten up against the cliff. It drained away and then the ancient Egyptians had come to give to the human spirit beauty and dignity. As she reflected on those first Egyptians, cries came from the minaret nearest to her and at once all the air was filled with the long, wailing notes of the muezzins calling the faithful to prayer. The kites, roused from sleep, floated up from the buildings in unhurried flight and began to glide with gentle, dilatory grace just above the roof tops. Harriet looking down on them, saw they were not as they seemed from below, a muddy brown but, catching the sun on their feathers, they gleamed like birds cast from bronze.

She was startled by another voice that joined with the muezzins, the voice of Madame Wilk. 'Come in, Mrs Pringle, it is forbidden to be on the roof.'

'I'm quite safe, Madame Wilk.'

'It is not for you to be safe, Madame Pringle. If you fall and are killed, the police will make trouble for me. So, at once, come in.'

Harriet went in and Madame Wilk banged the bolts into place, saying, 'Ah, I have too many worries.'

Harriet sat down to partake of a breakfast that was always the same. It began with six large, soft, oversweet dates served in a little green glass dish. The next course would be a small egg that might be boiled, fried or poached but always had the same taste of damp and decay.

Harriet was, like most of the pension guests, on the lookout for somewhere to live yet, as she thought of having to leave Egypt, of having to move once again to an unknown country, even the Pension Wilk seemed a desirable resting place.

On her way out, Harriet stopped beside Major Perry's table to ask, 'How did Madame Wilk get the idea we are in retreat?'

Perry, whose face had been drooping, reacted to the question like a bad actor. Puffing out a stench of stale alcohol, he laughed, 'Ha, ha, ha. You know what Cairo's like! Some surplus equipment was returned to the depot at Heliopolis and the locals got the wind up. Just the usual scare and rushing to the telephone.'

'I didn't know we had any surplus equipment.'

'Stuff to be broken up for spares. The desert's littered with it.'

'So there's nothing to worry about?'

'Nothing, girlie, nothing. When we get reinforcements, it'll be as right as rain.'

Harriet laughed. 'That's fine, only it doesn't rain here, does it?'

Guy and Harriet had arrived in Egypt during another 'Emergency', almost exactly a year before the present one. Then, as now, the Germans had reached Sollum and were likely to come further, but the fact did not mean much to the refugees who had suffered a much more acute loss. They reached Alexandria still mourning for Greece and their memories of Greece, and Egypt evoked in them disgust and a fear of its strangeness.

Their train had drawn into the Cairo station at midnight and those who had money in Egypt found themselves taxis and went to hotels. The rest, having nothing but useless drachma, waited about, bemused, not knowing where to go or what to do. Eventually an army sergeant took charge of them. Telling them that quarters had been requisitioned for them, he led them a long way through back streets to a building as discouraging as a poor law institution. Here they were shown one dormitory for the women, another for the men and a single cold shower to be used by both. The dormitories with their iron bedsteads, army blankets, dismal lighting and smell of carbolic, had a prison atmosphere but no one complained. The refugees felt they had to put a good face on things and look grateful, imagining, until the manager brought round the bills, that they were the guests of the military. They learned later that the place had been a brothel until closed down by the army medical corps and the brothel-keeper, put out of business, was free to recoup his losses at the expense of the refugees. They would have paid no more at a first class hotel and Guy, trying to make light of things, said, 'Now we know what it means to be "gypped".'

No food was served in the building and the new arrivals, gathered next morning in the hall, expected the sergeant to return and lead them to an army canteen. He did not come. No one offered them help of any kind. It came to them gradually that now they must look after themselves.

The Pringles, standing in the hall with the others, were surprised to see

Professor Lord Pinkrose near the door. He was reputed to be a rich man but, ever ready to conserve his wealth, he had joined the penniless crew that looked to the army for succour. And here he was, breakfastless like the rest, but having an air of knowing what he was about. With him were two men whom Guy had employed as teachers at the institute in Bucharest.

They were called Toby Lush and Dubedat. Toby, in his usual get-up of old tweed jacket and baggy 'bags', was clicking his teeth impatiently on his pipe stem. He could not stay still. Seeing the manager, he held to him, saying, 'We ordered a taxi for ten o'clock. Not here yet. Keep an eye out for it, there's a good chap.' The other man, Dubedat, elevated his thin hooked nose, his expression stern, disassociating himself from Toby's restless shuffling and gasping while Pinkrose, gripping his trilby hat, looked down at his feet. The hat, that was usually on his head, had left an indenta- tion upon his strange, dog-brown hair.

The manager detached himself from Toby who said, 'I think he'll fix things for us.'

Pinkrose, lifting his grey lizard face out of the folds of his scarf, sniffed. 'I sincerely hope so. I made an appointment for ten-thirty and would not wish to be late. It is impendent upon us . . . yes, yes, impendent upon us to show respect for the man who holds the reins.'

Harriet whispered to Guy, 'What do you think they're up to?'

Guy, adjusting his glasses to look at them, said, 'Why should they be up to anything?'

'Oh, they're up to something, all right.'

Seeing Guy beaming on them with such good will, she said, 'Have you forgotten that Pinkrose reported you as unfit for Organisation work?'

'Did he? Oh, yes, I believe he did.'

'You know he did. As for the other two clowns – they went out of their way to discredit you in Athens.'

'They behaved badly,' Guy agreed but his expression remained benign.

The brothel had not been air-conditioned and the refugees were drowning in the indoor heat. Guy's face glistened and his glasses kept sliding down his nose. A big, untidy man with books in every pocket, he could not but be amiable. Cast up here together in this wretched billet, he saw Pinkrose, Dubedat and Lush as companions in misfortune and bore them no grudge.

53

Making a sudden bolt out into the street, Toby Lush came back in a state of blustering excitement. 'It's here. It's outside the next door house. It's been there all the time.'

When the three were gone, the Pringles began to realise that they could not stand for ever, lost and purposeless, in the dismal hall. Others were beginning to venture out into the dazzle and unnerving unfamiliarity of the Cairo streets. They needed money. They had eaten in the army canteen at Alex' andria and that had been their only meal in four days. They needed food but, even more, they needed reassurance.

Guy said, 'I ought to report to the Organisation office, wherever that is.' Harriet thought it would be easier to find the British Embassy. They set out. Reaching a crowded main road, they felt hostility in the heat and tumult and became reckless. They stopped a taxi and were grateful to the driver for taking them in. He drove them to the Embassy where Harriet had to remain outside as hostage while Guy went in and borrowed the fare. They had stopped beside an ornamental wrought-iron gate but Guy was not allowed that way. A porter directed him to a small side building which was the chancellery.

Harriet, gazing through the gate at the dry lawns and flower-beds, wondered how plant life survived at all under this blaze of sun. In Athens, when they left, gardens and parks had been massed with flowers, In the olive groves, under the trees, the flowers stood as high as one's waist. Would she ever see the like again?

Guy, who had gone nervously into the chancellery, came out waving an Egyptian pound note. 'We have a friend here.'

'Who?'

'Old Dobbie Dobson.'

They went joyfully in to see Dobbie Dobson who greeted them just as joyfully. They had not known him well but now it seemed wonderful that they had known him at all. Taking both of Harriet's hands, he put her into a chair and smiled at her. The greetings over, the Pringles seemed to come to a stop. They wanted nothing more than to sit for a while in Dobson's air-conditioned office, among the furnishings of Spanish mahogany, the polished brasswork, the sense of order and richness, and regain themselves, but Dobson had to hear what had happened to them.

Pulling themselves together, they described their escape, making humour out of the hungry voyage, the vermin, the lice in the cabins, the passages boarded up because the freighters had been prisoner transports, the useless lifeboats, with rusted in davits. Dobson laughed with them.

'Well, well, you're safe,' he said. 'That's the main thing.'

Looking out at the lawn running down to the river, Harriet glimpsed the possibility of a settled life in Cairo. But it was only a glimpse. Such a life had not been offered them here and she was too tired and on edge to pursue the thought of it.

They had not seen Dobson for seven months and it seemed to them he had aged beyond that time. He was putting on weight while Harriet and Guy had grown sadly thin. He had lost his tufts of baby-soft hair and the skin was beginning to darken beneath his eyes. Only his diplomat's charm had remained untouched by this injurious climate. He said, 'Well, now, you'll be wanting money.'

Guy agreed he needed money but more than that he wanted to know how the Organisation stood in Egypt. Who was in charge?

'You probably know the director. His name's Colin Gracey. He was in Athens at one time.'

Guy stared at Dobson and Harriet stared at Guy. Dobson could not have spoken a more disastrous name but, knowing nothing of affairs in Athens, he was merely puzzled by their dismay. Guy was too discomposed to speak and Harriet explained that Toby Lush and Dubedat had bolted to Athens, fearing an invasion of Bucharest, and had made themselves so useful to Gracey, he had actually put Dubedat in charge of the institute.

'Oh, no!' To Dobson this seemed beyond belief.

'Yes. Gracey was supposed to be an invalid – he had some sort of back trouble – and he managed to get a flight to Syria, leaving Dubedat and Lush in charge. I will say that Guy won in the end, but that won't help him now.'

'So there was a struggle for power in Athens!' Dobson looked at Guy. 'I can't think Gracey will hold it against you. You'll have to see him, of course.' Dobson, with no wish to involve himself in Guy's situation, was now extending tact rather than friendship.

Before Guy need speak, an Embassy servant came in with cups of Turkish coffee. The concentrated caffeine in the small cups was as stimulating as alcohol to someone who seldom drank coffee. Guy, as he emptied his cup, sat up sharply, his expression decided. 'I won't see Gracey and I will not work for him.'

Harriet, worn out by strain and their three hungry days, could scarcely keep back her tears. 'What are we to do? Where can we go?' Her voice broke on these questions and Guy hung his head. Yet he remained obdurate. He knew his own worth and had expected to find here a respons/ ible director who would appreciate his qualities. Instead he was again sub/ ordinate to a man he despised. Having once overcome Gracey's hangers/on, he would not now come to terms with his cabal. He said, 'I'm as highly qualified as Gracey, which is something he doesn't like. The only qualifica/ tion he looks for is willingness to flatter him and do his work for him. I won't flatter him.'

Harriet said, 'But others will. Now we know where those three were going this morning. "The man who holds the reins" – Gracey! How on earth did Pinkrose know that he was here?'

'I told him,' Dobson admitted. 'Pinkrose rang the Embassy this morning, about ten o'clock, and he was put on to me.'

'And wasted no time going to see Gracey,' Harriet put a hand on Guy's arm. 'Darling, you'll put yourself in the wrong if you don't go too.'

Guy, seeing her eyes were wet, conceded a little ground. 'If he wants to speak to me, he can send for me. But I won't work for him.'

Harriet appealed to Dobson. 'Guy's in a reserved occupation. What happens if he refuses work offered him? Will he be placed under arrest?'

Dobson laughed. 'Nothing as dreadful as that, but he'll have no salary.'

Seeing them displaced, homeless, moneyless and futureless, Harriet put her face down into her hands and Dobson, touched by her desolation, turned his persuasive charm on to Guy. 'I really think, my dear fellow, you should just go and see Gracey. After all, he *is* your senior official. It would be the courteous thing to do.'

Guy, shaken by this mention of courtesy, raised troubled eyes and at that moment the servant returned and handed Dobson an envelope. Passing it to Guy, Dobson said, 'This is for you: an advance on salary, sanctioned by Gracey.'

'He knows I am here?'

'Yes. While you were paying off the taxi, I spoke to the finance officer and he got on to the Organisation office. I knew you would want some cash.'

Guy held the envelope for a few moments then put it into his pocket, saying, 'It's due to me. It does not change things, but I will go to the office. As you say, it would be courteous to do so. Where can I find Gracey?'

'The offices are on Gezira. They're rather splendid.'

This fact did not impress Guy. 'We'll have something to eat and see him after that.'

'Don't go too early. Offices here shut for the siesta and don't open before five.'

Coming out to the chancellery with them, Dobson squeezed Harriet's shoulder. 'Cheer up. You're safe and well. As they say in the RAF: "Any prang you walk away from is a good prang". And Egypt's not too bad. You probably think it's weird but it has a certain macabre charm.'

He recommended them to a restaurant at Bulacq, noted for its river fish, and waved them away. The restaurant was underground with bare wooden tables and the fish tasted chiefly of mud, but food was food, and the Pringles were restored. Harriet, over coffee, commended Guy to his face for his warmth, good humour and generosity, telling him he had only to be himself with Gracey and Gracey would be won by him. He could get anything he wanted. And he should stop and think how fortunate he was. His sight unfitted him for the army, that was true, but he could be directed into a much worse job. While other young men were fighting a war, he was only asked to teach and lecture. The times being what they were, personal pride was out of place. Guy was forced to agree. He said, 'Well, if he offers me something, I'll take it,' and seeing him relent Harriet began to imagine the meeting with Gracey would put everything right. And so it may have done had Gracey been in his office at five o'clock.

There were two girls, Armenians, in the outer office and they apologised for Gracey's absence. They admitted he was due in at five, but could not say when he would arrive. One girl said, 'Sometimes he does not come at all.'

Questioning her, Guy discovered that Gracey had gone out that morning with three English visitors, one of them a lord. He had not been back since. The Pringles, if they wished, could wait in the hope that he would come in for his letters.

It was evident from their manner of speaking that the girls had very often to apologise for Gracey. Waiting for nearly two hours, the Pringles realised that here, as in Athens, Gracey treated the Organisation as a mere extension of his social life.

'But it is a splendid office,' Harriet said, trying to soften Guy's resentment of Gracey's behaviour. 'A flat like this would be wonderful, wouldn't it?'

The office was at the top of a block of flats that jutted into the river at the northern end of the island. The river, reflecting light into the rooms, grew red with sunset and in the distance the pyramids came into view. It seemed to Harriet they could do worse than remain in Egypt and live in a place like this, but Guy said, 'Don't be silly. We could never afford to live here.'

The sun set, darkness came down, the lights were switched on and the girls prepared to leave the office. But the Pringles could stay.

'Sometimes Mr Gracey is very late.'

Guy decided they would stay another fifteen minutes. At the end of that time, when he was about to give up, Gracey strolled in and stopped at the sight of him. With no one to warn him that there were visitors in the office, he looked startled and seemed about to take to his heels. Guy stood up. Gracey, unable to escape, gave him a cold nod and said, 'Please sit down', then went into his office where he could be heard slitting envelopes and shifting papers about before calling to the Pringles to enter.

He had adopted an air of languid dignity, unsmiling and weary. At first glance his appearance was not much changed. His fair, classical head looked youthful and his long, delicate body moved with grace but gradually the youthful impression crumbled. His hair was more grey than gold and his face had dried and was contracting into lines. Egypt had aged him, as it had aged Dobson, but more than that: it had depleted what Dobson had retained. In Athens, a spoilt invalid made much of by Cookson and Cookson's friend, Gracey had been all smiles and charm. Now he did not smile.

'Well, Pringle, what are we to do with you?'

Guy was silent, leaving Gracey to answer his own question. Gracey, apparently having no answer, frowned as though it were inconsiderate of Guy to survive the Greek campaign.

During the afternoon, which they had spent at the Metro cinema, Guy had reflected on all Harriet had said at luncheon. He knew he was privileged to be reserved in a congenial occupation. Unlike most men, his chances of surviving the war were high. The least he could do was submit and accept what came to him. Having decided this, he had one moment of weakness as they set out for Gezira: 'If only it wasn't Gracey!'

Harriet said, 'You despise Gracey, so the greater the glory in swallowing your pride and obeying him. Your political beliefs should tell you that.'

'Nonsense. You're thinking of religion, not politics.'

'What's the difference?'

'Darling, you're being silly.'

Gracey said, 'I suppose you want to stay in Egypt?'

'Is there any choice?'

'No, not really. Men have been turning up from all over Europe. I've had to make jobs for them or get some other director to take them. They've gone to Cyprus, Turkey, Palestine, the Sudan – anywhere they could be fitted in. I've had my work cut out, I can tell you.' Gracey looked aggrieved at the thought of the effort expended on the men from Europe and his glance at Guy seemed to say, 'And, now, here's another one.'

'There's not much scope for the Organisation in Egypt,' he said. 'Here they have the Public Instruction system – the PI, as it is called – that's been employing English teachers for years. There's no point in duplicating their work. We have the institute, but that merely offers straightforward teaching. I can see no opening for a lecturer like yourself.'

'I'm prepared to teach.'

'The fact is, we're overstaffed. We've a number of excellent Egyptian teachers of English.'

Harriet said, 'I believe Lush and Dubedat came here this morning. May I ask if you've taken them on?'

Gracey, challenged, lifted his chin and looked remote. 'I owe a lot to them. They did yeoman service for me in Athens.'

'So you're employing them here! What about Lord Pinkrose?'

'Lord Pinkrose is not seeking employment at the moment. He feels he should take a holiday and as this is a sterling area, he has the means to do so. He has, I believe, a considerable private fortune on which to draw.'

'If you cannot employ me,' Guy said, 'I must be repatriated. That is in my contract.'

'Contracts, I'm afraid, don't count for much these days. I cannot re-patriate you. There's no transport for civilians. The evacuation ships, and they are few and far between, take only women and children.'

'Then I suppose I can be released from my contract and find other work.'

'There's no question of your being released. The Organisation holds on to its men. You'll just have to wait till I can think of something for you.'

'Very well.'

The strain between the two men was evident and Harriet made an attempt to improve the situation by asking about Gracey's health. Was his back any better?

'I'm glad to say it is. Much better.' Unable to resist the chance to talk about himself, Gracey relaxed slightly as he described his treatment by a French orthopaedic surgeon in Beirut. 'Most successful, I must say – but not at first. The spine was in a bad way. It did not respond to rest so he put me into a plaster jacket and that did the trick. I wore it for three months. Not very pleasant and not flattering to the figure, but I had to bear with it. I still get a twinge or two if I exert myself. I have to take care but so long as I *do* take care, and rest, and don't overdo it, I can jog along. So . . .' Gracey rose and extended a hand to Guy. 'Come back in a week. By then I hope I shall have something to offer you.'

Away from the office, Harriet said, 'I think he was glad to get rid of us. Perhaps he really doesn't know what to do with you.'

'It's his job to know what to do with me.'

'Oh darling, don't quarrel with him. He's probably not as bad as we think.'

Guy shrugged, bemused by the fact that Harriet, more critical of the human race than he was, was also, in her way, more tolerant. If he lost faith, he lost it completely. Harriet had not much faith to lose.

Returning to their dismal quarters, Harriet knew the thing they most needed was a place of their own. She spent the week going round small hotels and pensions, finding them filled by army personnel. She was near despair when she was offered a room in the Pension Wilk. Madame Wilk, however, required a month's rent in advance and the Pringles, handing over most of their money, faced a period of anxious penury. The pension provided meals, of a sort, but between meals, if you had no money to spend, there was little enough to do. A general evacuation still threatened and Harriet, fearing they might leave Egypt with all its sights unseen, persuaded Guy to take the tram-car out to Mena House. Guy would scarcely give the pyramids a glance. He found them neither beautiful nor useful and said he did not like them.

Harriet, becoming cross in the heat and glare, asked: 'What *do* you like?'

They had wandered into a 'dig' left idle by war and Guy, tripping on the uneven ground, gave a disgusted glance about him and pointed to some small trucks used for transporting rubble. 'I like those. They remind me of the tips on the road to Dudley.'

The pyramids observed, not much remained. The museum was

shut for the duration. Someone told them about the City of the Dead, a favourite gharry trip by moonlight, but Guy rejected it as 'a morbid show'.

When he returned to the Organisation office, he was told that Gracey had left Cairo. He had, in fact, left Egypt. Only one of the girls remained in the outer office and she looked embarrassed as Guy faced her, dumbfounded by Gracey's defection. He had gone to the office in hope of employment to fill his empty days, and now what was he to do? Where had Gracey gone? Gracey had gone to Palestine. As Palestine did not come under the authority of the Cairo office, Guy asked, 'Has he gone on holiday?'

'He say "on a tour of inspection".'

'What does that mean?' The girl shook her head. 'How long will he be away?'

'I do not know how long. Perhaps a long time. It depends.'

'On what?'

'On what is happening. The war, you know. If the Germans come too close, people go to Palestine.'

'I see. And who is doing his work while he is away?'

The girl shook her head again. Guy, at a loss, asked for a piece of pape and wrote the address and telephone number of the Pension Wilk. He asked her to let him know when she had news of Gracey's return. She looked sadly at the paper and said in her small, mournful voice, 'I am so sorry but after tomorrow I shall not be here. The office is closed when Mr Gracey is away.'

Until then the Pringles had scarcely given a thought to the emergency. The English residents in Cairo were flustered but to the refugees, still caught up in the tensions of the Greek defeat, the desert war seemed a trivial matter. Calamity for them was the German occupation of Athens and many of them wept as they heard the final broadcast from the Greek radio station: 'Closing down for the last time, hoping for happier days. God be with you and for you.'

The silence that followed was, for them, the silence of the civilised world.

Most of the refugees had no wish to stay in Egypt. Most of them went to Palestine and from there managed to make their way to India, Persia or South Africa. Some, it was rumoured, even managed to get back to England. Those who could not afford to travel on their own, began to talk about a possible official evacuation, seeing it as a solution of a vacuous life spent mostly in small underground bars, the only places they could afford where they were out of the appalling sun.

The bars, that had adopted names like the *Britannia* or the *George* to entice in the troops, sold Stella beer for which Guy acquired a taste. His closest friend in those dire days was Ben Phipps who had been a freelance journalist in Athens. Now, having reached a major war zone, he decided to offer himself to the London papers as a correspondent. He sent out eight cables to Fleet Street, claiming to be an expert on Middle East affairs, but replies were slow in coming.

Resentful of his own displacement, Ben Phipps was scornful of the English who lived richly in Egypt. 'A bloody good thing if the whole lot are given the boot. Let them know what it's like to live out of a suitcase.'

'What good will that do us?' Harriet asked.

Ben's small, black eyes jumped angrily behind pebble glasses. 'We'd all be in the same boat. That's what.'

Harriet had to agree that calamity had its uses. If they ended up together in Iraq or the Sudan, Gracey would have no more power than Guy.

Two days later a London evening paper cabled, appointing Ben Phipps its Middle East correspondent. A dramatic change came over him. He no longer despised the English who had done well in Egypt. He no longer hoped for a general evacuation. Though the Middle East situation had had for all of them as much structure and relevance as a cage full of flies, Ben now talked knowingly of desert strategy and the need to hold the Levant as bulwark against the loss of the Persian Gulf oil.

He left Cairo kitted out in khaki shorts and shirt and carrying the old portable typewriter he had brought from Greece. Guy and Harriet went with him to the train. 'Off into the blue, eh?' he said with relish, looking pityingly at the Pringles who would be left behind.

Guy, unable to believe his friend had gone, said he was sure he would be back in no time. But not only Ben Phipps had gone. One by one the remaining refugees found means to go elsewhere. Soon no one known to the Pringles was left in the bars. There was no one with whom to talk through the slow, dispiriting hours between meals. No one with whom to discuss the tricks by which the penurious supported life in Cairo. No one to ask for news.

This idle and purposeless life disturbed Guy and Harriet in different ways. Harriet longed for a home more spacious than the small, cluttered room at the pension but Guy, who had often in his youth had no home at all, only wanted employment and friends. Perhaps he wanted employment most. He was ashamed to be idle while other men were at war. He tried to outwit his workless state by planning lectures, concerts for troops, productions of Shaw or Shakespeare, but could do none of these things. He was without status, acquaintances and the means to carry out his plans.

Soon after Ben's departure, Guy picked up with Bill Castlebar who lectured at the Cairo university. Castlebar occasionally went to the bars but preferred the Anglo–Egyptian Union which he recommended to the Pringles. Because they had once or twice mentioned Dobson, he was uncertain where they belonged in the social hierarchy and gave his advice with a hint of irony. 'You may think you're a cut above the Union, but there are worse places. The Sporting Club has more to offer, of course – polo, racing, gambling, swimming. You'd meet the local nobs there but it costs a lot of money to play with them. Perhaps you can afford it?' Reassured on this point, he said, 'The Union's not smart but the conversation's a great deal livelier.'

'Can one get beer there?' Guy asked.

'Get beer! You can not only get it, you can get it on tick. *They let you sign for it.*'

Introduced into the Union, the Pringles sat under the trees and knew they had found their asylum. The Union, that shared the vast lawns of Gezira, existed to promote friendship between the Egyptians and their British rulers, but few Egyptians appeared there. The British scholastics, from the university lecturers who were fairly well off to the PI teachers who lived just above the poverty line, kept the place going. There was a club house and library and a belt of ancient trees of immense height that shaded the outdoor tables and chairs. As Castlebar pointed out, you could sit there all day and no one questioned your right. In a country where the ruling caste was expected to maintain aristocratic standards, the Union succoured the English poor.

Here Guy found company, the company usually being Castlebar and Castlebar's friend Jackman. He was immediately at home with them and Harriet accepted them, realising that they were exactly the sort of dissidents Guy would pick up wherever he went. He was entertained by Castlebar who wrote limericks, but had a much greater respect for Jackman. This puzzled Harriet until she learnt that Jackman had told Guy, in the greatest possible confidence, that he had fought in Spain in the International Brigade. Harriet felt an instinctive doubt of this claim and said, 'Why don't you ask Castlebar if it's true?'

'Castlebar knows nothing about it. Of course it's true, but he has to keep it dark. It wouldn't do him any good in a place like this if it got around.'

Six weeks passed without news of Gracey and Guy, existing in a state of desperate suspension, began to hate his director and to see Cairo as a centre of waste and imprisonment. He discussed Gracey with Castlebar and Jackman and they encouraged him in a revolt of ribaldry.

If they did not know Gracey, they knew about him. In Cairo, he lived as the permanent house guest of a rich Turk, Mustapha Quant (called by Jackman 'Mustapha Kunt') who maintained him in decadent splendour in a houseboat on the Nile. Their stories about Quant, Gracey and the parties given for male friends only were a delight to Guy who felt justified in ridiculing his director to all comers.

Harriet, made uneasy, said, 'Let's stop talking about Gracey,' but Guy had reached the point of anxiety in which talk was the only release. It was terrible to Harriet to see Guy's good sense overthrown. And if Gracey did not return, he might be held here in a despairing limbo until the war ended.

He exploded out of this condition one morning, coming from the shower, flapping his bath-towel about in his excitement, shouting, 'Listen to this.'

> There's Wavell of the desert,
> There's Tedder of the planes,
> But I'm Gracey of Gezira,
> I'm the man that holds the reins.
>
> I live in style with Mustaph,
> Our houseboat it is fine,
> But if Rommel looks like coming here,
> I move to Palestine.

'Don't you think it's funny?'

'Not very. And for God's sake don't put it around.'

'Of course I won't,' Guy assured her but when he composed another verse, he had to recite it to Jackman.

> They say Christ walked on water
> On the Sea of Galilee,
> But I'm Gracey of Gezira,
> No water walks for me.

The song, for Guy was now singing it to a music-hall tune of no origin-
ality, amused not only Castlebar and Jackman but anyone sitting near them
at the Union. Harriet, torn between pride in Guy and fear of reprisals,
begged those who heard the song not to repeat it. 'If if got back to Gracey,
Guy could be in real trouble.'

'Who would tell Gracey anything?' said Jackman, pulling his long nose
and shifting his thin backside about as he sniggered, acting amusement
without any amusement in his eyes.

People who barely knew Guy congratulated him on his temerity in
composing the song. The word 'temerity' alerted Guy to his own rashness
yet he remained defiant. Life was precarious and he might not have any
future to worry about.

Then the atmosphere changed. The British had retaken Sollum and were
chasing Rommel out of Egypt. Though Cairo seemed to them as empty
and crowded as a railway junction, they would have to settle down there.
Harriet started looking for a job.

Guy learnt of Gracey's return from Toby Lush. Toby, coming along the
crowded pavement with his trotting walk, saw Guy and was about to rush
across the road when Guy caught his arm. 'Where have you been?'

Toby sprang back, pretending to ward off a blow. 'Hey, old cock, don't
eat me.' His face slopping about like bilge water in his attempt to appease
Guy and also impress him, Toby said that he, Dubedat and Pinkrose had
gone on a sightseeing tour of upper Egypt. 'Pinkers hired a car and I did the
driving. Amazing what we saw. Gracey joined us two weeks ago and we
all came back together.'

'Perhaps now Gracey'll let me know what he has in mind for me.'

'He will, old cock, but you've got to realise he's a lot on his plate. Trouble
is, you said you didn't want to work in Cairo.'

'I said nothing of the sort.'

'Been a bit of misunderstanding, then, but don't worry. I'll put in a word
for you. And I say,' Toby became alert and encouraging, 'what's that song
you wrote: "Gracey of Gezira"? The old soul roared when he heard it
He said it'd be the institute's theme song.' The 'old soul' was Dubedat.

Aware, at last, of his own unwisdom, Guy said, 'Don't tell Gracey
about it.'

Toby spluttered on his pipe with joy, 'Don't worry. You know Gracey.
He's got a great sense of humour. He'll love it.'

When Guy went to Alexandria, Harriet, who had started work at the American Embassy, remained in Cairo. With two incomes, the Pringles could keep their double room at the Pension Wilk and be together at weekends. They regarded the mid-week separation as temporary. Either Guy would be permitted to return or Harriet would go to him.

At the Embassy, Harriet was known as the Assistant Press Officer. The title sounded important but she was merely a stop-gap employee and, sooner or later, the press office would be taken over by a team flown out from the States. The team was slow in coming. Harriet had been in her position for nearly a year when the latest, and most fearful, emergency arose in the desert. By then she had become as knowledgeable about the war as Ben Phipps. She was generally held to have inside information and people would stop her in the street to ask for news. But she was still temporary, and not only temporary but a member of an inferior race.

Having grown up in the belief that Britain was supreme in the world and the British the most fortunate of people, she had been shocked to find that to the Americans she was an alien who rated less than a quarter of the salary paid to an American-born typist. She protested to her superior, a Mr Buschman, saying, 'I'm not an alien – I'm British.' Mr Buschman liked this so much that he managed to get her a rise in salary. The rise was not great but it reconciled her to her alien degree and the working hours that had been imposed on the staff after Pearl Harbour. Entering the war with the enthusi-asm of late-comers, the Americans decided on an 'all-out' war effort. The other Cairo establishments closed from noon till five o'clock, but the Americans decided to work through the afternoon. Given an hour for luncheon, the employees returned to the Embassy when the whole city lay motionless in a stupor of heat.

Mr Buschman, a young married man, neatly built, not tall, with a flat, pale, pleasant face, was both fatherly and flirtatious with Harriet. He once tried to span her waist with his hands and nearly succeeded. Then he measured it with a tape and said, 'Twenty-two inches. I like that.' He asked her what she weighed. When she said 'Seven stone', he worked it out and said, 'Exactly one hundred pounds. I like that, too.'

And Harriet liked Mr Buschman. She particularly liked the way he called her 'Mem' as though she were Queen Victoria, and she felt an affectionate trust in him until the day when the German radio put out a threat to Cairo. At half-hourly intervals, a voice said, 'Tonight we will bomb Cairo off the face of the earth.' The threat was in English and Arabic and Harriet's translator, Iqal, bringing her this item, said, 'You see, Mrs Pringle, how they are seeking to frighten us!' Short and stout, with the heavy shoulders of a water-buffalo, Iqal shrugged so his shoulders rose in a hump behind his head. 'We are not much frightened, I think.'

The American staff did not seem frightened, either. Mr Buschman made no comment when he went through the news sheets that contained the repeated threat to destroy Cairo but when she left the office that evening, Harriet saw the Embassy cars gathered outside, prepared for flight. Next morning, the cars were not there. The Embassy seemed empty except for Harriet. Iqal and the Levantine girl typists. When Iqal came in with the first news sheets, Harriet asked him, 'Where is everybody?'

'You do not know, Mrs Pringle?' Iqal was eager to tell her what she did not know. 'Our American friends went for a night picnic in the desert, but now the danger is over, doubtless they will return.'

Iqal's grin held only a trace of irony. To him the actions of his employers were above criticism but Harriet was struck through by a sense of betrayal.

'Mr Buschman said nothing to me about the danger.'

'Nor to me, Mrs Pringle.'

Harriet had to realise that so far as Mr Buschman was concerned, she and Iqal were equally alien and equally dispensable. Now, with the Afrika Korps outside Alexandria, the Embassy cars were again assembled, packed and ready for a getaway, but this time she was less hurt by the sight of them. Mr Buschman remained, as he always was, cordial and kind, but she knew now that his cordiality had its practical side. He was concerned for the safety of the American staff but need not worry about aliens. The American staff had diplomatic protection and could leave, if they had to leave, in their own time. Their preparations were against the possibility of bombing, street-fighting or an Egyptian rising, all the risks of a base town caught up in active warfare.

The Americans, protected and prepared, remained calm. Only Iqal showed disquiet. On the morning of Madame Wilk's outburst, he said to Harriet, 'What do you British do with my country, Mrs Pringle? You come here to rule yet when the enemy is at the gate, you run away.'

'I haven't run away, Iqal.'

'No, but many have. And what of your officers who disport themselves at the Gezira swimming-bath! Where are they now?'

Harriet made a wry face, knowing that one of the sights at Cairo at that time was the queue of officers, half a mile long, waiting to draw their money from Barclay's Bank. Having confounded her, Iqal was at once contrite and good-humoured and showed her a news item he had been holding back. 'See here, Mrs Pringle,' he began to giggle wildly, 'here they say the Afrika Korps reach Alexandria tonight. They send a message to the ladies of Alexandria and this is what they say: "Get out your party dresses and prepare to defend your honour". Oh-ho, Mrs Pringle, oh-ho!' Iqal's thick dark finger quivered with excitement as he pointed to the item. 'These Germans are not deceived. Alexandria is a place of brott-ells.'

'How do you feel about a German occupation, Iqal?'

Faced with this direct question, Iqal at once became grave and declama-tory. 'You ask me, Mrs Pringle, how do I feel? That is an interesting consideration. What do these Germans promise us? – they promise freedom and national sovereignty. What are those things? And what are these Germans? They are invaders like all the invaders that have come here for one thousand four hundred year. They come, they go, the English no worse than others. But to govern ourselves! – that we have forgotten, so how do we do it? And why should we believe these Germans, eh? For myself, I am brushing up my German to be on the safe side, but all the time I am asking myself, "Better the devil we know". In their hearts, Mrs Pringle, the Egyptian people wish you no harm.'

'You mean, too many people are doing too well out of us?'

'Ah, Mrs Pringle, I see you know a thing or two.'

'Well, one thing I do know, the Germans won't get to Alexandria. The British always fight best with their backs to the wall, and we can't afford to lose the Middle East.'

'Can't afford? Deary me, Mrs Pringle, how many people can't afford? The French, the Poles, the Dutch – could they afford?'

'Don't forget, Iqal, we have the Americans with us now.'

At this mention of his employers, Iqal sobered and nodding in reverential appreciation of this truth, he whispered, 'Ah, it is so!'

Harriet worked in a basement area too large to be called a room. Mr Buschman sat at a desk between the French windows at the back. Harriet, who had an alcove to herself, was in charge of a map of the eastern hemisphere that covered the whole of one wall. Her daily job was to mark the potition of the combatants with pins. There were blue-headed pins for the allied forces, red for the Russians and Chinese, and black for the Axis. Recently, having had to order them, Harriet had obtained yellow pins for the Japanese.

On the morning when news came of Pearl Harbour, Harriet had gone to work in high spirits, seeing the war as more or less over. She found Mr Buschman in quite a different state. White-faced and trembling, he said over and over again, 'The bastards! The God-damn bastards!'

Harriet said, 'Well, it's something definite. You'll have to come in now.'

Mr Buschman struck his desk in rage. 'Definite? God-damn, it's definite all right. We'll make the bastards pay. We'll blow them right out of the water.'

But the Japanese were advancing and Harriet, sticking yellow pins into Wenchow and Gona, began to feel that the only change brought about by the American intervention in the war was the change in her working hours.

That day, leaving the office at one o'clock, she met Jakeman who asked her the usual question: 'Any news?'

Harriet shook her head.

'Where's Guy! Not still in Alex? I'd get him out of there if I were you.'

Jakeman drooping, with concave chest and shoulders hunched, kept his hands in his pockets as he talked. He had a thin, almost aesthetic, face, not unhandsome, but spoilt by a surly expression and the long nose that he was always stroking and pulling as though to make it longer. Looking at the ground in his hang-dog way, he said, 'I can tell you this, Rommel won't bother to take Alex. He'll cut it off by going round the back. When that happens, it'll fall of its own accord. No help for it. No supplies. Nothing. They'll be starved into surrender. You ring Guy and tell him to take the next train to Cairo. Here he'll have a chance. There – not a hope in hell. Tell him if he tries to stick it out, he'll only end in the bag. And a lot of good that'll do him, you or anyone else.'

Jakeman began to make off while Harriet was asking, 'What are we to do?' He looked over his shoulder to shout at her, 'When they get here, grab a car and race for the canal . . .'

'*If* they get here.'

'Nothing can stop them now.'

Harriet was the only guest taking luncheon at the pension. At the other end of the hall, almost invisible in the weak electric light, Madame Wilk sat at her table. Two tables away from Harriet sat Miss Copeland who appeared at the pension once a week. Today was her day. She would lay out a little haberdashery shop on one of the tables then, sitting in the silence of the deaf, she waited to be given her luncheon, tea and supper. After that she packed up and went to some mysterious living place. She sold sanitary towels to the younger women at the pension, passing them over, wrapped in plain paper, with a secrecy that suggested a conspiracy. No one knew how long she had lived in Cairo. Harriet, who was curious about her, had learnt that years before, when Miss Copeland still had her tongue, she used to tell people that she was related to an English ducal family. Some people got together and wrote to the head of the family on Miss Copeland's behalf, but there was no reply. She was now very old and her skin, tautly stretched over frail old bones, had the milky blueness of chicken skin. Each week it seemed she could not survive to the next, yet here she was, silent and pre-occupied, remote from the panic of the times. She went through her luncheon with the intensity of someone to whom a meal was a rare and wonderful treat.

Luncheon ended, as breakfast had begun, with six dates in a green glass dish. Harriet took her coffee over to Madame Wilk's table and whispered, although Miss Copeland was in no danger of hearing her, 'Does she know about the emergency?'

Madame Wilk gave her head a severe shake.

Miss Copeland's cottons, tapes, needles and pins were laid out this week, as every week, in orderly rows beside a red and white chequered Oxo tin for money, when there was any money.

'What's to be done about her?'

Madame Wilk spread her hands. 'God knows.' She and Harriet kept their heads together, fearing to disturb Miss Copeland's happy ignorance of events. She might have to be told, but not yet.

Harriet set out for work through streets coagulated with heat and empty of movement. Labourers and beggars lay in a sort of sun syncope, pressed against walls, arms over eyes, galabiahs tucked between legs to avoid any accidental exposure of the parts that religion required them to keep hidden.

Sweat trickled like an insect between her shoulder blades and soaked the waistband of her dress. She could smell the scorched smell of her hair. And about her there were other smells, especially the not altogether unpleasant smell that came from waste lots saturated with human ordure and urine. Cairo was full of waste lots: dusty, brick-strewn, stone-strewn, hillocky sites where a building had collapsed from age and neglect. The smell that came from them was nothing like the salty, pissy smell of an European urinal. It was rancid and sweet like some sort of weed or first war gas. Harriet thought of phosgene, though she did not know what it was like. She had read somewhere of soldiers mistaking the smell of a may tree for poison-gas.

On her solitary walks to afternoon work, Harriet had had odd experiences, induced perhaps by the mesmeric dazzle of the light. Once or twice, she had lost the present altogether and found herself somewhere else. On one occasion she was in a landscape which she had seen years before, when riding her bicycle into the country. It was an ordinary English winter landscape: a large field ploughed into ridges that followed the contours of the land, bare hedges, distant elms behind which the sky's watery grey was broken by gold. She could smell the earth on the wind. There was a gust of rain, wet and cold on her face – then, in an instant, the scene was gone like a light switched off, and she could have wept for the loss of it.

Once an old man, white bearded, of noble appearance, had stopped her and held out his hand. He was wearing priestly robes and a green fez. They talked for a while about life and her reasons for being in Egypt, then he asked her to marry him, saying he had had many wives in a long life but never one who would go out in the heat of mid-day without a covering on her head. She asked how it was his fez was green while all others were red and he said he had had it specially made for him to indicate to the world that he was a descendant of the prophet. He was a jocular old man and they parted with a lot of laughter.

Now, reaching Suleiman Pasha where the shop blinds were pulled down but doors were ajar in case custom should come, unlikely though it was, Harriet saw ahead of her a single living creature. It was a man in khaki shirt and shorts, a lost British soldier, hung over with baggage. When he reached the Midan, he sank down on the steps of an office block and began pulling the straps off his shoulders. Beneath the straps, under his armpits, in every crevice of his clothing the cloth was black with sweat. He was wiping his face when Harriet approached him.

The large buildings of the Midan threw one side of the square into shadow so deep it gave an illusion of darkness. Although the sky was a pure cerulean blue, the eye, reacting against excess of light, covered it with a dark film. The banks and office blocks, ponderously imitating western buildings, seemed as flimsy as theatre flats. The whole Midan might have been made of cardboard, not painted but blotted over and bloated with grey, black or umber dye, uneven and dimmed by dust.

Seeing Harriet, the soldier called out, 'Excuse me, miss. You English? I thought so. Strange how you can tell.' He plashed his hand over his pink brow, drew it down his cheeks and shook the sweat from his fingers. 'I missed the transport, Went to the barracks and they say I got to wait till seventeen hundred hours. Thought I'd look around but what a place! I was just saying to m'self "Where do you go now, chum? What's to see and do around here?"'

Harriet, looking about her, wondered what there was to see and do in the wide, empty streets of Cairo at this hour. She told him: 'There's the Rivoli cinema not far from here. It's air-conditioned and so chilly, you might catch a cold. I've caught cold myself there.'

'Can't be too chilly for me.' The soldier rose and looking her over said with jaunty fervour, "Spose you wouldn't come with me?'

She smiled, knowing to these lost men an Englishwoman, any Englishwoman, was not an individual but a point of contact with desirable life. 'I'm sorry. I have to go back to work, but I'll walk part of the way.'

'Right-e-o.' He put the straps back and with all his belongings lurching around him, went with her towards Fuad al Awal. Eyeing her with some curiosity, he said, 'Funny meeting someone from England, just like that! What you doing here, then?'

'Egypt's full of English people. My husband has a job here.'

'Oh, yes?' At the mention of a husband the soldier retreated into respectfu silence and Harriet, to start him talking again, asked how he had come to miss his transport.

'It was like this, see. Me and my mates went down into one of those bars and had a few beers and I passed out. Not in the bar, mind you. I went in – well, if you'll excuse me mentioning it – I went in the toilet. They didn't know I'd passed out, did they? I mean, I could've gone after a bint, couldn't I? Can't blame them, can you?'

'No, it could happen to anyone.'

'That's right.'

She could see how pained he had been at finding himself deserted and how much he needed company, but she was late already. Pointing to the cinema, she said regretfully, 'I have to go the other way.' Before she turned the next corner, she looked back and saw him standing like an eager dog, staring after her, hoping she would change her mind.

At the Embassy the only sign of life was the hopping of the hoopoes in and out of the garden sprays. Mr Buschman always played golf in the middle of the day and, coming rather late to the office, would put salt tablets into a large glass of water and drink it with a grimace. Lined up on his desk in different coloured boxes were pills and capsules which he called vitamins. Harriet had never heard of salt tablets or vitamins and Mr Buschman, amused by her innocence, said, 'They're sent out to us through the bag. They look after us, you see.' The vitamins were distributed among the American staff but not, of course, the aliens.

Looking over the news sheets, Mr Buschman laughed aloud. ' "Defend their honour" – that's rich!'

Harriet had tried to ring Guy from the pension and had been told that all the lines to Alexandria were engaged. She decided that if she could not reach him by telephone, she must go to him, and she said to Mr Buschman, 'I've been trying to get in touch with my husband but can't get hold of him. He ought to leave Alexandria . . .'

'Don't worry, mem. He'll leave when he's ordered to leave.'

'There's no one to order him. The director's gone to Palestine, the office is shut – but he doesn't know this. He's alone up there. He'll just wait expecting to receive orders that won't come, and he'll be trapped.'

Harriet gulped and Mr Buschman, putting a hand on her shoulder, said, 'Hey, hey, mem, don't cry. Give the girls his number and tell them to ring it every five minutes till they *do* get through.'

'But, Mr Buschman, if they can't get him, I'll have to take a day off and go up to Alex and tell him how things are.'

'You do just that, mem,' Mr Buschman gave her shoulder a squeeze and his kindness, his concern, his ready willingness to help her, rayed from his face like love. Much moved, Harriet asked him to come over and look at the wall map. She pointed to the two sets of pins, one in the desert, the other in the Ukraine, converging on the Middle East like two black claws. 'You see what it is, Mr Buschman: it's a giant pincer movement.'

Mr Buschman stared at the map and slowly shook his head. 'Looks like it. But don't forget, mem, that's only a map. There's a mighty big bit of territory between those pincers.'

'Yes, they've a long way to come but the Germans move quickly.' Harriet had seen the German news films in Bucharest. She had seen the golden-haired boys standing up in their tanks, singing, 'What does it matter if we destroy the world? When it is ours, we'll build it up again,' as they drove with all speed on to Paris. She thought how quickly they could eat up that almost unguarded territory between the pincers. 'If the Ukraine collapses, what's to stop them? We can't even keep them out of Egypt.'

Nonplussed, Mr Buschman stared, rubbing his hand across the back of his neck, then went back to his desk leaving Harriet unassured. She saw the Middle East cracking between the pincers like a broken walnut and asked herself: what would happen then? She tried to work out on the map the strategy of defeat. The British troops, she supposed, would retreat into Iraq and make a last stand in defence of the Persian Gulf. But suppose there were no troops? Supposing the whole of 8th army was caught between the converging pincers and not one man remained to retreat and defend what was left? What would they do then? There was almost relief at the thought of it. Responsibility would cease. They would not have to run away again.

The exchange girls, unable to reach Guy, told Harriet: 'It's the business men. They ring all the time because they are nervous. And they're already talking to each other in German.'

Harriet decided to appeal to Dobson. When she left her work, other people were returning to theirs. It was the rush hour and the most oppressive time of the day. Heat, compacted between the buildings, stuck to the skin like cotton wool. The roads were noisy with traffic and the workers, unwillingly roused out of their siestas, were rough and irritable. Bunches of men hung like swarming bees at the tram-car doors, clinging to rails and to each other. When a car swerved round a corner, several were thrown off but falling lightly, they picked themselves up and waited to get a handhold on the next. The richer men, to avoid this rabble, fought for taxis and Harriet, knowing she could not compete, decided to walk down to the river.

The pavements were more crowded than usual. Some of the men were so new to commerce that they still wore the galabiah but most of them had managed to fit themselves out with trousers and jackets. Some had even taken to wearing the fez. Many were pock-marked or had only one seeing eye, the other being white and sightless from trachoma; many were enervated by bilharzia, but they were all rising in the world, leaving behind the peasants and the back street balani from whom they derived.

Harriet stopped to look in the windows of a closed-down tourist agency. She saw, dusty and cracking with heat, the posters that used to draw the rich to Egypt: the face of the Sphinx, the lotus columns of Karnac, the beautiful and tranquil Nile with the feluccas dipping in the wind. She sadly thought, 'Goodbye, Egypt', but at that moment a familiar sensation came into her middle and she knew she was in for another attack of 'Gyppy tummy'. The sensation, that was not altogether pain, appeared in her mind as a large pin – not an ordinary pin but, for some reason, an open safety pin – which turned slowly and jabbed her at intervals. She thought over what she had had for luncheon. In this country one ate sickness. She could not blame Madame Wilk who was always telling the cook to wash his hands. The cook would reply, 'Sa-ida, we wash our hands all the time. It is our religion to wash our hands.' And so it was. Harriet had seen the men at the mosque putting a finger or two into the pool and giving a token splash inside their galabiahs. Madame Wilk said, 'What am I to do? I can't follow them when they go places.' Nor could she. So Egypt was not only the Sphinx, the lotus columns, the soft flow of the Nile, it was also the deadening discomfort and sickness that blurred these sights so, in the end, one cared for none of them.

Harriet reached the Embassy's wrought-iron gates as the sun was dropping behind Gezira and a mist like smoke hung over the river. Passing into the mist, she realised it really was smoke. The atmosphere was heavy with burning. Inside the Embassy garden, she saw a bonfire and the Embassy men and women, Dobson and Edwina among them, bringing out trays and bags of papers. Servants were feeding the papers to the fire and the gardeners were poking them about with rakes to keep them alight. This activity was solemn, yet not quite solemn. Edwina was making some remark and everyone laughed. They had their immunity, after all. Whatever happened, they would get away alive.

Dobson looked towards her and she waved to him. He crossed to the gate with a smiling amiability as though the paper burning was a social ceremony and Harriet might be welcomed in. Instead, as she was about to speak, he came out to join her and suggested they stroll along the embankment. 'My eyes are watering from the smoke. Let's get out of it.'

Dobson's air was, as it always was, insouciant and she said, 'Just now I was thinking of the prewar tourists who seemed to be immune to bacillary dysentery. And you, you're immune to the enemy.'

Dobson laughed. 'One of the perks of the profession.'

'Well, I want your help. Guy's not immune, as you know, and he's on the outskirts of Alexandria where he'll have little idea of what's going on. I can't get through to him on the phone. What are we supposed to do?'

Dobson came to a stop and stood with his back to the embankment wall. At this end of the river walk a group of banyans had grown from the path and dropping their branches down, had rooted themselves on all sides. There was a whole complicated cage of banyans, their silvery, tuberous trunks looking immensely old. The intertwining of branches to roots and roots to branches had left a central cage and Dobson stepped into it, looking up at the knotted roof as though seeing the banyans for the first time. While he stood there, apparently reflecting on Guy's position, a rain of charred paper fragments came floating down and with half his attention on the paper, he said, 'I suppose Gracey's in touch with him?'

'No,' Harriet spoke sharply to regain Dobson's whole attention. 'Gracey's gone, probably to Palestine. Anyway, we've no means of contacting him. The office is shut.'

'Oh!'

Smoke darkened the sunset but the smoky air was rich with the rose colours of evening and through it, wavering like a child's kite, a half sheet of headed paper sank and settled, just out of reach, in the banyan branches. Peering up at it, Dobson said, 'Oh, dear!'

'Is it a fact that Rommel is only one day's drive from Alex?'

'So it seems, but there's no immediate cause for anxiety. If Alex is evacuated, the military will bring the English civilians out, I'm pretty sure.'

'But there may not be time to evacuate the civilians. And if the town is cut off, no one will get away.'

Dobson smiled. 'We've got a navy, you know.'

Harriet was not sure whether he was laughing at her or not. Probably in the face of the fall of Alexandria, Guy's fate seemed to him, as it would to most people, a minor matter. But it was not minor to her and Dobson, all in all, was a kindly man. After a moment's reflection, he said, 'I'll tell you what I'll do. If I can get the Embassy line cleared this evening, I'll give him a tinkle and advise him to be on the alert.'

'Thank you. But much better to tell him to come to Cairo.'

'I can't very well do that. Not my territory, you know, but I'll warn him that the situation's serious.'

And that, she realised, was as much as she could hope for from Dobson who now had to get back to his bonfire. But the bonfire was dying in the twilight and the girls were going home. Dobson paused inside the gate to say, 'Though there's no cause for panic, I really think you'd do well to leave Cairo. Most of the women and children are being packed off. There's a special train taking anyone who wants to go. It leaves about nine tomorrow morning.'

'But if there's no cause for panic . . .'

'No *immediate* cause. No one's being forced to go at the moment, but there could be a God-almighty flap if and when they are. If you leave in good time, you'll be spared the turmoil. We just want to clear the decks, in case . . . Then, if the situation rights itself, you'll have had a free holiday in the Holy Land.'

Harriet said nothing.

'I'd get to the station early, if I were you. Bound to be a bit of a crush.' Dobson smiled, taking her silence for acquiescence. Good-natured though he was, he could be self-important in office and now, satisfied that he had disposed of her, he nodded her away. 'Goodbye. And perhaps we'll meet at Philippi.'

3

It took a couple of days for the convoy to disperse. It had arrived during a lull in the fighting. When they leaguered, the gunfire had stopped but next day, at first light, the men were awakened by a thudding uproar that seemed to be less than a mile away. Simon, sitting up in alarm, was taut with protest: the noise was too close and he was not prepared for it. Surely he should have been given time to brace himself against an onslaught like this? He got out of his sleeping-bag to see what was to be seen and there was nothing but rising billows of smoke on the horizon. The guns must be three or four miles away.

Realising this, his nerves subsided but he was dispirited by the arid desolation around him and suffered, like everyone else, from fear of what would happen next. Those who could locate their units were the lucky ones. They were packed into trucks to be delivered to friends, in places where they knew the routine of life. They went cheerfully and the other men said to each other, 'Lucky buggers!' Half the trucks went with them so the remaining men, with gaps in their leaguer, felt exposed to the unknown.

At mid-morning, having nothing much to do, they were distracted by signs of activity nearby. Traffic today was mostly driving westward. Different sorts of transport trucks were bringing up supplies and waiting to deliver on to an area a hundred yards west of the convoy's camp. Simon, asking the sergeant what was going on, discovered that this area was to form a service depot for the battle a few miles up the road. Engineers took over the area and put down oil barrels that marked tracks for the lorries. The lorries then moved on to the mardam to deliver their goods. Service lorries came next. Gradually, as though the positioning of the black barrels gave meaning to the desert, the enclosed sand was occupied by vehicle workshops, tank repair units, dressing stations and supply dumps.

The men who were still in the camp stood and watched as the empty sand flats filled with men and materials. The service units seemed aware of an audience and moved about like stage hands, displaying their efficiency. Simon and the others, grouped together to hide the embarrassment at their enforced idleness, saw the supply base grow before them.

The Spitfires and Hurricanes went unheeded until a plane of a different kind dived over the camp and spattered the ground with bullets. The men threw themselves down, trying to dig themselves in, for the first time aware that here, idle and useless though they were, they could die as easily as the men at the front. Simon, being the only officer among them, ordered them to get spades from the lorries and dig slit trenches. They did this with enthusiasm. The sand digging was easy enough, the trenches were completed in an hour and their occupants, again with nothing to do, stood deep in them, resting their arms on the mardam, bored by their own inactivity and envious of the activity of others.

The traffic changed direction again. Trucks that had gone up to the front were returning with wounded and taking on supplies. Smoke and dust hung in the growing heat. Seeing the orderlies and stretcher-bearers moving, as grey as ghosts in the dusty distance, the men of the convoy grumbled resentfully. Couldn't they go and offer a hand? Simon consulted with the sergeant but the men were untrained in the work in progress and the trained men would have no use for them.

The gunfire was an unending reverberation against the senses. The distant smoke clouds rose so thickly that the sun was a white transparent circle behind haze, but the loss of light did not bring any diminution of heat. By mid-afternoon most of the men had lost interest in the service depot and dropping down into the trenches, slept until sunset when the canteen truck came round. The sound of the guns was dying out. The trucks, leaving the depot, were going eastwards again and the men of the convoy relaxed into a new friendliness, feeling they had survived an ordeal.

The sergeant came over to Simon and said in a sociable way, 'In case you don't know, sir, my name's Ridley.' The fact they were among the remnants left in the camp had brought them together and Ridley, become confiding, said he had seen Major Hardy leaving the camp soon after daybreak. According to Ridley, the major had driven off to divisional headquarters on a ploy of his own.

'Been sick, see,' Ridley said. 'Jaundice. The brass-hats all get it, comes from all the whisky they put down. Well, he was in hospital a long time and when he came out, he found he's been replaced, which doesn't surprise anyone. What he wants, if you ask me, is to get on to staff but he's a toffee-nosed old bumbler and I bet they don't want him.'

'What do you think will happen to the rest of us?'

'Can't tell you that, sir, but let's hope we stick together.'

At dawn next day, the guns started up again and the service units were out sweeping and tidying their areas as though attempting to make a habitat of a bit of desert. The men of the convoy, expecting another day of tedium, watched disgruntled till the canteen truck came round. While they were eating their sandwiches, Major Hardy's staff car came into the leaguer. This was indeed a diversion. The sergeant, who knew everything, had said to Simon, 'We won't see his nibs again.' They all stood and watched Hardy's legs come out of the car as though his emergence were a special entertainment laid on for them. Standing beside the car, he called Simon to him. He was a changed man. Until then, keeping his distance, he had had the ruffled atmosphere of one who nursed a grievance.

'Boulderstone,' he said, addressing Simon with easy confidence. 'This area will be evacuated at six a.m. tomorrow. The trucks are to move to another camping site a few miles back. Any questions?'

'Yes, sir. Are you coming with us, sir?'

'I am. I am now your commanding officer.'

Before Simon could make any comment, Hardy dismissed him and returned to the car where he sat examining papers for most of the daylight hours.

Next morning, taking his place in the leading lorry, Simon found Arnold at the wheel. He was surprised that Arnold was still with the remnants left in camp. He said, 'I thought you went with the trucks.' Arnold had gone with the trucks but his unit had moved. No one could tell him where it was and so, after dark, when the men were asleep, Arnold had made an unobtrusive return to the camp.

'And you're staying with us?'

'Looks like it, sir.'

'Splendid.' Arnold was someone Simon knew. Arnold had given him help on the outward trip and could be relied on to help him now. Arnold, known and helpful, brought a sense of continuity to a disrupted world.

They sat together in comfortable silence, awaiting the order to move. It did not come. Time passed and the cool of daybreak took on the sting of morning. At last, Simon jumped down from the cabin, intending to approach Hardy but was stopped by the sight of the major, face drawn, hands shuffling through the paper that lay, disordered, on the car bonnet. He gave Simon a look of such rancour that Simon made off to where Ridley stood with a sardonic smile on his narrow, kippered face.

'What's the hold-up, sergeant?'

'If you ask me, sir, the old fucker's lost his notes of the route.'

Whatever Hardy had lost, he had now found and coming over to Simon and Ridley, fussily important, he ordered Ridley's truck into the lead. Climbing back into his cabin, Simon found Arnold drooping under the heat from the roof. As they were about to start out, the canteen truck came round and the men, getting down for their tea and bully, could see Hardy haranguing the sergeant.

Everyone was eager to be off. The patch of desert where they had leaguered was like most of the desert elsewhere, yet it had become hateful to them. They seemed to imagine that, once on the move, their world would change. By the time they set out, the track was under mirage and the convoy went at a crawl. Heat fogged the distance so there was no horizon, nothing to separate the silver mirage fluid from the swimming, sparkling white heat of the sky. They might have been moving in space except that objects – petrol cans, scraps scattered from falling aircraft, abandoned metal parts – stood monstrous and distorted out of the mirage.

The wind, blowing hot into the cabin, roused Simon to painful awareness that here he was and here, for God knows how long, he would have to remain. Pushing the sweat streams back into his hair, he said, 'It's so bad, I suppose it can only get better.'

'Oh, surprising how you get to like it, sir.' Arnold, though he was no longer in the lead, peered from habit out of the windscreen for sight of the piles of stones, trig-point triangles or oil barrels with which the engineers marked the line of firm sand.

It was late afternoon before the mirage folded in on itself and dwindled away. Arnold gave a murmur of satisfaction, seeing them still on the track, and Simon said, 'Good show, eh?'

Arnold smiled and Simon, wanting to know more about him, asked, 'You come round the Cape? What was it like?'

'Not bad. We didn't see much till we stopped at Freetown. Then at

Cape Town, they took us a trip up Table Mountain. It was smashing.'

'The scenery, you mean?'

'The scenery wasn't bad, either. But it was the flowers. Never saw anything like them.'

'We weren't allowed ashore. They'd had the British army by the time we arrived and we just had to stay on board. It was a big ship – the *Queen Mary*. A liner.'

Arnold, too, had come out on a liner but could not remember what it was called. The lower deck had been packed like a slave ship, the hammocks slung so close it was impossible to move without rocking the man on either side, but he had discovered there were splendours higher up. Sent to the saloon deck with a message, he had looked in through an open door and seen a real bed, gilt chairs with tapestry seats and a carpet on the floor.

He commented without envy, 'The officers had it good.'

'Only the brass hats. There wasn't elbow room in our cabin. They'd put in extra bunks and your face nearly hit the one above. Did you have any special friends on the ship?'

Arnold nodded but paused before admitting their names. 'Ted and Fred. Chaps I dossed down with.'

That, it seemed, was the most Arnold would give away for the moment. They drove a few miles in silence then Simon questioned him again, wondering if he had felt about Ted and Fred as Simon had felt about Trent and Codley. Arnold said, 'Ted and Fred were all right,' and another mile passed before he explained how the three had been drawn together. They had occupied three hammocks, in a cubby beside the engine. 'You see, I had the middle place.' Only that fact, he believed in his humility, had admitted him to the team. They had taken possession of two square yards of deck space and each morning, first thing, one of them would go to the space while the other two queued in the canteen.

'Ted and Fred: they were special, weren't they?'

Arnold gave an embarrassed grunt and excused his emotions by saying, 'They were my mates.'

'What happened when you reached Suez?'

Arnold had had better luck than Simon. His relationship with Ted and Fred had survived for nearly a month in Egypt. There had been no emergency in those days, so the three went to a base depot for acclimatisation before being sent to a camp at Mahdi where they shared a tent and waited for their movement orders. If no order arrived by mid-day, they were free to get passes out of camp and take the tram-car into Cairo. They usually went to a cinema but often enough they just walked about, grumbling to each other. They were browned off, not only because they were there, but because they felt no one cared whether they were there or not.

Ted and Fred were town-bred boys and did not find Cairo as strange as it seemed to Arnold. He had grown up in the Lake District and, wandering aimlessly through fetid, filthy, noisy, sun-baked streets, he longed for his own green countryside. Months passed before he was reconciled to the desert but now he said, 'The desert's all right when you get to know it.'

They had been nearly a month at Mahdi when Ted, who was the boldest of them, said to the sergeant, 'What are we here for, sarge, mucking about in camp?'

The sergeant seemed to like his cheek. 'You'll find out soon enough, my lad,' and a week later, when two men were needed to make up the comple-ment of an out-going truck, he picked on Ted and Fred. Arnold, who had visited the zoo on his own, came back as the truck was moving off. He ran after it, shouting, 'Where are they taking you?'

Ted and Fred, looking at him over the back flap, could only shrug their ignorance. Ted grimaced, comically rueful, but Arnold knew they were gratified at being chosen while he was not. The truck turned out of the compound and that was the last he ever saw of Ted and Fred.

'I bet you missed them?'

Arnold stared ahead for a minute or two before he whispered, 'I didn't know how I was going to go on living.'

'Were you on leave in Cairo?'

'Not leave, exactly,' Arnold had developed amoebic dysentery in the desert and had been sent back to base hospital. While he was away, his company had been 'whacked up' giving covering fire during the evacuation of Gazala.

'Suppose I was lucky, really. A lot of my mates copped it.'

'What do you think happened to the rest?'

Arnold shook his head. 'Could have been sent to join other battalions. That happens when a company's badly whacked up. Anyway no one knew where they were.' And so Arnold was displaced and, like Simon, uncertain what lay ahead for them.

When they stopped to brew up, Simon drank his tea standing beside

Arnold, feeling not only that their uncertainty was a bond but that there was sympathy between them. But he feared their attachment could not last. They could be separated by circumstances: even if they had the luck to remain in the same unit, they would be divided by rank.

He asked, 'What about Ridley? – How did he lose his outfit?'

Simon learnt that Ridley had been wounded during the retreat from Mersa Matruh. Discharged from hospital, he found his company had been broken up so, like the other men left in the convoy, he belonged nowhere.

As they started again, the staff car pulled out from its position between trucks and Hardy, his head out of the window, shouted that he was taking the lead. He turned inland and they drove for an hour before being signalled to stop. When the convoy came to a standstill, Ridley jumped down from his truck and, coming to Simon, whispered fiercely, 'Christ, if we leaguer here, we're sitting ducks.'

Simon thought Ridley was right. The flat, bare mardam offered no protection and there was nothing in sight but a group of trucks some distance south. There was nothing to mark this stretch of desert, but Simon supposed it had some meaning for Hardy. Feeling that Ridley expected him to act, he went to the major and asked, 'Are we to camp here, sir?'

'No. Tell the men to stand to. I've something to tell you all.'

Papers in hand, the men drawn up in front of him, Hardy did his best to convey amiable authority. 'I've called a halt so I can put you in the picture. We're a mixed lot, as you know, and some of you are new to the desert. Others are not at their best, having returned from sick leave, but I think we can make ourselves useful. Orders are that we join with another detachment to form a mobile column. There's a number of such columns down south – Jock columns they are called, after Colonel Jock Campbell, VC, who thought them up. Clever man. As I said, we'll be at the southern end of the line – away from the big dogfight, I'm afraid, but with a job to do. We're to swan about and sting the jerries whenever and wherever we get the chance.'

'Sounds exciting, sir,' Simon said.

'Could be. Could be.' Not wanting to overdo the amiability, Hardy jerked up his head and asked, 'Any questions?'

'I'll say there are,' Ridley whispered to Simon then, raising his voice, he adopted an obsequious whine quite different from his usual sardonic tone. 'Do we go south straight away, sir?'

'No, we'll stick around here for a few days and wait for supplies. We need extra officers and, of course, artillery.'

'This stinging the jerries, sir: how're we to set about it?'

'Ah!' Hardy examined his papers and seemed relieved when he found the answer. 'It'll be a matter of swift raids and counter-attacks.'

'I *see*, sir,' Ridley respectfully said though, in fact, the answer did not tell them much. There was an uneasy silence then everyone listened, awed, as Ridley managed to bring out another question. 'Sir, how'll the column be made up? Number of trucks, guns and the like, sir?'

'I think I can answer that,' Hardy, his manner stern and competent, consulted his papers again but this time the answer was not to hand. Giving up, frowning his annoyance, he made a blustering attempt to extemporise. 'There'll be gunners, naturally. Artillery officer, of course. Enough infantry for close protection. Four lorries, I'd say – could be six. And . . . and so on.'

'What about hardware, sir?'

'Hardware? I suppose we'll have to take what we can get.'

'Plenty lying about, sir.' Ridley, with satisfaction in his own knowledge, began to advise on things they might find useful, but Hardy would have none of this. Cutting through Ridley, he said, 'Carry on, Boulderstone.'

'Sir. Where are we making for, sir?'

The major had marked his command by putting on an impressive pair of field glasses. He now raised them to look at the only trucks in sight and after long contemplation said, 'Yes, those are our chaps.'

He pointed into the south-west and as the men looked with him, their faces shone red with the setting sun.

Hardy seemed pleased with himself and shouted, 'Get a move on, Boulderstone. No time to waste.'

The trucks filled. Simon was in the lead again. They set out to find company and cover before the night came down on them.

4

Dobson had been right. There was going to be a scramble for the special train. To make matters worse, the train was late and those packed together on the platform were in a state of agitated anxiety, expecting tumult.

Cairo had become the clearing house of Eastern Europe. Kings and princes, heads of state, their followers and hangers-on, free governments with all their officials, everyone who saw himself committed to the allied cause, had come to live here off the charity of the British government. Hotels, restaurants and cafés were loud with the squabbles, rivalries, scandals, exhibitions of importance and hurt feelings that occupied the refugees while they waited for the war to end and the old order to return.

Now they were all on the move again. Those free to go, or of such eminence their persons were regarded as sacrosanct, had taken themselves off days before. It was said that the officers of General Headquarters had left in staff cars but, whether that was true or not, there were still officers at Groppi's. Now it was the turn of the English women and children who had obstinately remained in spite of warnings. The warnings had become urgent, and most of them had decided to leave.

Harriet was not among them but she was not far from them. Where she stood, awaiting the Alexandria train, she could look across the rail at the vast concourse packed on the platform opposite. She saw people she knew. She saw Pinkrose, hanging on to his traps and pushing first this way, then that, trying to find a position that would give him an advantage over the others. In his determined search and frequent mind changings, he thrust women from him and tripped over children, and so enraged the volatile Greeks,

Free French, Poles and German Jews that they shouted abuse at him and blamed him for their fears. Hearing none of this, aware of nothing but himself, he struggled back and forth, losing his hat, regaining it, clucking in his agitation.

The train was sighted and a groan went through the crowd. The train came at a snail's pace towards the platform. The groan died out and a tense silence came down on the passengers who, gripping bags and babies, prepared for the battle to come. As the first carriages drew abreast of the platform, hysteria set in. The men who had been castigating Pinkrose for loutish behaviour, now flung themselves forward, regardless of women and children, and began tugging at the carriage doors. The women, suffering the usual disadvantage of having to protect families as well as themselves, were shrill in protest, but the protest soon became general. The carriages were locked. The train, slow and inexorable as time, slid on till it touched the buffers at the end of the line.

The scene was now hidden from Harriet by the arrival of her own train. Hardly anyone was risking the move to Alexandria and choosing among the empty compartments, she heard the clamour as the special train was opened up. She also heard the gleeful yells of the porters throwing luggage aboard. 'You go. Germans come. You go. Germans come.'

Iqal might have his doubts about the German promises but the fellahin had heard there were great times ahead. The wonder was, Harriet thought, that they were all so tolerant of the losers. Even when poor, diseased and hungry, they maintained their gaiety, speeding the old conquerors off without malice. No doubt they would welcome the new in the same way.

Harriet's train moved gently out. The uproar died behind her and she passed into the almost silent lushness of the Delta. Here was a region of dilatory peace that lived its own life, unaware of war and invaders. All over the Delta that stretched north for a hundred miles, black earth put out crops so green the foliage was like green light. Now, in high summer, this vibrancy of green was exactly as it had been when the Pringles first arrived. Then it had been Easter. Greece was aflower with spring but in Egypt there was neither spring nor autumn, only the heat of summer and the winter's soft warmth.

Flat, oblong fields were divided from each other by water channels, and each produced crops without respite. Vegetables, flax, beans, barley, tobacco, cotton: all lifted their rich verdure repeatedly out of the same blackness for which Egypt had once been called the Black Land. Between the crops there were fruit trees: mangoes, pomegranates, banana palms, date palms, and sometimes a whitewashed tomb, like a miniature mosque, or a white house with woodwork fretted like a child's toy.

Men, women and children went on working without looking at the train. Their persistence was leisurely and the train, too, was leisurely. Harriet was able to watch a water buffalo trudge a full circle, turning a water wheel that had outworn generations of buffaloes.

When, a year ago, she first saw the Delta, it was evening. The refugee ship had arrived early in the morning but people were not allowed ashore. They had to be questioned and given clearance. They were hungry. They had been told to bring their own food but in Athens the shops were empty of food, and there was none to be found. Harriet had bought some oranges on the quay and these had kept the Pringles and their circle of friends going for three days. Oranges had been the main diet in Athens for some weeks before the end and that was how they had existed: on oranges, wine and the exaltation of the Greek spring.

Berthed by the quayside at Alexandria, the passengers saw nothing but cases of guns and ammunition. No food. Then two soldiers had come to stare up at them and the passengers shouted at them in all the languages of Europe. The soldiers came to the edge of the quay, asking what it was the refugees wanted. 'Food,' shouted Harriet.

Food? – was that all?

The men went into a shed and came back with a whole branch of bananas. They broke off the fruits and threw them up over the ship's rail and everybody scrambled for them. Harriet caught one and took it to share with Guy who sat where he had sat for most of the voyage, placidly reading the sonnets of Shakespeare.

'Half each,' she said and he smiled as she peeled off the green skin and broke the pink flesh, then watched as she bit into it.

'What does it taste like?'

'Honey,' she said and the sweetness brought tears into her eyes.

Allowed to land, they were taken to an army canteen for bacon and eggs and strong tea. 'Tea you could trot a mouse on,' said Guy. The sun was low when they boarded the train and they journeyed into a country stranger than any other, yet suffocatingly familiar. The heat, the airless quiet, the rich oily colours reminded Harriet of old biblical oleographs seen at Sunday school.

It was the 'Land of the Pharaohs', a land she had known since childhood.

'Look, a camel,' someone shouted and they all crowded to the window to see their first camel of Egypt lifting its proud, world-weary head and planting its soft, splayed feet into the sandy road. The workers were leaving the fields. A string of them wandered along the road, slowly, as though it did not matter whether they went home or not.

The sun set and twilight merged and darkened the fields. Half-way between Cairo and Alexandria, the train stopped at Tanta. A Greek girl called out, 'My God, look at Tanta!' They looked and experienced the first shock of Egyptian poverty. Tanta station was in a culvert overhung by the balconies of gimcrack flats where washing was strung on lines and rubbish was heaped for the wind to blow away. Fat men in pyjamas lay in hammocks or stood up sweating and scratching and leering down on the women in the train. Many of the refugees were Athenians, used to a city of marble. In Alexandria, where it rained, the bricks had been baked but there was no rain in the Delta. Tanta was the dun colour of unbaked clay.

Beggar children whined up at the train, banging on it to demand attention. As the train pulled out, they ran beside it, their bare dirty feet slapping the ground until they were lost in the twilight. Then darkness came down and there was nothing to see but the palm fronds black against the afterglow of sunset.

Here was Harriet at Tanta again. The same fat men sprawled on the balconies, the same children whined at her, the same smell of spice, dung and death hung in the air, but none of it disturbed Harriet now. Tanta was a part of Egypt. It was the nature of things, and her only thought was to get the journey over. If asked, she would have said she did not dislike Tanta as much as she disliked Alexandria. Though she deplored her mid-week separation from Guy, she dreaded the time when her job would end and she would have to move from Cairo. Built on a narrow strip of land between a salt lake and the sea, Alexandria, she felt, was depressing and claustrophobic. Castlebar, who went each week to tutor the son of an Alexandrian Greek banker, had said to Guy, 'You'll enjoy it. The fashionables are quite amusing,' but Guy was not among 'the fashionables'. His college was not even in Alexandria. It was beyond the eastern end of the long Corniche that ran from the Pharos, all round the old port, and stretched in an endless concrete promenade, until it was lost in desert. Guy was in the desert. He taught English at a business college where the sons of tobacco and cotton barons wanted to learn a commercial language. When Guy organised a series of lectures on English literature, a deputation of students came to tell him that they did not need to know about literature. They did not want English, as Guy understood it. They wanted something called 'commercial English'.

Alexandria was famous for its sea-breeze but the breeze could often bring in a summer mist. When Harriet left the train, she found the sun hidden by a moisture film that increased the greyness of the streets. The townspeople were queuing up outside banks or hurrying from shop to shop, buying as though against a siege. There was unease in the air, the same unease that Harriet had felt in Athens when the Germans reached Thermopylae. In Cairo people were saying that the rich business community of Alexandria had appointed a reception committee to prepare a welcome for Rommel. That was probably true but the rich were stocking up before the invaders came to empty the shops. Cars, packed with supplies like the cars outside the American Embassy, stood ready for those who thought it wiser to flee. Some of them were lagged with mattresses as a protection against aerial bombardment.

Harriet took a bus along the Corniche. There was a drabness about the streets and she felt that some bright constituent was missing. She realised that the young naval men, who went about in white duck, as light-hearted as children, were missing from among the people on the pavements. She supposed that shore-leave had been stopped.

That day no one had time to lie on the beach. The long grey sea edge, usually full of bathers, was deserted except for a few small boys. The vacuous greyness of the town depressed her. She realised she had become acclimatised to Cairo's perpetual sunshine and rumbustious vitality. Here the long sea-facing cliff of hotels and blocks of flats had a winter bleakness as though all life had moved away.

In Cairo, the German occupation was still merely possible; here, apparently, it was a certainty. She decided she would stand none of Guy's heroics. She would take him back to Cairo that very night.

In normal times, Guy would have been on leave. The college had shut for the summer but, feeling he had no right to take leave, he had remained to conduct a summer course in English. Only a few students, eager to excel or to gain his favour, had enrolled but they were enough to give him a sense of purpose. He would argue that the school was part of the college curriculum and he could not abandon it. She would argue that it was not and he very well could.

Again calamity presented itself as a solution. I would deliver Guy from Alexandria and from his wretched lodgings. If she had to come here, they would live not in one of these expensive Corniche flats but in the same sleazy hinterland where he was living at the moment. Not much caring where he lived, he had taken a room in a Levantine pension of the poorest kind, a place so dark and neglected, everything seemed coated with grime. One day, watching him as he talked to the landlord, she had seen him rub his hand on the knob of a bannister then pass the same hand over his forehead. She had berated him, telling him he might pick up leprosy, smallpox, plague or any of the killer diseases of Egypt. Guy, who believed all disease was a sickness of the psyche, said, 'Don't be silly. You only catch what you fear to catch,' and, fearing nothing, he saw himself immune.

When she left the bus at the end of the Corniche, she had still to walk half a mile to where the college stood isolated in a scrubby area of near desert that was now being built up. The building had once been a quarantine station for seamen. Staring out to sea, grim faced, lacking any hint of ornament, it might have been a penitentiary. And for Guy it was, in a way, a penitentiary. He had been exiled here for his song, 'Gracey of Gezira' – or so Harriet believed. He had brought his exile upon himself.

No one, not even a boab, was in the hall. She walked unchecked down to the half-glazed door of the lecture hall and, looking in, saw Guy at a desk, bent over a book. The shutters had been closed against the sun and had not been opened when mist covered the sky. The amber colour of the electric light made his face sallow and he looked very drawn. He had lost weight and his cheeks, that had been smooth with youth when they married, only two years before, now showed a line from nostrils to chin. Time and the Egyptian climate had told on them both.

From the silence, she guessed they were alone in the building and she was reminded of another time of danger when Guy, who had been the beloved mentor, waited in vain for his students. During their last days in Bucharest, with the Iron Guard on the march, the students were wise to stay away.

As she opened the door, he turned his head and at once he was young again. He jumped to his feet, animated by surprise and pleasure. 'Well, this is the nicest thing that's happened to me for a long time.'

'I've come to take you back to Cairo.'

He laughed, treating her statement as a joke. She looked at the book on his desk. It was one she had given him for his last birthday and she said, 'Good heavens, you're not trying to lecture them on *Finnegans Wake*?'

'Not all of them, but I have two exceptionally brilliant chaps who are interested in English for its own sake. Pretty rare in this place. I promised them a seminar on Joyce. I'm certain that Joyce got a lot of his funnier pieces from students at the Berlitz School. I get the same sort of things here. Look,' he pulled some students' papers out of his desk and read, '"D. H. Lawrence was theoretically wrong" – Joyce would have loved that. And here,

Thou wast not meant for death immoral bird . . .

'Darling, you've got to come to Cairo, at least for a few days.'

'You know that's impossible. I have my summer school and . . .'

'Which you're keeping open for only two students?'

'Well, I had ten to begin with. They thought if they humoured me by joining the class, I'd repay them by marking up their exam papers. When they found it didn't work, they faded away. But there are two left and they're exceptional.'

'Well, exceptional or not, the fact is you're keeping this place open for a couple of students? Here you are, at a time like this, waiting to discuss *Finnegans Wake*?'

'Why not? What do you expect me to do?'

'I expect you to have some sense. Don't you realise the Germans are less than fifty miles from Alex?'

'Oh, darling,' he took her hands and squeezed them. 'Little monkeys' paws! You aren't frightened, are you? You weren't frightened in Greece when we had nothing in front of us but the sea. Here we have the whole of Africa.'

'I'm frightened for you. A lot of good having the whole of Africa if you're cut off here. If you're waiting for orders, you'll wait for ever. There's no one to give orders. Gracey's bolted, as usual. So, for that matter, have Toby Lush, Dubedat and several thousand others. I saw Pinkrose going off on the special train this morning. The least you can do is come to Cairo. If you hang on here, you'll end up in Dachau. In Cairo, we stand a fair chance of getting away.'

'Don't worry, darling. We've always got away before.'

'That's the trouble. You're overconfident. We've got away twice – but it could be third time unlucky. They move so fast, you could be caught before you knew they had reached Alex.'

'I can't argue now, darling,' Guy put an arm round her shoulder and led her to the door. 'The students are due any minute. You get back to Alex. Get yourself something to eat and I'll see you later. I'm going to the Cecil to meet some men.'

She asked suspiciously, 'What men? What time?'

'Six o'clock. You'll find Castlebar there. And I'm having supper with a chap you don't know. Called Aidan Pratt. If you get there before I do, introduce yourself. Be nice to the poor fellow. He's very shy.'

'All right. Six o'clock. And be prepared to come back with me.'

Guy laughed and shut the door on her.

The sun was breaking through the mist and the promenade was in sunlight when she reached the bus stop. Guy had said, 'I can't argue now', implying, she hoped, that he would argue later, but later there would be Castlebar and this man she did not know and Guy, always high-spirited in company, would be too volatile to discuss unwelcome reality. He had an impulse to take risks, and then there were the two students, the ambitious swots who roused his old obstinate loyalty and could detain him there until it was too late.

'Bloody students!' She saw them as voracious creatures who would devour him if they could. And, in time, he would be devoured. She felt rage that he should be wasting his learning on this wretched place.

As there was no bus in sight, she decided to walk the length of the Corniche and so pass the dead centre of the day. Walking, that in Cairo meant bathing in sweat, was pleasant enough here where the sea wind tempered the heat, but the walk was monotonous. It was a dull shore with rocks that were rotting like cheese. At one point where the sea washed under the cheesey, crumbling rock shelf, holes had been cut so the waves, beating through them, made a booming sound. Or so it was said. Harriet had never heard it. The holes were very ancient and were no longer a diversion. Today the water splashed through them with a half-hearted plip-plop that she thought a fitting comment on the wartime world. The sun was dropping and the light deepening. This was the evening when the conquerors of the Afrika Korps were to force their pent-up ardour on the ladies of Alexandria.

The conquerors had not yet arrived but there was a British soldier leaning against the sea wall. He looked like a man with all the time in the world but his baggage showed he was waiting for transport.

She stopped to lean beside him, staring with him at the flat, almost motionless sea where no ships sailed, and said, 'You off to the desert?'

He muttered, 'Ya.' He was older than the soldier she had met in Cairo and he did not marvel at meeting a young Englishwoman.

'I suppose you've no idea what's happening out there?'

'Nope. Heard nothing for days.'

'Do you think Rommel will get here?'

'He'll get here if he can, won't he? If not, not. There's no knowing, is there?' He spoke dully, sodden with boredom, so, knowing she would get no response from him, she walked on. The barrage balloons were beginning to rise over the town. By the time she reached the harbour, there were a dozen or more kidney shapes hanging in mid-sky. She had an hour to get through before going to the hotel so walked on till she was opposite the Pharos, then she sat on the wall, her legs hanging above the sand, and watched the pleatings of ruby cloud that were forming round the horizon. The Pharos, newly painted, reflected the sky. The scene absorbed her so it was some minutes before she realised she was an object of prurient excitement among the boys on the shore below. They were dodging about in their ragged galabiahs, the eldest not more than ten or eleven, bending down, sniggering, as they tried to see up her skirt. She shouted 'Yallah' but they would not be driven off. She lifted her legs over the wall and sat the other way but the boys ran up the steps to stare at her from the road. At last, sick of their antics, she jumped down and went to the Cecil.

The atmosphere inside the hotel was forlorn. The cosmopolitan patrons had gone with the rest and even the bar, the venue of British naval officers, was empty except for three army captains who stood together, constrained and sober, and another who sat by himself. This last was near the door, watching for someone, and she guessed from his vulnerable air, his expectation and his disappointment when she came in, that he was waiting for Guy. He must be the shy Aidan Pratt. From her experience of Guy's acquaintances, she guessed that this man had asked Guy to dinner not simply for the pleasure of his company. He had a need of his own. He wanted to confide in Guy, or ask his advice, or get something from him. Guy had probably promised him the evening and he, supposing he would have Guy's company to himself, had not bargained for her, or for Castlebar. Guy was, as usual, double-booked, and not only from forgetfulness. His engagements crowded upon each other because he brought down on himself more dependence than any normal person could support.

Knowing the man would not welcome her company, she wandered back to the foyer and sat there as the lights came on inside and the twilight deepened outside. Guy did not appear and, feeling solitary and exposed, she returned to the bar and approached Aidan Pratt. When she spoke, his surprise was almost an affront.

'Guy Pringle suggested I join you here.'

He stared with animosity until she explained that she was Guy's wife, then he stumbled to his feet, attempting to recoup his discourtesy with a smile. He was a heavy, handsome young man with limp and oily black hair. He was still in his early twenties, but his eyes were contained in hollows of brownish skin that aged him. They were large eyes, very dark, and his smile did not dispel their desolation. His aura of depression repelled her. She, too, had hoped to have Guy to herself. He was, she realised, another victim of Guy's reassuring warmth. Each one imagined himself the sole recipient. Guy would remake the world for him, and for him alone. They clung to him and, in the end, he evaded them or asked her to protect him from them. 'You answer the telephone, darling . . .' Deeply buried, there was in him an instinct for preservation and the instinct might save him in the end.

Aidan Pratt asked her what she would drink. From the bar, he looked intently back at her, perhaps wondering if he could confide in her, treat her as a surrogate for Guy, and she realised she had seen him before. When he brought back her drink, she asked if they had met somewhere. He shook his head but his smile took on vitality as though her question had pleased him.

When he sat opposite her, she felt his whole personality on edge. His face was moist, not from heat, because the bar was air-conditioned, but from nervousness. His uniform of fine gaberdine was expensively tailored but he fidgeted inside it as though troubled by its fit. She asked where he was stationed. He was on leave from Damascus.

'Damascus? Then how did you come to know Guy?'

'Doesn't everyone know Guy?' he gave a laugh. 'Last time I was here someone told me a story: two men were wrecked on a desert island. Neither knew the other but they both knew Guy Pringle.'

'Yes, I heard that story in Cairo.'

'I met him here, in this bar, on my last leave. Next day I went out to the college and we walked to Ramleh, talking all the way there and back. A memorable day. We arranged to meet here again the following evening. I waited three hours before I discovered he wasn't even in Alex. He'd gone to Cairo for the weekend.' As Harriet showed no surprise, he asked, 'Does that sort of thing often happen?'

'You remember the bread-and-butter fly that lived on weak tea and cream? If it couldn't find any, it died. Alice said, "But that must happen very often" and the gnat said, "It always happens".'

'Always? He makes a habit of letting people down?'

'He doesn't mean to let them down. He takes on too much. People persuade him to do what he hasn't time to do so, inevitably, *someone* is let down.'

Aidan's mouth tightened and he said with slight hauteur, 'As you are here, I suppose we can depend on him tonight?'

'Yes, he'll turn up sooner or later. I want to take him back to Cairo.' She thought it an odd time for anyone to come here on leave and said, 'Things are pretty bad, you know.'

'You mean, worse than usual? Isn't it the same old romp as last time? They reach Sollum and then they're driven back?'

'They're much nearer than that. They said they'd reach Alex tonight.'

'Obviously you didn't believe them or you wouldn't be in Alex yourself. Still, you're right. He oughtn't to stay out where he is. A lot could happen before he got wind of it.'

'I'm glad you agree with me. How long are you staying here?'

'Not long. I could only get forty-eight hours so I return tomorrow.'

'I envy you. I wish we were safely in Damascus.'

'Oh, Damascus isn't all that safe. We have our troubles. The Free French are in control but a good many Syrians don't want them. We often hear pistol shots. People get killed,' he paused and dropped his voice. 'Friends get killed. A friend of mine looked out to see what was happening and a bullet went through his head.'

He glanced at her to see how this information affected her, and quickly glanced away. The loss of a friend and, she would guess, no ordinary friend! So this was the tragedy he was nursing within himself! She said, 'I'm sorry,' but of course it was Guy he wanted. Only Guy would hear the whole story because only Guy could give the true, consoling word. She added, 'Very sorry,' and as she spoke, he made a gesture, so poignantly conveying his loneliness and heartbreak that she knew she had, indeed, seen him before.

She was puzzled by the familiarity of that gesture. He stared down at the floor. There was nothing more to be said but then, at the most opportune moment, Guy entered the bar.

His glasses pushed into his hair, his arms stretched over an insecure burden of books and papers, he hurried to them, saying delightedly, 'So you found each other all right!' He bent to kiss Harriet. 'I didn't tell you who he was. I knew you'd recognise him and I wanted to surprise you.'

Looking again at Aidan, Harriet did recognise him. 'Of course, I knew I'd seen you before. You're the actor, Aidan Sheridan.'

Aiden, revivified by the arrival of Guy, made a denigratory movement of the hand. 'I was Aidan Sheridan. Now I'm Captain Pratt of the Pay Corps.'

He could not suppress Harriet's admiring memory of him. 'I saw you play Konstantin in *The Sea Gull*. I went with a friend to the gallery and we sat on a narrow plank of wood and gazed down at you, spellbound. It was all new to me – I'd never seen Chekov before. I was very young and at the end I went out crying.'

Aidan flushed darkly and caught his breath. He was moved by her memory and several moments passed before he could say, 'I was young, too. It was my first big role. At that age it is bliss to have a dressing-room to oneself. On my first night, sitting in front of the mirror I said to myself, "Now it's all beginning!"'

Guy beamed on his wife and friend, letting them discuss Chekov for a while, but eager to have a part in the felicitations, he soon took over to compliment Aidan on other parts he had played: Henry V, Romeo, Oswald . . .

'Did you play Hamlet?'

Aidan shook his head. 'That was to come.'

Guy, knowing he had asked the wrong question, hurried on to another subject: his own production of *Troilus and Cressida*. Describing it, he longed to be in the theatre again and said, 'I must produce another Shakespeare play.'

'Gracey would never let you,' said Harriet.

'If it's for the troops, he couldn't very well refuse. Or why not a Chekov play? Why not *The Sea Gull?*'

'Really, darling, for troops?'

'Well, why not? The men get sick of those concert parties. One of them told me they'd welcome a real play. They're not fools. They want something to think about. *The Sea Gull* is about wasted youth. It would have meaning for them.'

Aidan sombrely agreed and Guy turned excitedly to him. 'You would play Konstantin, wouldn't you?'

Startled by the suggestion, Aidan gave an ironical sniff. 'My first youth is passed. Trigorin would be more up my street these days.'

'Then, would you play Trigorin?'

'You're not serious? I couldn't act with amateurs.'

The statement had a finality that shocked Guy into silence. Harriet laughed and Aidan again blushed darkly, this time with shame, realising that his vanity had betrayed him.

'But you are an amateur,' Harriet spoke with friendly reasonableness, not wishing further to deflate his unhappy ego. 'You are an amateur soldier among professionals, aren't you?'

'I suppose I am.'

Guy, having made a rapid recovery, said, 'But you would help and advise, wouldn't you?'

'Willingly, if I'm around. But I can't get here as often as I would wish.'

Harriet, wanting to put a stop to this talk of productions said, 'And quite probably Guy won't be here, either.' She looked at Guy, insisting that he listen to her. 'Be sensible. Jackman says Alexandria will be cut off. Rommel will simply march round behind it and it will fall of itself. They could be here tomorrow. Come back to Cairo, just till we know what's going to happen here. '

'Darling, you know I can't abandon my students like that.'

'What students? Did those two turn up this afternoon?'

'No, but that doesn't mean . . .'

'It means *they've* abandoned *you*. I bet they're taking German lessons.'

Guy laughed. 'If the worst happens, I'll jump on a jeep. The army will take me out.'

'The army won't get out. It'll be surrounded, too.'

'Then it'll be another Dunkirk. The navy will rescue us.'

Dobson had said the same thing and Harriet, for the moment, let the matter drop. Guy asked Aidan if he had met Catroux who was, according to gossip, the illegitimate son of a royal personage. Did Aidan think this was the truth? Aidan discussed Catroux with avid interest, as though the general were his own achievement or an important part of his own life. Harriet could imagine that the name of Catroux dominated Syria as other names dominated Egypt. There had been Cunningham, Ritchie (the troops sang 'Ritchie, his arse is getting itchy'), Freyberg, Gott. Now there was Auchinleck. She saw them as larger than life, archetypal heroes, who had power over other men, and over civilians, too. When they decreed that Egypt should be evacuated, everyone must pack and go. The war had deprived poeple of free will. They must do what they were told.

Aidan, while talking, came to a sudden stop and gazed with unbelieving displeasure as yet another intruder arrived to claim Guy's attention. Castlebar had come to the table. Harriet could feel, almost like a physical force, Aidan's will to remove Castlebar but Castlebar was not to be moved. Confident of Guy's welcome and not unwelcomed by Harriet, he sniggered a greeting and sidled round the table to seat himself on a chair with his back to the wall. Guy, happy in the belief that Aidan and Castlebar would be drawn to each other, introduced the one as 'the famous actor' and the other as 'the famous poet'. Ducking his head, Castlebar gave Aidan a sidelong stare of dislike which Aidan, more directly, returned.

As Guy went to the bar to buy drinks, Castlebar put a packet of Camels on the table in his usual manner. The packet was placed central to his person, the open end facing him, a cigarette pulled out and propped up so it could be taken and lighted from the one in his mouth. Thus, there was no wasted interval between smokes. His thick, pale eyelids hid his eyes but all the time, he was observing Aidan as he might an enemy.

The two men were physically alike. They had the same heavy good looks but Castlebar was some ten years older. His sallow skin was falling into lines, his hair was greying and his full, loose mouth sagged as though pulled down by his perpetual cigarette. His lips were mauve and had the soft, swollen look of decay. Harriet, sensing their distaste of each other, supposed that Castlebar resented Aidan's youth while Aidan saw in Castlebar a debased analogue of himself.

Guy, certain that his friends were enjoying each other as much as he enjoyed them, began to plan a whole evening for them all: a few drinks here, then to Pastroudi's for a bite and on to Zonar's for coffee and drinks then, if they wanted to go on drinking and talking, they could come back to the Cecil where Aidan was a resident. Neither man interrupted this exuberant programme but at the end, Castlebar said, 'Sorry. Nothing I'd like better but I'm going back on the early train.'

'Take the later train.'

Castlebar shook his head, stared down for some moments then stammered, seeming to force his voice through impeding teeth, 'Don't want to hang about here. Not even for love of you, dear old boy. My Greeks were in a panic. They had packed and would leave at the first sound of the guns. They thought I was mad to come up here but they owed me a bit – a whole quarter's tuition in fact. Thought I'd better make sure of it.'

Harriet fervently said, 'Thank God someone's got some sense.' She gave an ironical laugh as she looked at Guy. 'Castlebar may drink too much and smoke too much, but he's not taking silly risks.' She turned to Castlebar, 'Can't you persuade Guy to come to Cairo. He thinks the navy will rescue him.'

'The navy?' Castlebar lifted his eyelids and gave Guy a startled stare. 'Don't you know the navy's gone?'

'Gone?' Harriet was alarmed. 'Gone where?'

'No one knows. The Red Sea, I'd imagine. My Greeks were in a state about that. They say the whole Fleet upped anchor this morning and deserted the town.'

'Good heavens, that shows you ...' Harriet turned on Guy but Guy, adept at dodging her anxieties, jumped to his feet and the others watched him as he went to make much of a big, stooping, paunchy fellow who had just entered the bar.

'Who's he found now?' Castlebar spoke with indulgent exasperation. 'Your husband's crazy. Here he is sitting with friends who hang on his every word, but he's not satisfied. As soon as he sees someone else, he rushes over to them.'

'It's Lister. I met him at Groppi's. His job's in Jerusalem but he comes here all the time to fill up with food.'

Aidan, his face contracted as though with pain as he saw Guy bringing Lister to the table, said to Harriet, 'He gathers people as he goes.'

Lister, limping on a stick, smiled as he joined the company, his round blue eyes giving an impression of innocent, almost infantile, amiability, but Harriet knew he was more complex than he seemed. In the midst of his fat, pink, glossy face there was a cherub's nose and a very small mouth covered by a fluffy moustache. He was wearing a pair of old brown corduroy trousers and a shirt that had faded to yellow, and only his cap and the crown on his shoulder indicated that he was not a civilian but an army officer. He sank into a chair as though the few steps from bar to table had exhausted him, and pushed his right leg under the table, out of the way of harm. Getting his breath back, he lifted Harriet's hand, brushed it wetly with his moustache and asked, 'How is my lovely girl?'

'Not too happy. We've just heard that the navy's left Alex.'

'Good God!' Lister's little mouth fell open. 'What next? You'd scarcely believe it, I didn't know till I got here that there's a flap on. No one tells us anything in Palestine. I'm in Intelligence but there hasn't been a signal from GHQ ME, for a week.'

Harriet said, 'The rumour is that GHQ ME has left Egypt. They've been too busy evacuating themselves to send you a signal.'

'That's probably it. Jerusalem's packed out with evacuees, but it's always like that when the Germans cross into Egypt. To tell you the truth, you're safer here. Palestine's a cul-de-sac and if we move on to Syria, we'll meet the German 6th army on its way down from Russia. Where do you go then? Better off here, I say. You can always go down the Nile.'

Castlebar sniggered. 'You mean, *up* the Nile.'

'Yes. This must be the only country in the world where south is up,' Lister's big, shapeless body quivered as though he had made an enormous joke.

Guy, putting out his hands to Lister and Castlebar, urged them to tell some limericks. Between them, he said, they had the best collection he knew. 'Come on, let's have a flyting.'

'Oh!' Lister, choked by his own laughter, flapped a hand in protest. 'I'm too far gone. Been at it all day. I can't remember anything.' His nose, that was still the nose of infancy, glowed with the drink he had taken. 'Took a taxi from the station to Groppi's, rang Harriet (I'd've given you a fine repast, m'girl), had lunch at the Hermitage, went back to Groppi's for a few cream cakes, then I thought why not pop up and see old Pringle? Knew I'd find you in the bar.'

Aidan, pushing his chair back from the table, looked at Lister in frowning distaste. Castlebar, as he noted this, gave Harriet a sly grin and said to Lister, 'Bet you intend a visit to Mary's House?'

'Oh, oh, oh!' Lister averted his eyes as though deeply offended but his laughter overtook him, his body collapsed in on itself and tears ran down his cheeks. When he had recovered enough, he said, 'Did you know: when they got a direct hit, all the chaps taken to hospital said, one after the other, "I got mine at Mary's House", and a little sweetie of a nurse said to the doctor, "Mary must've been giving a very big party."'

It was an old story but they all laughed except Aidan, whose frown grew darker. The drinks were renewed and Castlebar was persuaded to speak a few limericks. His poetry was a mild mixture of nostalgia and regrets but his limericks had a dexterity and obscene wit that convulsed Lister who soon attempted to rival them. Lister's humour was scatological and Harriet, bored, said as soon as there was a pause, 'Darling, don't you think we should eat?'

'Yes,' Guy had a couple of inches in his glass, 'when I've finished this,' but he made no attempt to finish it. Washing it slowly round and round, he gained time by leaving it unfinished.

He invited Lister to Pastroudi's but Lister, shaking his head, tittered mysteriously and left them to guess where he was going. When it seemed the 'flyting' would end, Castlebar insisted that Guy must contribute to it. 'Do Yakimov,' he urged and Lister agreed. 'Oh, oh, must have Yakimov.'

Yakimov, dead and turned to dust in the dry Greek earth, led a post mortem life in Guy's repertoire of comic characters. Harriet, hungry but resigned, listened with fear that the performance might fail and pride that it did not. She was the only other one of the party who had known Yakimov in life and so the only one who, watching Guy's rounded, sunburnt features take on Yakimov's slavonic mask, marvelled at the impersonation. The change, for her, verged on the supernatural. For the others, there was a funny story. Guy imitated Yakimov's delicate, fluting voice, but the voice was not as exact as the face. 'Ee⁄a knew a lay⁄dee who played a most unfair game of ... cro⁄o⁄o⁄quet. She would put her skirt over her balls and move them about with her foot, *just* wherever she liked ...'

Here the laughter began. Harriet had heard the story so often, both from Guy and Yakimov himself, she could have reproduced every intonation. She ceased to listen but, instead, watched the two inches of beer going round and round as Guy spoke. If in a hurry, he could open a throttle in his throat and put down a pint without pausing for breath. If he wanted to linger, no one could make his beer last longer.

When he recovered from his mirth, Lister bent forward to say in a half-whisper, 'Heard a strange story at Groppi's this morning. You know Hooper, the one that married a rich girl who paints a bit? Well, she took that boy of theirs into the desert and she was so busy with her painting, she didn't notice the kid had picked up a live hand-grenade.'

Harriet sat up, realising she was about to hear of the tragedy she had witnessed – when? With all that had happened since, it seemed an age ago. She said, 'I was there. I saw her bring the boy in. We all realised he was dead, but the Hoopers couldn't believe it.'

Lister opened his eyes, amazed. 'So – is it true? – Did they really try and feed him ...' He circled a finger over his cheek. '... through some hole in his face?'

'Yes.'

'A weird story!'

Castlebar sniggered. 'Egypt's a weird place. Feeding the dead's an ancient custom, but it still goes on.'

'Goes on, does it?' Lister asked with awe.

'Oh yes, they all go up to the City of the Dead, taking food to share with the corpse under the floor. They set up house there and stay till the dead relative's got used to the strangeness of the afterlife. I like it.'

'Yes,' Lister, too, liked it but he could not keep his laughter back. He and Castlebar laughed together while Aidan, who had been shocked by the feeding of the dead boy, regarded them with horror. Guy was putting down his beer. The party had to break up. Castlebar was catching his train. Lister, with his secret intention in mind, began determinedly to get himself to his feet. He could scarcely put his right foot to the ground. 'Gout,' he explained and bending unsteadily over Harriet, he kissed her hand again. 'Look me up when you come to Jerusalem. You don't need to stay in that ghastly refugee camp. I'll use m'influence and get you a room at the YMCA. We'll have some fun. I'm the life and soul of the YMCA smart set. I'm always in trouble because I keep a few bottles in the wardrobe.'

Castlebar and Lister left the bar together and Guy, reluctant to part from them, went with them as far as the foyer.

Aidan said in disgust to Harriet, 'What extraordinary people! Why does

Guy waste his time with fellows like that? And repeating limericks to each other! An odd occupation!'

'The English do become odd here. Ordinary couples who'd remain happily together in Ealing or Pinner, here take on a different character. They think themselves Don Juans or tragedy queens, and throw fits of wild passion and make scenes in public . . .' At Aidan's movement of enquiry, Harriet laughed. 'No, not Guy and me. We're only apart from circum- stances. We're thought to be an exemplary pair.'

'But Guy? With those people, he was not himself. He was acting the fool, wasn't he?'

'Yes, in a way. But what's he to do? He's stuck at that commercial college, wasting his talents. He's not allowed to leave the Organisation and Gracey can't, or won't, give him a job worthy of him. Other men are at war, so he must take what comes to him. He cannot protest, except that his behaviour is protest. He must either howl against his life or treat it as a joke.' As she spoke, protest rose in her, too. 'This is what they've done to him – Gracey, Pinkrose and the rest of them. He believes that right and virtue, if persisted in, must prevail, yet he knows he's been defeated by people for whom the whole of life is a dishonest game.'

Aidan looked at her with new interest. 'He's not happy, and I don't think you are, either.'

'Can one expect to be happy in these times?'

'No. We have no right . . . no right even to think of happiness,' Aidan sighed and looked to the door for Guy's return, and Harriet began to feel curious about him, wondering what she would make of him if she knew him better.

The three of them set out for Pastroudi's restaurant. Alexandria had been blacked out by the military and the darkness enhanced the disturbing emptiness of the streets. A shudder passed through the air and the ground seemed to move beneath their feet. Harriet, unable to account for this phenomenon, came to a stop and said, 'Is it an earthquake?' She had experienced one in Bucharest but this, she realised, was something different. The shudder and vibration were repeated and went on as though a distant steam-hammer was pounding the earth. The two men, walking indifferently through it, made no comment until Harriet asked, 'What is it?'

Aidan told her, 'It's a barrage. They're preparing an attack.'

'Who? Them or us?'

'It's very close. Probably us.'

Guy spoke as though the vibration was a commonplace. 'I'd guess twenty-five pounders, wouldn't you?' He looked to Aidan who said, 'And the new six pounders. I'd say, 5.5 inch howitzers, too.'

Harriet, surprised that Guy should have heard of a twenty-five pounder, asked how far the barrage was from them.

Guy laughed. 'At least forty miles. I don't think Rommel will make it tonight.'

Aidan said seriously, 'If they break through, they could make it before daybreak.'

'But they won't break through. I must say, I'd like to take a troops' entertainment out to our chaps.'

Harriet said, 'Darling, really, you're mad!' She did not know whether Guy's courage came from his refusal to recognise reality, or a refusal to run from it, but the idea of taking an entertainment to men engaged in a desperate delaying action seemed to her typical of his mental processes.

The moon was pushing up between sea and sky, throwing a long channel of light across the water. The promenade was a spectral grey in the moon glimmer. Not a soul, it seemed, had come out to enjoy the cool of evening, but when they pushed through the heavy curtains into Pastroudi's, they found the restaurant crowded, noisy and brilliantly lit. The Alexandrians were eating while there was still something to eat. Uncertainty and fear raised the tempo of chatter into an uproar. Aidan had booked a table but they had stayed so long at the Cecil, the table was lost to them. They had to wait in a queue and while they waited, the air-raid warning rose. As the wailing persisted, people shouted to each other that it must be a false alarm. The Luftwaffe would never bomb a town that was about to fall into German hands. The warning added a sort of hilarity to the noise. No one took it seriously until the manager strode through the room shouting, 'What do you do? You know the regulations. Downstairs, everyone. M'sieurs, m'dams, into the kitchens, I beg you.'

His alarm infected the diners and they began pushing their way down into the hot and clotted, greasy atmosphere of the basement. The kitchen staff and waiters, fitting themselves in between stoves and sinks, left the central space clear for the customers. The lights were switched off. The wailing ceased and there was an interval of attentive silence before people began to complain that the precautions were unnecessary. They had left their food for nothing. It was, as they had said, a false alarm. A man called them all to go back to their dinners but before the fret and grumbles could lead to action, a bomb fell. It was a distant bomb, but a bomb, nevertheless. The silence was the silence of fear, then a moan passed over the kitchen.

Guy said, 'That was the harbour. They're bombing the French warships.'

Ah, that explained the raid. And who cared what happened to the French ships that had lain there immobilised since the fall of France? Then a second bomb fell, much nearer, so close, in fact, that the pots and pans rattled and cries went up. People began struggling towards the stairs as though hoping to find some other, safer, place, and Guy put his arms round Harriet to protect her and she pressed to him, less afraid of the bombs than of the fear around her.

A third bomb fell, further off, a fourth, so distant it could just be heard, and at once the panic died. The raiders had passed over. People relaxed and took on the gaiety of relief, telling each other that they could now go back and eat in peace. But the manager was on the stair and would not let anyone pass. They had to wait for the All Clear before the lights were switched on and they could return to their spoilt food.

Harriet was due back in her office next morning and had to catch the last train. Leaving the restaurant, Guy was intercepted by a man who wished to gain favour for a stout youth who came lagging after him. The son had to take a book-keeping examination and the father pleaded for him. 'I feel, Mr Professor, sir, he should have an extra understanding of this subject.' The subject was not part of Guy's curriculum but he listened patiently and gave what advice he could. The conversation ended with an invitation to cakes and liqueurs. When could the professor come? Any day of that week or the next week or the week after would be suitable. The whole future was open to him so there was no excuse, no chance of escape. Harriet made off before the invitation could be extended to her.

In the hall she could hear the man shouting, 'So, then, you come Thursday week, professor, sir?'

'If Rommel doesn't get here first.'

'Very funny, professor, sir. You make a joke, eh? You make a joke?'

Passing out through the black curtains, they found the city adazzle with moonlight. Harriet was reminded of another night of full moon, the night of Hugo Boulderstone's twenty-first birthday. Just as tonight, they had left the blacked-out restaurant and entered this startling light that cut the buildings into shapes of silver and black. Harriet remembered Hugo's face white in the moonlight and the voice that told her they would never see him again.

Now Guy, his head full of productions and plays and all the theatre talk of the dinner-table, stopped to declaim, 'On such a night as this . . .' and pausing, turned expectantly to Aidan Pratt who took the lines up, speaking them in a voice so charged with emotion and melodic resonance that his two listeners marvelled:

> In such a night
> Troilus methinks mounted the Trojan walls
> And sighed his soul out to the Grecian tents
> Where Cressid lay that night . . .

At the end of Jessica's speech, he bowed to Guy, inviting him to continue.

Guy, in his rich, pleasant voice, said, 'In such a night stood Dido with a willow in her hand . . .' and broke off to add, 'And on this very shore'.

'Somewhere further west,' Aidan gravely amended and Harriet turned to hide her laughter.

Walking towards the station, Guy persuaded Aidan to recite other speeches from other plays, adding others himself and so, quoting and counter-quoting, the thought of the invaders was lost in the poetic past. They left the sea behind and came into the gimcrack district near the station where a whole family might occupy a corner of a room. One of the last bombs had fallen here. Three houses had collapsed together on to the basement where people had been sheltering. Some of them had survived but were trapped inside. They were calling through cracks in the masonry, pleading to be released.

Neighbours, mostly of the balani poor, stood in the road before the ruin, grinning with embarrassment because the pleadings were in vain. No one had the means to move the vast mountain of rubble heaped on top of those who cried.

Guy, Harriet and Aidan, coming upon this scene, felt they should act or conduct action but realised they were as helpless as the rest. Seeing a police-man at the rear of the crowd, Guy asked what was being done for the prisoners. When would they be released? The man put on a show of official competence on hearing an English voice and said, 'Bokra'. Guy did not think this good enough. Something should be done there and then. The policeman said that the civil authorities had no rescue team and no machinery for lifting heavy material. They usually depended on the good will of British servicemen, but now the servicemen had gone away. The people in the basement would have to wait and see if help came. In an earlier raid, survivors were similarly trapped and had been still crying out a week later.

'What happened in the end?' Harriet asked but no one had the answer to her question.

The survivors, overhearing what was being said, set up a more furious wailing and the policeman, going to the rubble, shouted in to them to be patient. Very soon, perhaps that very night, the whole German army would be here to dig them out. At this, the prisoners began to curse the British for bringing the house down on their heads.

Guy said to Aidan, 'If we organised these fellows into a gang, they could clear the site by passing the stuff from hand to hand.' When the policeman returned, Guy repeated this plan in Arabic and the bystanders, realising what he had in mind, wandered off in all directions.

Soon there was no one left to form a gang and the policeman, twisting his face into a grimace of pity, apologised. 'Those very poor men, effendi. Those men not strong.' Guy had to agree. The fellah, weakened by hunger and bilharzia, could not do much. The policeman said, to reassure him, 'Bokra police come. Bokra all very nice.'

Harriet said, 'Bokra fil mish-mish,' and the policeman could not keep from laughing.

Guy appealed to Aidan, 'What's to be done?'

'Nothing, I'm afraid.'

That being so, they had to go on, with the cries of the abandoned prisoners dying away behind them.

Harriet's train was about to leave and she had no time to argue with Guy but, leaning out of the carriage window, she pressed him, 'Darling, when will you come to Cairo? Tomorrow?'

'No, not tomorrow. I'll come at the weekend.'

Aidan was smiling with satisfaction that, at last, he had Guy to himself. The train began to move. Before it was under way, Harriet heard him beginning to tell Guy about his friend in Damascus who had gone out to see what was happening and died with a bullet in his head.

5

The Column did not form itself as rapidly as had been expected. The infantry was there but the guns and gunners had not arrived. Hardy was also expecting another lieutenant. Simon, who for the moment was in charge of both platoons, told Ridley that he had heard there was a serious shortage of artillery. Ridley mournfully agreed. 'We could be hanging about here till Christmas.'

Simon oversaw the digging of slit trenches and he envied the men because they had this occupation, but the digging was easy and the job quickly done. After that, boredom was general. They were occasionally strafed by a passing Messerschmidt but they were too far back to rate serious attention by the enemy. There were no diversions and nothing to do but camp chores. The day's events were the visits from the mobile canteen and the Naafi truck that sold cigarettes and beer.

Early in the morning, the men kicked a ball about – there was a belief that the enemy never attacked men at play – but as the heat increased, activity lost its pleasure and the players flagged. After the mid-day meal, the old soldiers would fit up a ground sheet or blanket to form a bivouac and the newcomers soon copied them. Everyone in camp slept through the afternoon. Simon, who had regarded sleep as a time-wasting necessity, now discovered it could be bliss. Whenever he had nothing better to do, he would get into his sleeping-bag, which protected as much against heat as against cold, and hiding his face from the light, would sink into sleep. Sleep devoured boredom. Sleep devoured time. Here, he thought, they were all like the Cairo beggars who at noon gave themselves thankfully to oblivion.

But there were enemies that could deprive one of sleep. The flies were the worst. The newcomers became, after a while, inured to the bite of mosquitos and sand-flies, but nothing could repel the tormenting flies that buzzed and hit one's face and dragged their feet over sweaty flesh. Simon told Ridley of the black blanket of breeding flies he had seen on the Red Sea shore and Ridley described the fly traps that the men constructed from wire. 'At Mersa,' he said, 'we caught the buggers by the million.' When the traps were full, there would be a mass burning of flies but the flies lived off the dead and the stench of the pyre would linger about the camp for days. For this reason fly burnings were now forbidden.

After sleep came the evening and the men longed for evening as a parched man longs for water. When the sun touched the horizon, the pressure of heat lifted and the flies disappeared.

At the end of their first day at the new camping site, Hardy's driver put a folding table and chair outside the HQ truck and Hardy sat down with his radio to listen to the news. When Simon came within hearing distance, Hardy said, 'You can get yourself a chair from the truck, Boulderstone,' and so, each evening, Simon joined Hardy beside the radio set. After a while, attracted by the sound of the radio, the men began to collect at a distance, at first respectfully standing but, as the entertainment became a habit, seating themselves in groups, smoking and even occasionally making a comment which Hardy ignored. He sometimes grunted or gave, when a news item disturbed him, a bitter, coughing laugh, but he said nothing to Simon who, isolated at the table, would have preferred to be with the men.

The Column was joined by a gunner officer called Martin and a third chair was put out at sunset. Martin was a sandy Scot with an inflamed skin and a bristling red moustache. As he was a captain, Hardy could not ignore him altogether but neither man had much to say. On his second evening, Martin brought a bottle of whisky to the table and sent the driver to find glasses. When he poured drinks for himself and Hardy, he made a grudging movement in Simon's direction but Simon said he only drank beer. That was Martin's first and only gesture towards Simon who was then ignored by both officers. With them, but apart from them, Simon wondered if there was any creature in the army more wretched than a subaltern who had no contact with his seniors and was not allowed to consort with his men.

Talking to Ridley about the non-arrival of the guns, he said, 'We might have been living it up in Cairo all this time. Why were they in such a hurry to get us out here.'

Ridley, solemn with the consciousness of his own wisdom, said, 'We've got to be here. That's the point, see.'

'Even if we're doing nothing?'

'Lots of chaps out here are doing nothing, but they've got to be here. What'd happen if they wasn't?'

Simon laughed. 'I see what you mean.'

'After all sir, it's experience.'

'Pretty dreary experience, sarge.' Simon's early apprehension had begun to fade. So little had happened that he began to think that nothing ever would happen and he wrote home to say what an odd business it was, living here in the desert, like nomads, with nothing to do. In his opinion, they were worse off than the nomad Arabs who sometimes passed the camp. The Arabs had tents, and tents were homes of a sort, but the army men slept under an open sky. For several nights Simon was worried not only by the lack of cover but by the intrusive magnificence of the Egyptian night. The stars were too many and too bright. They were like eyes: waking in mid-sleep, finding them staring down on him, he was unnerved, imagining they questioned what he was doing there. And there was the vast emptiness of the desert itself. The leaguered trucks formed a protective pale but as there were only four trucks, they could not join up. Between them could be seen dark distances that stretched for ever – and what might not come out of the distance while they slept? Some men found the space about them so threatening, they would seek refuge under the lorries. This was a fool thing to do, Ridley told them. There were freak rain storms, even in summer, and lorries had been known to sink into the wet sand and smother the men while they slept.

But in spite of their fears, the dawn came too soon for them. The guards, whose watch had been spent in the last bitter hours of the night, had the job of rousing the camp. Their shouts of 'Wakey, wakey' sounded a note of heartless relish for the men dragged out of sleep. Getting themselves up in the steel-cold daybreak, they could see no reason in their lives.

The first warmth of sunlight lifted the spirits. For a while the sand was the colour of a lightly cooked biscuit, stones threw shadows as long as sword blades and the whole desert was as airy and exhilarating as an endless seashore. Simon thought, 'If only the sun would stand still . . .' but the sun inched up and up till its heat was an affront to the human body. The water ration those days was a gallon per man and this had to serve for washing, shaving, washing of clothes, cooking and drinking. Simon was tempted at times to drink the lot and leave himself unwashed.

Hardy, speaking as though he had given the matter long thought, told Simon to find himself a batman. 'Got any preferences, Boulderstone?'

'I'd like to have Arnold, sir.'

'Arnold?' The choice seemed to surprise Hardy. 'You think he could cope?'

'I've found him very capable, sir.'

'Indeed? I don't know much about him but Ridley thinks he's a bit of a wet.'

Simon said, 'He's all right, sir,' and Arnold was granted him. He understood Ridley's doubts about Arnold but he also understood Arnold. What he knew of him, he had discovered by direct questioning. Unquestioned, Arnold was not one to reveal himself. Simon had several times found him gazing at some desert creature – a spider or lizard or a beetle rolling a ball of dung before it – and realised that his interest went beyond curiosity. On the last occasion, Simon asked, 'What did you do in civvy street, Arnold?'

'Student, sir.'

Simon had to ask three more questions before he discovered that Arnold had studied Natural History at Durham. He had taken his degree a week before the outbreak of war. He not only observed the desert creatures, he was forced to observe the games the men played with them. The men would catch a couple of spiders – not tarantulas that were dangerous to handle, but the big white spiders, of fearful appearance but harmless – and goad the creatures into fighting each other. Or, a more popular and spectacular sport, they would pour petrol round a scorpion and light it so the creature was ringed with fire. They would then gleefully watch its attempt to break out until, in the end, unable to endure the heat, its sting would droop slowly and penetrate the scales on its back. While the other men whooped with joy, Arnold would watch as though he shared the creature's agony.

Simon thought it wretched sport but he recognised the men's need for some sort of diversion in this God-forsaken wilderness. Arnold, helplessly shifting his feet or twisting his hands together, felt only for the animal world. Usually he was silent but once he burst out, 'Why do you do it? Why do you do it?'

The men laughed at him and said, 'Look what he'd do to us if he got the chance!'

'And why not? We don't belong here. This is his habitat – his home, I mean. We've no right here. He has to defend himself against us. Why not leave the poor things alone?'

Arnold was a joke. The men said, 'Poor old Arn, he's sand-happy,' but the officers were less tolerant. The outburst had been talked about and Martin said to Simon, 'I don't know why you want that squit as a batman. You can't trust those quiet types and that one, he's nothing but an old woman.'

Ridley was held to be the most knowledgeable man in camp. He was in Signals and so had the means of picking up information. At work in the HQ truck, he gossiped with other transmitters, picking up and purveying all the rumours, scandals and jokes of the line. When not at work, he talked to the drivers of the supply trucks that visited the camp and if they had nothing to tell him, he usually had something to tell them.

Simon, for some reason, was a favourite with Ridley who would come to him first with any news worth passing on. Ridley was ready to help Simon because Simon accepted help and advice with gratitude and humility. Ridley could sort out the noises that came from the forward position and could tell Simon which was the sound of a field gun and which a medium or ack-ack. He warned Simon about mine fields and uncharted areas where a jerry can or an old baked beans tin might be a booby trap, set to blow your head off.

Simon was troubled by this information and not understanding why, he brooded on it until suddenly, like a returning dream, he remembered the dead boy in the Fayoum house. All the incidents of that day had become remote for him and the people he had met seemed to him beings of an unreal world. He now knew the real world was the fighting world where his companions had a substance and significance that set them apart from the rest of mankind. Only Edwina had circumstance in his world because she was Hugo's girl and Hugo was constantly in his mind. One day, feeling he now knew Ridley well enough, he asked him, 'Could you discover the whereabouts of a Captain Hugo Boulderstone?'

'With respect, sir – a relation of yours?'

'My brother.'

'Ah!' Regard for this near relationship lengthened Ridley's long face. 'Shouldn't be difficult. Not what you'd call a *common* name.'

Soon after, Ridley discovered that there was a Captain Hugo Boulderstone attached to the 6th New Zealand Brigade at Bab el Qattara. Simon eagerly asked, 'What chance of getting a lift down there?'

'Couldn't say, sir. You'd have to bring it up with the major.'

Simon brought it up that evening, beginning, 'Do you think, sir, I could get a lift down to Bab el Qattara? I'd like ...'

'Don't be a fool, Boulderstone,' Hardy interrupted him, 'You can't get a lift anywhere. You're not out here on a sightseeing trip.'

Next day Ridley had word that the Bab el Qattara box had been evacuated and German forces had moved in.

'That doesn't sound too good, does it?' said Simon.

'There's no knowing. Chaps think the Auk could be up to something.'

Two field guns and two anti-tank guns and their gunners joined the Column which was now complete except for the lieutenant due to take over the second platoon. He arrived next day when Simon was helping Arnold, whose job it was to collect rations from platoon headquarters. Simon and Arnold were both on-loading the section's water-cans and sacks for supplies when a staff car drew up a few yards from the truck. Simon had thrown off his sweat-soaked shirt: his shorts needed a wash and his desert boots were covered with sand. Arnold looked no better than he did and the lieutenant, fresh from the discipline of base camp, eyed the pair of them with acute distaste. Wearing his best gabardine, carrying gloves and cane, he had obviously got himself up to present himself to the officers of the Column. Extruding his superiority, he shouted, 'I say, you fellows, is Major Hardy about?'

Recognising the voice rather than the man, Simon said, 'Good God, it's Trench,' and would have embraced him, had not the new arrival taken a disgusted step back.

'Who the devil are you?'

'Don't you recognise me? I'm Simon Boulderstone. Where've you been? We've been waiting for you.'

Trench's fair hair had bleached white under the Egyptian sun. With his fine, regular features and military moustache, he could have posed for a portrait of the ideal young officer, but at that moment he lacked the calm assurance for the part. Instead, disconcerted, he looked Simon over to make sure he had not lost officer rank then, smiling sheepishly, he gave a halting account of his movements since leaving the ship at Suez. He and Codley had been taken to Infantry Base Depot to await a posting. Giving Simon a reproving glance, he muttered, 'How is it you're doing what you're not supposed to do?'

'What do you mean?'

'*You're loading a truck.*'

Simon laughed. In that moment it was revealed to him that Trench was an ass. His friend, whom he had admired beyond all other men, was one of those asses who thought familiarity with the men was 'bad for discipline'. He was a 'spit and polish' officer, a sort of man Simon despised.

'You need to get some service in.' Simon said. 'When you've been out in the blue for a bit, you'll be glad to do anything to break the monotony.' He turned to Arnold and winked at him. 'OK, Arnold, carry on. Don't forget oranges and cheese. Try and bag some fresh meat this time. If they offer you pilchards again, tell them where they can stuff them.'

Arnold saluted with uncustomary smartness. 'Sir. We could do with some Cruft's Specials, sir.'

They'll let you have plenty of those.'

'And it's our turn for jam, sir.'

'Good show.'

Arnold's manner was deferential and Simon, seeing him off, gave him every possible attention, apparently forgetting that Trench was waiting to be led to Major Hardy. The truck went off. Simon, turning away from it, saw Trench with surprise. 'You still there? Come along then, I'll take you to the HQ truck.'

They walked together in silence, both knowing that the old intimacy was lost to them. Some time passed before they thought about it again or understood how, or why, it had ever existed.

The Column, completed, was ordered to prepare for a move and Hardy made an inspection of weapons. As he walked with Martin between the ranks, Ridley asked in the obsequious whine he reserved for senior officers, 'Think we'll get a scrap, sir?'

'Could be. Could be.'

'Make a nice change, sir.'

Hardy was giving nothing away but Simon felt his apprehensions revive. Bored during the waiting days, he would have wished for action.

Now action threatened, he thought longingly of boredom. Doing his best to appear calm, he asked Ridley, 'What's it like, being under fire?'

'You don't feel so much at the time. It's the thinking about it, is worst.'

'You mean, you get your blood up?'

'That's right. Couldn't've put it better m'self. Back here you think you don't hate jerry, but when you go in, it's different. P'raps you see a pal cop it – a decent bloke, p'raps, what's done you a favour. You think "Right you bastards, I'll get you for that" and so you go in fighting mad. You get to hate them like hell. You got to, y'see, you wouldn't be no use if you didn't.'

The thought of being injected with hate, as with a drug, did nothing to reassure Simon. Hate could make you reckless but recklessness did not make you safe. During the night before the dawn departure he woke several times. Hearing the other men stirring and muttering, he knew they were as tense as he was.

Next morning delay would have been welcome, but this time they started as the first cherry red strip of light appeared between the black earth and the black sky. Simon felt no inclination to talk. He was beside Arnold in the leading truck and the leading truck was the one that copped it if they struck an uncharted minefield. As the strip widened, the desert was flushed with red. Simon had been provided with a compass for this journey which took them over sand flats as featureless as mid-ocean. The sun rose and the hours passed. Soon enough they were in the dusty glare of noon, the most painful hour of day, with mirage stretching like water over the track. A hill appeared in the distance, not high but unique in this part of the desert.

Simon stirred himself to ask what it was. Arnold said, 'It's the Ridge, sir.'

The Ridge, as they drew near it, could be seen in detail, a long, narrow outcrop of rock, its flanks fluted as though innumerable rivulets had run down it for centuries. Simon had been told that they were going south of the Ridge so he imagined the journey would soon be over. As they came level with the rock, a wind sprang up and ran along the rock base lifting the sand like the edge of a carpet.

'We're in for a bit of a storm, sir,' Arnold said. 'Think we should call a halt?'

Simon was uncertain but as they rounded the eastern end of the Ridge, the sand had thickened like a fog in the air and Arnold advised him, 'If we brew up now, sir, it could be all over by the time we're finished.' He put up the flag and the Column was halted. Simon, running back to consult with Hardy, was thankful to find they had done the right thing.

They drank their tea, bunched together with backs to the wind, waiting for the storm to die down. Instead, it grew worse and Ridley said morosely, 'Could go on for days.'

Breathing sand, eating sand, blinded and deafened by sand, the men crouched by the trucks for shelter and picked sand from their noses and the interstices of their ears. Ridley became more gloomy. 'Known this go on for *weeks*,' but at sunset, when the air glowed as though the sand had become incandescent, the wind dropped and the world became visible again. In the slanting light the Ridge with its fluted sides looked like a monstrous millipede. Beneath it, there was a large encampment and Simon would have been glad to leaguer to its rear but Hardy decreed that they make another mile before darkness fell. As they moved off, guns opened up behind them and Simon, his stomach muscles contracting, felt he should have written home before leaving camp. He thought of his mother first, then remembered his wife. He should have sent letters to both of them, preparing them for whatever happened to him, but in terms that made light of it all. He tried to think of his wife but the few days of their honeymoon had disappeared into the past. He made an effort to recall her face and saw instead the long, fair, drooping hair of Edwina Little. Troubled by his infidelity, he took out his wallet and gazed at the photograph of Anne and all he could feel was that her face was not the right face. He wanted to see the laughing, sunburnt face that had leant towards him from the balcony in Garden City but the truth was, no face could distract him now. The whole of the pleasurable world had dwindled out of sight, leaving him with nothing but a sense of loss and an awareness of the danger he was in.

The Column leaguered in a service area where supply dumps and transports were camouflaged with nets. It looked safe enough, rather like a vast workshop, but the trucks had just drawn up when the guns started again and hammered their senses as they sat round Hardy's radio waiting for the news. The newsreader announced that later in the evening there would be a commentary on 'The Alamein Line'. Simon asked Hardy, 'What's that, sir?' and Hardy, who would not admit ignorance, said, 'If you pay attention and listen, Boulderstone, you'll find out.' This admonition was so familiar to Simon, it occurred to him that Hardy had been a school-master in his civilian days. The commentator told them that the Alamein Line stretched from the coastal salt lakes to a mysterious hole in the desert called the Qattara Depression and his description suggested that there were bodies of well-armoured troops in close formation for forty miles. None of the officers questioned this but Simon, who had seen nothing of such a line, spoke to Ridley before going to his sleeping-bag. 'I say, sarge, you heard that about the Alamein Line. Where exactly is it?'

Ridley, as much at a loss as he was, gave the matter thought and said, 'This is it, I reckon. There's the South Africans up north and a couple of Indian divs down south, and the Kiwis are under the Ridge, and our chaps are in between. They're a bit thin on the ground but it's a line all right.'

Ridley seemed satisfied but Simon, who had pictured the front as a carnage of gun-fire, bursting shells and barbed wire hung with the dead and dying, felt disappointment as well as relief. 'It's not much of a line, sarge.'

'It's all we've got. Still, it's not what we've got but what they haven't got that'll make the difference. It said on the intercom today that the Auk's trying to make an army out of remnants. That's it – remnants. The Auk's a great bloke but I don't know I fancy his chances.'

'Do you fancy anyone's chances, sarge?'

'Ah, now, sir!' Ridley pulled himself up and spoke with confidence, 'We'll do for them, yet – you wait and see.'

Driving next morning into open desert, the guns booming behind, the Column was as exposed as a fly on a window-pane. Arnold, peering out for markers, also kept an eye on the sky but it was not till mid-morning, when they had stopped to brew up, that enemy aircraft observed them. Ridley was carrying tea mugs over to the officers when three Italian Macchis buzzed the trucks. Before any of the men could drop to the ground, bullets were spitting about them. The officers sprang back and Hardy, the eldest of them and the most alarmed, lost his balance and fell, his voice rising in a thin, protesting cry, 'Oh, my wife and kids!'

The Macchis, having strafed the Column from end to end, flew off. No one had been hit. Ridley helped Hardy to his feet and everyone behaved as though the fall had been an unfortunate trip-up and said, 'Bad luck, sir.' Simon, thinking he alone had heard Hardy's cry, decided it must never be mentioned, not even to Arnold.

Driving on, they came into a region where rocky outcrops, miniatures of the great Ridge, rose, one after the other, out of the flat mardam. These outcrops changed in colour, the usual Sahara yellow taking on a tinge of pink and the pink growing and deepening until the rocks and sand had the faded rose colour of old red sandstone. Hardy called a halt between the rock ridges and the Column leaguered in a wide, flat area, like a rose pink ballroom aglow with sunset. In the distance, when evening cleared the air, a dramatic range of high ridges could be seen on the horizon. Hardy, consulting his maps, told the officers that the range marked the terminal of the line. Beyond it was the Depression and the Depression, it seemed, could not be crossed. So the Column need go no further. 'Tomorrow,' he said, 'the men'll make slit trenches and dig in the vehicles.'

They had arrived.

6

Rumour came to Cairo of a battle fought inside Egypt at a railway halt called El Alamein but, it seemed, nothing had been settled. The Germans were still a day's tank drive away and their broadcasts claimed they were merely awaiting fresh supplies. Any day now the advance would begin again. Egypt would be liberated and Rommel and his men would keep their assignation with the ladies of Alexandria.

Though the situation had not changed, the panic had died. Those who were, or believed themselves to be, at risk, had gone. Those who remained felt a sense of respite but were warned they might have to leave at short notice. They were advised to keep a bag packed.

When Harriet, returning for luncheon, found a note at the pension to say Dobson had rung her, she supposed the evacuation order had gone out. She took out the small suitcase, the only luggage she had brought out of Greece, and put together a few toilet articles. The suitcase was already packed. She could leave in minutes, but she did not intend to leave without Guy. She thought of a dozen arguments to bring down on Dobson when he telephoned again and his voice, when she heard it, startled her. His tone was jocular. Instead of ordering her to the station, he invited her to meet him for drinks at Groppi's: 'Come about five-thirty.'

'You sound as though you had good news?'

'Perhaps I have,' he spoke teasingly. 'I'll tell you when I see you.'

Back at the office, she looked through the news sheets, but they gave no cause for rejoicing. Whatever Dobson would tell her, it could have nothing to do with the war.

That morning she had heard that her job at the Embassy would not last much longer. The promised team from the States was about to fly to Egypt.

Mr Buschman, not caring to tell her himself, had sent her a typed note. Dispirited, she went to the wall map where the black pins converged upon the Middle East.

She had taken it over during the great days of the Russian counter-offensive when everyone was saying that the Russian winter would defeat Hitler as it had defeated Napoleon. Marking the Russian advances, she rejoiced as though pushing the enemy back with her own hands. Guy had picked up a new song from one of his left-wing friends and repeatedly sang it to what was, more or less, the tune of *The Lincolnshire Poacher*:

> To say that Hitler can't be beat
> Is just a lot of cock,
> For Marshal Timoshenko's men
> Are pissing through von Bock.
> The Führer makes the bloomers and his generals take the rap,
> But Joe, he smokes his pipe and wears a taxi-driver's cap.

In the desert, too, the Germans had been in retreat. The British troops, who had been making a hero of Rommel, now turned their admiration on to Stalin and the Russian generals. But that had all passed. Harriet, bringing the black pins closer to the Kuban river, thought, 'A few more miles and they'll have the whole Caucasus.'

Inside Egypt, the black pins stretched from the coast to a hatched-in area of the desert named on the map 'Qattara Depression'. When Mr Buschman wandered over to see who was where, she asked him what this Depression was. He stood for some moments, rubbing his small, plump hand over the back of his neck, and then gave up: 'All I know is, it's the end of the line.'

'But why is it the end of the line? Why don't they come round that way? If they did, they could surround the whole British army.'

'Too right, mem. They surely could.'

Harriet asked Iqal about the Depression but he had never heard of it.

'How is your German these days?'

He smiled an arch smile, the runnels of his face quivering so he looked like coffee cream on the boil. 'I brush it up now and then, but I don't know! These Germans should make more haste.'

'I told you they wouldn't get here.'

'That is true, Mrs Pringle, and perhaps you spoke right. But on the other hand, perhaps not. It says in the broadcasts they regather their forces and then they come – zoom! So what is one to think? See here, Mrs Pringle, they exhort us, "Rise against your oppressors" they say, "Kill them and be free".'

'You don't think the English are oppressors, do you?'

Iqal raised his great shoulders. 'Sometimes, yes. Sometimes, no. When they break through the palace gates and tell my king what to do, what would you call them? Are they not oppressors?'

'We're fighting a war, Iqal. If the Egyptians really felt oppressed, they would turn on us, wouldn't they?'

'Ah, Mrs Pringle, we are not fools. My friends say, "Time enough when the Germans are at the gate – *then* we cut the English throats".'

'Oh, come now, Iqal, you wouldn't cut my throat?'

Iqal giggled. 'Believe me, Mrs Pringle, if I would cut your throat, I do it in a kind and considerate manner.'

'You wouldn't hurt me?'

'No, no, Mrs Pringle, indeed I would not.'

Harriet reached Groppi's when the sun was low in the sky. She passed through the bead curtain into the brown, chocolate-scented cake and sweet shop as the great round golden chocolate boxes were reflecting the golden sky. The garden café, surrounded by high walls, was already in shadow. It was a large café, sunk like a well among the houses, with a floor-covering of small stones and it disappointed people who saw it for the first time. A young officer had said to Harriet, 'The chaps in the desert think Groppi's is the Garden of Sensual Delights – but, good grief, it isn't even a garden!'

It was, she said, a desert garden, the best anyone could hope for so far from the river. It was a garden of indulgences where the Levantine ladies came to eye the staff officers who treated it as a home from home.

The ground was planted, not with trees, but with tables and chairs and coloured umbrellas. But under one wall, where there was a strip of imported earth, zinnias grew and an old, hardy creeping plant spread out and up and covered lattices and stretched as far as the enclosure that stood at one end of the café site. This creeper sometimes put out a few copper-coloured, trumpet-shaped flowers that enhanced the garden idea. But this display, and there was not much of it, would have died in an hour without the water that seeped continually through the holes in a canvas hose. In spite of the water, the mat of leaves hung dry and loose, shifting and rustling in the hot wind. Only the tough, thick-petalled zinnias thrived in this heat.

When Harriet entered, the safragis were taking down the umbrellas, leaving the tables open to the evening air. At this hour people were crowding in, searching for friends or somewhere to sit. Dobson must have arrived early for Harriet found him at a vantage point, in front of the zinnias. He had seen her before she saw him and was on his feet, beckoning to her, his smile so genial she wondered if he had news of a victory.

She asked, 'Has anything happened?' He did not answer but waved her to a chair. Whatever he had to tell, he was in no hurry to tell it.

A safragi, his white galabiah given distinction by a red sash and the fez that denotes the effendi's servant, wheeled over a gilded trolley laden with cream cakes. Harriet asked for a glass of white wine. Dobson urged her to choose a cake, saying, 'Do join me. I think I'll have a *mille feuille*. Good for you. You've lost weight since you came here.'

'I really hadn't much weight to lose.'

Dobson put his fork into his *mille feuille* and said as the cream and jam oozed out, 'Yum, yum,' and put a large piece into his mouth then asked, as he sometimes did, about her work at the American Embassy.

'Coming to an end, I fear,' Harriet gave a wry laugh. 'Perhaps we're all coming to an end. Iqal was joking about cutting our throats – perhaps not just joking. He seemed to resent that occasion when the ambassador drove a tank through the palace gates.'

Dobson, putting more pastry into his mouth, swayed his head knowingly, swallowed and said, 'We're always having trouble with Farouk. He's a fat, spoilt baby, but he's a clever baby. The other day H.E. waited over an hour for an audience. He thought the king was with his ministers but instead he had a girl with him.She put her head out of the door and seeing H.E. there in all his regalia, she went off into screams of laughter and slammed the door on him. When he eventually got in, he found Farouk sprawled on a sofa, languid and irritable – post coitum, no doubt. He thought, with the hun so close, he could tell us to clear out. H.E. explained why we must hold Egypt at all cost. Farouk scarcely bothered to listen and at the end, he sighed and said, "Oh, very well. Stay if you must. But when your war's over, for God's sake, put down the white man's burden and *go*".'

Dobson, having told his story, looked over the garden as though expecting another guest. Harriet hoped she would now hear why he had invited her here, but before anything more could be said, two Egyptian women stopped to speak to him. He jumped up, became at once diplomatically effusive, and they talked together in French. The women, dressed in an embellished version of Parisian fashion, wore black dresses to which they had added brooches, necklaces and sprays of flowers. Their skirts ended an inch above the knee but their sleeves, as required by the prophet, came down to their wrists. They flirted with Dobson, their eyes enhanced by eye-veils, and moved their heads, giving small, rapid turns this way and that so their earrings danced. Harriet had heard that Dobson, the only bachelor among the senior diplomats, was regarded in Cairo as 'quite a catch'. One of the women invited him to a cocktail party and he accepted as though overwhelmed by the thought of it, but when the women moved away, he fell back in his chair with a long, exhausted sigh. 'My policy is to accept everything and go to nothing. Where's that husband of yours?'

'Are you expecting him?'

'Certainly I'm expecting him. I rang him first thing this morning and asked him to be here at five-thirty. It's now nearly six and I ought to be back in my office.'

'You want to see him about something? Is it important?'

'It is for him.' Dobson laughed, making light of Guy's nonappearance but it was an aggravated laugh. Harriet looked anxiously towards the entrance, fearing that Dobson would go and the important matter be nullified, all because Guy could never turn up on time. She said to excuse him, 'People make too many claims on him so he ends up with more engagements than the day will hold. The result is, he's late for everything and made later by all the telephone calls he makes to explain why he'll be late.'

Dobson thought this very funny. 'How does he get away with it?'

'If he didn't get away with it, he'd have to learn not to be late. People spoil him and make him worse than he need be.'

The afterglow of sunset was taking on the green of dusk. The evening star appeared as from nowhere, radiating long rays of white light, and the coloured electric bulbs were lit among the creepers. All about, in the high house walls, windows were thrown open and people looked down on the brilliant garden.

Harriet said, 'When we first came here from Greece, those lighted windows frightened me. I thought, "What a target we are!"'

But at that moment, the lights meant nothing but the passing of time, and her fear was the fear that Guy would not turn up at all.

Dobson said, 'Ha, here he is!' forgiving Guy on sight for being three-quarters of an hour late.

Guy, lost between the tables, was dishevelled as ever. He had broken his glasses and mended them roughly with adhesive tape. At least, Harriet consoled herself, he hasn't brought anyone with him.

When Dobson waved to him, he came over at a hurried trot, breathlessly explaining how someone or something had detained him. Dobson, all irritation gone, said, 'Don't worry. Don't worry at all. What are you going to drink?' When at last the table was resettled, he said impressively, 'Now, then!' They were going to hear what this meeting was all about.

'I've received a telegram from Bevington.'

'Our chairman?'

'Lord Bevington himself.' Dobson started to laugh so that his body was shaken by a sort of nervous hiccups. 'I remember when Bevington came here on a visit. It was my night on duty at the Embassy and I'd just got my head down when the boab looked in – huge, coal-black fellow – and croaked at me, "De lord am come!" Dear me, I said to myself, it's the day of judgement . . . Well, now! first things first. Colin Gracey has been given the push.'

'He's leaving the Organisation?'

'You needn't be surprised. Pinkrose cabled the London office and accused him of neglect of duty, incompetence, cowardice in the face of the enemy and, most heinous crime of all, going to Palestine without letting Pinkrose know. He also, as a make-weight, said he had evidence of immoral practices.'

'Really!' Harriet was interested. 'What immoral practices? The house-boat? Mustapha Quant?'

'Probably. A Turk was mentioned.'

Guy looked troubled. 'They can't simply take Pinkrose's word for it. There must be an official enquiry.'

'There has been an enquiry. In any case, Pinkrose's complaints were only the last of a series made by British residents. Pinkrose carried most weight because he is known to Bevington who cabled the Embassy for confirmation. I cabled back that Gracey had indeed fled and the office was shut. This clinched it. We were informed that if Gracey returned he should be handed a letter ordering him to Aden which is, I believe, the Organisation's Devil's Island.'

Guy took off his glasses and, the tape giving way, the lenses fell apart. He asked, 'But who will replace him. Are they flying someone out?'

'No.' Smiling blandly, Dobson watched Guy fidgeting with the broken frame then said, 'Bevington has chosen a London appointed man – the only one left in Egypt.'

'Guy?'

Dobson turned his smile on to Harriet who threw back her head and laughed with delight. Dobson looked to Guy for a similar reaction but Guy, though he had flushed with pleasure, looked disturbed. 'Is this really fair to Gracey?'

'You don't have to worry about Gracey. He's not likely to take himself to Aden. Even before he left here, he was enquiring about a possible passage to the Cape, saying that the exigencies of life in a war zone were telling on his health.'

Guy still did not seem satisfied and Harriet, taking the glasses out of his hand, said, 'Forget Gracey. What you have to think about is the Organisation. If Bevington has chosen you for the job, it's up to you to do it. Don't waste concern on Gracey.'

As he reflected on this, Guy's expression lightened and he realised that he had before him a whole new area of activity on which to expend his energy. All he had to do now was settle matters at the Commercial College. As Harriet had suspected, when the need came, these matters could be settled easily enough.

Guy said, 'I've a couple of excellent Greek teachers who can take over the English department. I'll be back here as soon as they're installed and my first aim will be to get the Institute on its feet.'

'And,' said Harriet, 'you'll have to tidy yourself up. Here,' she returned his glasses, neatly mended with tape, and said, 'Order a new frame for them,' then she took his hand and said with affectionate pride, 'I don't know how you do it, but you always win in the end.'

Dobson had to leave them but, standing up, he said, 'I don't know how you feel about that pension of yours but I have a room free in Garden City. It was Beaker's room and he's left a few sticks in it. If you like to look at it . . .'

'Goodness, yes. How wonderful!' Overwhelmed by the day's good fortune, Harriet could not speak above a whisper.

It was arranged that next evening, when she left work, she was to look at the room.

Dobson said, 'Bless you both', and made off through the garden, walking with a backward tilt as though his heels were lower than his toes. Looking after the short, plump figure, Guy said, 'There, I always said Dobson was a really nice fellow.'

'Have I ever said anything else?'

The Organisation men, feeling themselves inferior, had been inclined to jeer at the diplomats who, in times of danger, saw the Organisation as another and unnecessary problem.

Now Guy said, 'I'm afraid we felt they were another order of being – but, really, they're not bad when you get to know them.' He was rapidly taking on confidence and vitality as he considered the responsibilities that lay ahead. The lines on his face had faded and he was alert with a new consciousness of authority. Harriet thought, 'He may one day be eminent.' Guy, catching her considering glance, said, 'We'll have more money now, so let's have a Pernod on the strength of it.'

Dobson told Harriet that the flat belonged to the Embassy. He explained why it was divided into two parts and led her through the baize door into what had been the harem quarters. He usually let these rooms to Embassy staff but if no Embassy person needed accommodation, he was free to let to friends.

'So I had Professor Beaker and now . . .' he gave Harriet a humorous little bow, 'I hope to have Guy and Harriet Pringle. What could be nicer! But you better look the room over before deciding. It's not at all grand. The main part is protected because the servants' rooms are above it, but this wing is immediately under the roof. I'm afraid it gets rather hot.'

When he opened the door, the heat, as though too big for the room, rolled out and wrapped itself round them like an eiderdown. The servants had not bothered to pull down the blinds so heat came in, not only through the ceiling, but also the window. The woodwork, which had been sun-baked for a century, seemed to crackle with heat and the floor shook as they walked upon it.

The room was furnished with a divan bed, two chairs and a hanging cupboard. The professor had rented this furniture from a store in the Muski and the Pringles could add to it if they wished.

'I know it's not much, but it's rent free. You only have to pay your share of the housekeeping. So – what do you think?'

Harriet, trying to think of some adequate expression of gratitude, gave a little sigh and Dobson, mistaking her hesitation for uncertainty, said, 'I'll leave you to consider and look around.'

Harriet, left to herself, absorbed the atmosphere of the room that was square and not very large. The window looked out on the leaves of a tree that filled the whole window space. The heat muffled her but, entranced by the thought of living here with Guy among congenial people, she did not mind the heat. She sat on the edge of the bed and stared at the tree then, hearing a telephone ringing, she was struck with fear that someone else was wanting the room and she hurried back to Dobson to lay claim to it.

Dobson, his call finished, came into the living-room and she said at once, 'It's a wonderful room.'

'Oh, hardly that, but if you want it, it's yours. I'm sorry Edwina's not here. She's out with one of her young men, but do sit down. Hassan has squeezed some limes for us. Will you have gin and lime, or just plain lime and water?'

'Lime juice! What luxury!'

Dobson, thinking she referred to the work of squeezing the limes, said, 'Oh, it's not so difficult. We have a little machine thing.'

Settling down with his gin and lime, he asked if she had heard any amusing gossip lately. Unable to think of any, she put her question about the Qattara Depression.

Dobson, being able to answer it, looked pleased. 'The Depression is just an immense salt pan but it's got the jerries foxed. They know if they tried to cross it, their tanks would sink into it. Tweedie, the military attaché, drove out to take a shufti and he said you can see the German engineers climbing down to it and poking sticks into the surface. Until they find a way across it, it acts as a strategic terminus.'

'But couldn't they go round it?'

'Too far. Five hundred miles or more. Tweedie thinks they're over-stretched as it is.'

'You think that's why they've come to a stop? You don't think they're simply waiting for the Caucasus to collapse? If the German panzers came down through Persia, they'd meet up with Rommel and surround the British forces. 8th Army could be wiped out.'

'Dear me,' Dobson laughed. 'You certainly believe in facing up to the worst.'

'If Hitler got the Baku oil and the Middle East oil – what would happen then?'

Dobson cheerfully considered this possibility – Harriet realised that cheerfulness was a form of diplomatic courtesy – but she could see he was bored by her suppositions. 'I imagine our troops would have withdrawn to Upper Egypt long before that happened. We'd battle on.'

'For ever? Like the Hundred Years War?'

'It's possible,' Dobson spoke as though the war was a tedious subject, better not discussed. Harriet finished her lime juice and said she must go. Taking her to the door, Dobson said in the tone of one making a confession, 'I may say that, in my cable to Bevington, I mentioned that Guy was the only Organisation man in Rumania who stuck it out to the end.'

'Thank you, Dobbie. Guy needs a friend.'

'Needs a friend! But no one has more friends.'

'There are friends and friends. There are those who want something from you and those who will do something for you. Guy has plenty of the first. He's rather short of the second.'

'Do you mean that?'

'Yes. He collects depressives, neurotics and dotty people who think he's the answer to their own inadequacy.'

'And is he?'

'No, there is no answer.'

The next day, when Harriet brought some of her belongings to the flat, she found Edwina in the living-room. The two girls had met at parties but had talked only once, during a dance at Mena House when they happened to be in the cloakroom together. Edwina, putting on lipstick of a violent mulberry colour, caught Harriet's gaze in the looking-glass and winked at her as though they shared a joke. She said, 'This colour's a bit much, isn't it?' Harriet did not think so and Edwina said, 'Some people say I'm fast, but I'm not really. I only want a good time.'

And why not? Harriet asked herself. Drawn to Edwina's easy good-nature, she would have talked longer but Edwina, besieged by all the excitements awaiting her, threw her lipstick into her bag, saying, 'Well, back to the fray. Let's have a chat some time,' and was gone. The time did not come. Though they were the same age, Harriet and Edwina did not meet on common ground. Edwina was unmarried and reputed to be the most eligible girl in Cairo. Even the plainest English girls were sought after and Edwina, a beauty even if not a classical beauty, had so many invitations to dinners and parties, she could not, with the best will in the world, find time for other girls.

Now she greeted Harriet like an old friend, saying, 'Oh, I'm so glad you've taken the room. What fun it will be, having you here!' Pushing the sun-bleached hair away from her eyes, she observed Harriet with such warm and welcoming admiration that Harriet felt the world would change for her. 'Yes,' she said, 'what fun!' and life, that had been dark with war and defeat, for a moment took on the brilliance of Edwina's good times.

Edwina said, 'How sad, I have to go and change but we'll see such lots of each other now we're sharing a flat, won't we?'

Of course. Of course. Harriet, going to her room, heard Edwina singing under the shower. Putting her things into the hanging-cupboard, she noticed a dry, herbal scent in the air, like the scent of *pot-pourri*. She thought it came from the dried-out wood then saw that the window had been opened and noises, gentle and monotonous, told her that there was a garden outside. She heard the hiss of water and realised that the water was drawing the scent from dry grass. And there was a thin thread of pipe music repeating the same phrase over and over again.

She took a chair to the window and standing on it, tried to look through the tree's dark, glossy, ovoid leaves but they grew too thickly and there was nothing to be seen but the blur of sunlight beneath the lowest branches. The sun was sinking and its rays, piercing in between the leaves, filled the room with a dusty glow. Close to the tree, she saw that its head of leaves was dotted with green fruits that here and there were taking on a flush of orange or pink.

Looking into the tree, feeling protected by its presence, hearing the delicate pipe phrase endlessly repeated, she felt comforted as though by the prediction of happiness to come.

When she returned to the living-room, Dobson wandered from his room, naked except for a bath-towel worn round his waist like a sarong. 'We're very informal here,' he said.

She asked about the garden outside her window and was told it belonged to the owner of one of Cairo's big stores. 'A very rich man,' Dobson said with satisfaction.

'Someone's playing a pipe out there.'

'That's the snake charmer, a frequent visitor. He's a bit of a joke among the safragis who say he can always produce a sackful of snakes because he brings them with him. He charms the same snakes every time.'

Harriet was pleased to hear that the snakes were not killed but led this enchanted life, perpetually charmed by pipe music.

At the end of the week, when she left the pension and brought the last of her things to the flat, Dobson asked, 'And when are we to be joined by the great man himself?' Edwina entering, as he spoke, wanted to know who the great man was, saying, 'Why have I not met him?'

Harriet said, 'You'll meet him soon. He is my husband.' She expected him to turn up for supper that evening and had told him he would see Edwina, but Edwina was dressed for some much more sumptuous occasion than supper at the flat. Waiting for her escort, she asked Harriet to join her on the balcony. The French windows had been opened and the first cool air of evening was drifting into the room. Outside there were some old wicker-work sofas and chairs. Sitting in the the mild, jasmin-scented twilight, looking over the palms and sycamores and mango trees that grew in the riverside gardens, Harriet felt that she and Guy had at last found a home in Cairo.

Edwina had brought out the grocery lists which she made for the senior safragi, Hassan, and showing them to Harriet, said, 'You can take a turn at the housekeeping if you like, but you have to keep an eye on Hassan. He expects to make a bit here and there, but it mustn't be too much. Also, he's inclined to pay more than he need at the market to show what a great house he works for, so you have to keep a check on prices. They all take advantage any way they can and Hassan's no worse than most.'

'There are just the four of us: you, Dobbie, Guy and me?'

'No, there's one more: Percy Gibbon,' Edwina seemed to regret the addition of this fifth person but said no more about him. 'I do look forward to meeting Guy,' she sighed. 'I wish I had a nice husband like that. Dobbie says he's a pet.'

Harriet, flattered, wondered if, among the young, expugnable officers who took her out, Edwina could ever find one she would wish to marry. Lulled into a sense of well-being by Edwina's amiable chatter about food and market prices, Harriet forgot that her companion was going out and felt a sense of shocked deprivation when Hassan came out to announce,

'Captain come, sa'ida,' and Edwina jumped to her feet. Again she lamented that she must go but she was eager for the evening's entertainment. Standing a moment against the light of the room, she gathered together her sequinned scarf and her little, glittering evening bag, then smiled and went away, leaving behind her scent of gardenias.

The snake charmer did not return for several days but Harriet, coming back from the office one afternoon, heard a more complex and powerful music filling the flat.

Dobson's room led off the living-room, the door stood ajar and as she paused near it, Dobson looked out and said, 'You haven't seen my gramophone, have you?' He invited her into a room that was larger than the other bedrooms but as sparsely furnished. The only thing remarkable in it was an old-fashioned box gramophone with a horn of immense size. The horn, made of papier maché, lifted itself towards the ceiling, opening in a mouth that was more than four foot wide.

'I've never seen anything like it.'

Dobson was delighted by her astonishment. 'Magnificent, isn't it? It must be the only one of its kind in the Middle East. I bought it from Beaker who got it before the war, when you could get anything sent out. He didn't want the bother of transporting it to Baghdad so I was happy to take it from him. It's hand made, of course. The needle is amethyst so it will never wear out.'

The record had ended and lifting it, holding it delicately by the edges, Dobson turned it over, saying, 'I'll put it on again so you can hear the quality of the sound.'

The gramophone had to be cranked up by hand. Dobson, in his siesta garb of a towel round the middle – worn not from modesty but to ward off stomach chills – turned the handle so his fat little belly protruding above the towel edge, his narrow soft shoulders and his soft pale arms, all quivered with the effort. He looked, Harriet thought, as plump and bosomed as a woman but he was quite unabashed by the fact. Placing the needle to the moving record, he stood back and the music unrolled like velvet about the room.

Harriet, not knowledgeable about music, guessed it was Mozart.

'Yes. The Clarinet Quintet. Exquisite, isn't it?'

All through the late afternoons and evenings of mid-summer the questing notes of the clarinet filled the flat as Dobson played and replayed his new record.

135

Harriet's job might end any day now. It ended, as things were liable to do these days, without warning. Harriet was at the map, advancing the black pins across the Kuban river at Krasnodar when Iqal came up behind her and said in a hurried whisper, 'Important gentlemen have come from America. I warn you, one is about to enter.'

She turned and said, 'I think he's entered already.'

The man, as neat looking as Mr Buschman but younger, seemed oddly pale and composed among the hot, sunburnt people in the basement. He was dressed as Mr Buschman dressed: a dark blue poplin suit of elegant cut, a white silk shirt and a narrow black tie. Mr Buschman had not returned from golf and the new arrival came straight to Harriet with hand outstretched. 'As you see, we are here at last. We touched down half an hour ago.' Unmoved by the ancient world, unmoved by war, he smiled with sublime self-assurance, showing perfect teeth. Seeing the map, he asked, 'How's it going?'

'On and on and on.'

'It'll go better now.'

'You're going to blow them right out of the water?'

He was much amused. 'You've said it, mem.'

Harriet put the pins down. 'The Germans have crossed the Kuban river. You might like to mark it up.'

'Oh, give them to my secretary. She's in the john at the moment. She'll just love playing with those little pins.'

Harriet said goodbye to everyone and turned her back on the map as she would, if she could, have turned her back on the whole weary conflict.

Guy, when he entered the Institute as Director, found in the hall a notice that said Professor Dubedat and Professor Lush would, on alternate evenings, give lectures on Shakespeare, Milton, Wordsworth and other outstanding figures of English literature. Apart from this promise, little remained of the cultural activities that had once filled the six rooms and lecture hall of the building in the centre of Cairo. The place had a run-down appearance. Three Egyptian teachers remained to take dwindling classes and these, when they heard that a new Director had arrived, came to Guy with complaints and questions.

'Where, may I ask, sir,' one of them asked, 'are these professors called Dubedat and Lush? Of their lectures we have not heard one word.'

Guy did not know. He called a meeting of all the remaining staff – a Coptic secretary, the two Greek women who looked after the library and the three teachers – and gave them a talk, impressing on them the importance of the work he required them to do.

Harriet, sitting at the back of the hall, wondered again at Guy's ability to stimulate enthusiasm and make possible what before had seemed impossible. She had felt the same wonder when, producing *Troilus and Cressida* in Bucharest, he had overcome the apathy of the stage-hands and infused the cast with his own energy. And that had been simply for one evening's entertainment. Now he had a task much more worthy of his spirit. He told the staff that he was working on a new curriculum for the autumn term when there would be not only classes in English but lectures by such notables as Professor Lord Pinkrose, the famous poet William Castlebar, Professor Beaker from Baghdad and half a dozen of the English professors at Fuad al Awal University.

As Guy brought out these names, Harriet was astounded to realise he knew them all and had already approached them. Even Pinkrose had written from the King David Hotel, Jerusalem, to say that when it was safe for him to return to Egypt, he would be pleased to repeat the lecture that he had given at Phaleron before a brilliant audience on the day Germany declared war on Greece. Guy read this letter aloud with such emphasis that the audience, deeply impressed, broke into applause. Then, the library! Up till now the librarians had followed the out-of-date procedure of keeping the books guarded behind a counter and handing them out on request. All that would change. The library shelves would be thrown open to borrowers to pick and choose and browse at will. Guy was making a list of a thousand recently published books which he intended to order and which, sooner or later, would turn up. He laughed and said, 'Later rather than sooner, I imagine,' and the audience applauded again.

The English librarian, a Miss Pedler, was among those who had gone to Palestine, and the library had been kept open by the Greek women, both married to Egyptians, who now began calling out the names of books that the library needed.

'Write them down. I'll see we get them.'

Guy said he intended setting up a library of gramophone records which would be lent to musical groups in the forces as well as the Institute. He planned a weekly Institute evening when there would be music, poetry readings and plays.

'And dancing?' one of the teachers excitedly asked.

'*And* dancing. One very important thing – we will need more teachers. Put it among your English-speaking friends. Tell them the work is regular and the pay good.'

The Egyptian teachers laughed, throwing themselves about in their chairs and shouting, 'Professor Pringle, sir, we have had no pay since Professor Gracey went away.'

Guy said that would be put right. No one mentioned the German advance or questioned his certainty that the Institute would remain and the British remain with it. Harriet, who might once have feared that Guy promised more than he could perform, was now confident that what he said he would do, he would do.

Walking back to Garden City, he asked her, 'Was I all right?'

'You were splendid.'

Guy had been so absorbed by his new authority that Harriet had had no chance to ask him what he thought of the move to Dobson's flat. When she spoke of it now, he said, 'The room's all right but that tree is a nuisance. It cuts off the light.'

'I love the tree. What do you think of Edwina?'

'She seems a nice girl. A bit of a glamour puss.' Guy laughed at the thought of Edwina and Harriet felt she could be thankful that glamour was an abstraction which did not much affect him.

'What do you think of Percy Gibbon?'

'That fellow who sits at the table and never speaks?'

'Yes. I feel he resents our being there.'

Guy laughed again, unable to believe that anyone could resent his being anywhere. 'I suppose he's shy, that's all.'

Guy was too busy to observe the life of the flat. There was scarcely time in the day for all the tasks he had set himself. He had a trestle-table sent from the Institute so he could work at home. The table was put up in the Pringles' bedroom where it was very much in the way. Guy, whose sight was poor, could not bear the room's penumbra and, looking round, found the room next to them was empty. He asked Dobson if he might put the table in there. The room was so small that Dobson had not thought it tenable for long, and said, 'Use it by all means, my dear fellow.'

Spreading out his papers in the spare room, Guy heard the door open and, looking round, found Percy Gibbon regarding him with malign disapproval. 'This is where I do my exercises,' Gibbon said.

Guy genially replied, 'Carry on. You won't disturb me.'

Percy did not carry on but slammed the door violently as he went.

During the time they had been in the flat, he had once spoken to Harriet. When she had said at the breakfast-table, 'I heard a rumour that we've lost the Canberra,' he lifted a face taut with reproof and said, 'If you heard that, you should keep it to yourself.'

Later, Harriet said to Dobson, 'I don't think Percy Gibbon likes us. He seems to feel we have no right to be here.'

'He's the one who has no right to be here. He asked me to let him stay for a few days while he found a place of his own. That was a year ago, and I can't get rid of him. He complains about his room, about the servants, about everybody and everything. I've suggested, very tactfully of course, that he'd be happier elsewhere, but he says he hasn't time to look for another place.'

'He's pathetic, really. He's in love with Edwina.'

'Surely you're joking?' Dobson laughed aloud at the thought of Percy in love but Harriet, who had seen him looking at Edwina with desperate longing, could only pity him.

7

Simon first felt the Column had taken on identity when he heard one of the men refer to it as Hardy's. Soon Ridley and Arnold and all the rest of them were calling themselves Hardy's Lot, speaking of Hardy as though he were another Popski and they his private army.

If Hardy himself had had any qualities on which to hang reverence, they would have made a hero of him, but everything about the major discouraged worship. He had little contact with the men and his remote manner suggested a self-sufficiency in which they had no faith. Simon had been right in suspecting that Hardy had been a schoolmaster before the war. According to Ridley, he had been the headmaster of a small prep school in Surrey. Simon, who had had a form-master not unlike the major, realised that Hardy was a timid man whose silence and withdrawn manner hid nothing but inefficiency. The form-master, Bishop, kept his distance with the boys and they did not know what to make of him. Some of them were ready to believe he was a superior person but when he left after only one term, the school porter told them, 'Poor chap, he wasn't up to it.'

Having known Bishop, whom he did not like, Simon felt he already knew Hardy and oddly enough, for that reason, did not dislike him. Instead, remembering the lost papers and the shuffling hands, Simon felt protective towards him. He could imagine Bishop in the same position and felt that Hardy, a middle-aged man, uprooted from a regular job, was worse off than any of them.

The day after they had leaguered among the pink rocks at the southern end of the line, Simon supervised the digging of slit trenches. One of the men called Brookman, a big, heavy fellow who had told Simon that before the war he had been in 'the fruit', was giving out his usual street-trader's patter.

Throwing a rock to his butty, he shouted, "Ere y'are, gran, you can eat 'em with no teeth.' The butty pitched the rock back and Brookman, leaping into the air, let out a thin, anguished howl: 'Oh, my wife and kids.'

This gave rise to so much laughter, Simon could see how the story had gone around. Ridley, of course, was the culprit. To Brookman, Simon spoke sharply. 'Cut it out, Brookman, anyone can be caught off balance. You're a married man yourself, aren't you?'

Brookman, startled by Simon's unwonted severity, mumbled, "Speck you're right, guv,' and there were no more jokes about Hardy's wife and kids.

They were supposed to be in the front line but the only thing out in no-man's-land, apart from the junk yard litter left by earlier fighting, was a small hill in the middle distance. At night, yellow flashes of fire and Very lights marked the German positions to the north, but there was no sight of the enemy during the day.

Simon's nerves had subsided but at the same time, he felt a sense of let-down at the thought of returning to the sleepy boredom of the earlier camp.

Seeing Hardy with his field glasses up, he asked him, 'Why don't they come on, sir?'

Hardy continued to stare towards the German lines as though he might find the answer out there, then he said, 'I suppose they had to stop sometime. Jerry's only flesh and blood, after all.'

'But if they could get this far in less than a month, why not finish the job?'

'My guess is, they made it too fast. If they've outrun supplies, they could be stuck for some time to come.'

A few mornings later, while the dew still hung on the camel thorn, half a dozen enemy trucks were sighted, travelling slowly and cautiously round the base of the hill. They were first seen by Ridley who ran to Martin. Martin gave the order to open fire and Ridley, coming over to Simon, grinning his self-satisfaction, said, 'This is it, sir. Get your head down and cover your ears.'

Simon followed Ridley into a slit trench and, bending his head against the sand, protected his ears. The sound that came to him through his hands was the most fearsome he had ever heard. The gunners, who had had little to do till then, made up for their inactivity. As the firing persisted, Simon felt physically pummelled by the uproar but imagined he was taking it well until, the action over, he found to his consternation that his cheeks were wet. While he was scrubbing away his tears, someone put a hand on his shoulder. He swung round, angry and ashamed, but it was only Arnold.

'It's all right, sir. It takes you like that first time.'

'What happened?'

'We got one truck and the others made off double quick.'

Climbing up from the trench, Simon could see the solitary German truck smouldering at the foot of the hill. Three bodies were sprawled about it and he said to Arnold, 'What about those chaps? Shouldn't we do something to help them?'

'Nothing we can do, sir. The others hauled the wounded on board before they scarpered. Those chaps have had it.'

Simon, sent out to investigate, took Arnold and three men with him. This was his first venture on foot into open desert and though the area ahead was much like the area of the camp, he had a disturbing sense of offering himself as a target. He could imagine all the guns of the Afrika Korps trained on his party and he said to Arnold, 'Walking ducks, aren't we?'

'On a job like this, sir, they usually leave you alone.'

Whether this was true or not, the burial party went unmolested to the truck and examined the bodies. The Germans, though newly dead, were already stiffening in the heat. Simon looked at them with awe. They were not simply the first dead Germans he had seen, they were the first Germans: and, more than that, they were the first dead men he had seen in the whole of his life. One lay face down and when turned over, Simon saw he was a youth very like Arnold. Going through the uniform pockets, he found the usual things: identity papers, letters, snapshots of mum and dad, but no girl friend or wife. Too young for that, Simon thought and said to the men, 'All right, get on with it.'

The graves were not deep. No point in remaining longer than need be out here, yet, because it was customary, the men tied some sticks together to form crosses and placed one at each head. And, Simon thought, what a fool business that was! You killed men and marked the spot with the symbol of eternal life. Walking back, he said something like that to Arnold who replied, 'They'd have killed us, given the chance.'

'That's what they said about the scorpion.'

'I know, sir, but you don't have to kill scorpions. The other's different – it's what we're here for.'

Following the attack on the enemy trucks, there was a long period when no enemy was seen. Ridley had discovered that the New Zealanders had been moved to an encampment near the Ridge and Captain Hugo Boulderstone was still with them. As the days passed vacuous with sun, heat and the drone of flies, Simon decided to make another application for leave to visit his brother. The major, his glasses trained, as usual, on nothing, turned fiercely at Simon's request.

'You mad, Boulderstone, or something?'

'I just thought, sir . . .'

'It's not your job to think. Your job is to stand by and await orders.'

Going back to his bivouac, he murmured to Ridley, 'The major does great work with those field glasses.'

Ridley, inflating his cheeks, let the air break through closed lips but that was his only comment. Now that Hardy was in command, Ridley did not openly criticise him and Simon felt the need to justify his remark.

'I asked for leave to visit my brother and he jumped down my throat.'

'Not surprising, sir, if you don't mind me saying so. They say on the intercom the Kiwis are up to something.'

'An attack?'

'Could be, but don't worry, sir. Might be no more than a twitch.'

A few days later, waking before dawn, Simon heard the rumble of distant artillery and the thud of aerial bombardment, and knew this was the attack. He imagined Hugo in the midst of it. He sat up on his elbow and saw Ridley, wearing nothing but his drawers, peering between the leaguered lorries in the direction of the hill. A waning moon, a big, lop-sided face, cast a dismal half-light over the camping area. Going to Ridley, Simon whispered, 'What's up?'

Ridley whispered back at him, 'Don't know, sir, but it's my belief jerry's up to something over there.' He nodded towards the hill where lights, faint, as from a dark lantern, were moving on the upper slopes.

'Think I should wake the major, sarge?'

'No point. Can't do much before sparrow-fart.'

But Simon, unable to contain his information, went to where Hardy lay and finding him awake, excitedly reported what had been seen.

'Who saw these lights?'

Simon had to admit that Ridley saw them first. 'But I confirmed it, sir. I thought you'd want to know at once, sir.'

'Quite right, Boulderstone. When it's light we'll let them know we're here.'

Rising before dawn, prepared for the noise of gunfire, Simon stood with the other officers beside the HQ truck, seeing the hill appear in the sudden, startling whiteness of first light. They could see black figures moving quickly as though to take cover before day would reveal them.

Martin shouted an order to the gunners: 'All right, give them half a dozen rounds.'

As the guns opened up, the figures fell out of sight. Hardy, surveying the hill through his glasses, said, 'No sign of life now. Probably only a patrol but I'll get through to air reconnaissance and advise a check.'

Soon after, a Leander, slow and sedate like an elderly mosquito, went over the Column and several times circled the hill. Half an hour later the report came that the hill was still occupied and there were signs that the enemy was turning it into a miniature fortress. The ground before it on the east, had been disturbed as though mines had been laid, and store puts for weapons had been dug on the western side.

The guns started again and continued their fire at intervals during the afternoon. After the four o'clock brew-up, Simon and Trench were ordered to report to Hardy. The HQ truck was dug into the shelter of a rock ridge and Hardy and Martin were lying on top of the ridge, both training field glasses on the hill.

Simon and Trench, standing a couple of yards apart, did not look at each other as they waited. Though circumstances forced them to associate, they did not do it willingly. Each felt in the other an awareness that something was wrong, though neither could have said what it was. Even now, sharing the anxiety of the summons, antagonism was alive between them.

Hardy, turning his head to look at them, gave a long sigh of dissatisfaction, saying, 'The enemy's still in position. I hoped our fire would rout them but there's more of them than we thought. The trouble is, we're short of ammunition.' He said something to Martin then slid down from the ridge and spoke to his two lieutenants. 'There's nothing for it, I'm afraid, but to send in the infantry. Make a direct attack, give them a blow, a real knock-out, that'll drive them off the hill.'

Both young men said, 'Yes, sir,' sounding as enthusiastic as they could.

Simon, glancing obliquely at Trench, saw him staring at his feet, his fine, long mouth half open, obviously uncertain what was expected of him.

Hardy said, 'You'll lead your platoons into action tomorrow, starting out before dawn.'

Simon again glanced at Trench and seeing his lips quiver, thought, 'He's more scared than I am.' For a moment, he felt a gleeful sense of triumph then his own fear came over him. When they met later for the evening meal, Simon, for the first time since Trench joined the Column, felt able to speak freely to him. 'Do you think we should leave letters or write out cables, or something?'

'You mean, for our people?'

'Yes. I've got a wife, too. What do you think?'

They had heard of men writing letters, letters that often enough proved to be letters of farewell, and they self-consciously considered whether or not to do the same thing. Trench decided, 'I don't think we should. It's a bit like asking for it.'

'You're probably right.'

Sharing the immediacy of the attack, their antagonism seemed to have gathered itself together and vanished like the mirage. They began reminding each other of incidents during their days on the *Queen Mary* and almost at once their old sense of intimate understanding came back. Remembering their laughter on board ship, they started to laugh again, recalling Codley's jokes. Their excitement was like a renewal of love but it was a febrile excitement. They could not put from their minds the fact that at daybreak they would be under fire. Yet the laughter, like alcohol, gave them a sort of courage and they were still together, scarcely able to bear the thought of being separated, when Hardy came round the camp. He stopped beside them. 'Boulderstone? Trench? Try and get some sleep before the balloon goes up.' He spoke kindly, as he might to his own children, and both men were emotional with gratitude and a willingness to obey him to the end.

Simon did not expect to sleep but he was sleeping when the guard's voice roused the camp. 'Wakey, wakey, you lazy bastards.' Sitting up in the darkness, he found Arnold standing beside him and asked, 'For God's sake, Arnold, what time is it?'

'Three ak emma, sir.'

The reason for waking at that hour was too shocking to contemplate.

The men rose groaning and swearing at the intense cold. Simon, in a daze, could not contemplate the ordeal ahead but maintained a sort of half sleep, stumbling as he pulled on his sweater. Hardy was also up and when the two platoons assembled he came, fully dressed, to tell them that Martin and his artillery would accompany them and give them covering fire. The sappers would go in first to check whether or not mines had been laid at the base of the hill.

Waiting for the all clear, the men silent behind him, Simon had to swallow down the nausea that rose from the pit of his stomach. If it forced itself up, where, he wondered, could he go to vomit unseen? But it remained what it was, a phantom nausea, a sickness of the nerves, and as soon as they moved, he forgot about it.

The enemy seemed to be on the alert. Repeated gun flashes dotted the German positions and the men, who were in close order, instinctively kept closer than need be as they marched into no-man's-land. The moon had set and they moved by starlight. There was little to see and Simon thought it unlikely that anyone had seen them, yet, a few hundred yards from their objective, a flare went up from the hill-top, blanching the desert and revealing the two close-knit platoons. Immediately there was uproar. Red and yellow tracer bullets, like deadly fireworks, passed overhead and machine-guns kept up their mad, virulent rattle. Simon shouted, 'Run for it,' but the men had not waited for an order. They were running for their lives through the shrieking, whistling, rustling, thunder-filled air.

Pelting towards the hill, Simon told himself, 'We're running straight into it,' but the hill itself was cover. Simon's platoon had arrived without loss and he called to Trench, 'What about your chaps?' Trench's breathless voice came to him from the darkness, 'All right, I hope.'

There was no let up by the gunners on the hill but now Martin's artillery was sounding a reply and Simon, crouching with his men, waiting for the barrage to cease, began to hope that the guns would settle the matter. Then Martin came over and, speaking under the noise, instructed him to take his platoon to the left of the hill and advance upwards till battle was joined. Trench and his platoon would go to the right. In a low, grumbling tone that suggested the whole business was something of a bore, Martin told both the young men, 'The order is: to accept no more casualties than the situation justifies.'

Simon's voice had become a croak as he asked, 'Casualties, sir?'

'Pull yourself together, Boulderstone. D'you imagine there won't be casualties? Now – go in and show fight.'

The firing had stopped but as Simon started to move off, Martin seemed to change his mind. He said, 'Wait.' No sound came from the hill and for an elated moment Simon imagined the enemy had been wiped out, then the machine-guns began again.

The sky broke and a livid light showed them to each other. Looking from one drawn face to another, Simon thought, 'We're mad to be here.' Ridley, head hanging morosely, was waiting to fix up a field telephone. Martin was also waiting, no one knew for what. Arnold gave Simon an affectionate, reassuring smile as though he had been through all this before and he knew it would be all right.

'Now,' Martin whispered, 'get on with it. Give the hun a bloody nose. Should be a piece of cake but if you hit a snag, send a runner back and we'll sort you out. *If we can.* Off you go, and good luck.'

Glancing back, Simon had a glimpse of Trench's face miserably contracted and he thought, 'Poor old Trench.' He, himself, was revivified now action had begun. Reaching the left flank of the hill, he drew his revolver and ordered his men to fan out. They made their way crabwise up the grey, cinderous lower slopes. Their feet, sinking into the ground, made little noise but the defenders were prepared for them. As the first of them came in sight of the machine-guns, hand grenades showered down on them. They bent double, drawing together for mutual protection while Simon shouted, 'Fan out . . . fan out,' not expecting to be obeyed.

A palisade of flat stones and rocks had been built at the crown of the hill. Seeing a head rise above it, a hand lifted to pitch a grenade, Simon fired, and was amazed to see the man leap up and fall backwards. His shot, his first shot with intent to kill, had found its mark. He had wounded someone, or even killed him. Either way, he'd put one jerry bastard out of action. The satisfaction intoxicated him. In his excitement, he lost all sense of danger and did not hear Arnold shouting, 'Keep down, sir. For God's sake, keep down.' In an ecstasy of joy, he rushed into a fusillade of machine-gun bullets, thinking he had discovered the thing he had wanted all his life.

His euphoria faltered when a bullet whined past his ear. He realised the ground about him was bouncing with bullets and Arnold's cries suddenly made sense. He threw himself down behind a rock and saw that the other men had taken cover. The cover was not much. The upper slopes of the hill were littered with rocky outcrops but so low that the men were lying behind them with heads down. The battle now settled into a give and take of rifle fire, then a howl of anguish went up. The Germans had hurled a mortar bomb. Arnold, dodging from rock to rock, reached Simon and lay down beside him. 'Three chaps hit, sir. Two badly. One of them a gonner.'

'Who is it?'

The dead man was Brookman and Simon asked himself how many casualties the situation *did* justify? The machine-gun fire, having died down, opened up on the right-hand side of the hill. He realised that Trench was getting it and he was free to act. He said to Arnold, 'Run back. Tell Martin we've been under heavy fire but there's a lull. Say I propose to rush the enemy lines. Ask for further orders.'

Arnold went down the hill in leaps and Simon ordered the others to fix bayonets and wait. If they went in soon, they could draw the fire off Trench. Here was an opportunity to rush the palisade and perhaps behind it there was no more than a token force. He became impatient of the delay and looking down the hill, saw that Arnold had just started the ascent. Bent low, he was taking it cautiously. Simon shouted to him to hurry and, eager to comply, he straightened himself, ran forward, threw up his arms and fell.

Simon called to him, but he did not move. Screaming his name, Simon ran down to where he lay, white faced, eyes open. He had been hit in the chest. In spite of the fixed stare, Simon believed that something might still be done for him. Testing his weight, finding him light enough to carry, Simon lifted the thin, young body on to his shoulder and went at a half-run down to the foot of the hill.

Astounded by the sight of him, Martin shouted in fury, 'You damned fool, what do you think you're doing?'

'It's Arnold. He's my batman and driver. He's been shot in the chest.'

'Put him down at once and get back to your men.'

'You'll look after him, won't you?'

'Get back, I tell you. You could be court-martialled for this.'

By the time he reached the hill-top, the Germans had leapt the palisades and had met his platoon in hand-to-hand combat. Coming face to face with a blond, pink-skinned German youth, Simon fired in a fury, saying, 'Damn you. Damn the lot of you,' and the pink face opened and spilt out redness, like a pomegranate.

This was hatred, all right. Simon felt he could do battle with the lot of them but the defenders had already had enough. They turned, scrambled back over the palisade and stumbled down the western side of the hill. Their trucks awaited them and as the victors bawled after them in triumph, they piled in and drove towards the main German positions.

Returning to base, Ridley caught up with Simon to say, 'Not a bad show, sir.'

'Not too bad, sarge.'

'You heard, sir? Mr Trench copped it.'

'Dead?'

'Dead as mutton, poor bloke. They say, just before he was hit, he was putting up a tremendous fight.'

'Just what I'd expect,' Simon said, ashamed that he had expected nothing of the sort. He could not understand now his earlier contempt for Trench. Trench and Arnold had been his friends and he had lost them both. He wondered, as Arnold had wondered when Ted and Fred went from him, how he could live without them.

The engagement had cost the Column eight men, all told. The bodies were brought back and buried before supper. Hardy said to Simon, 'You acted unwisely, leaving your men, but I understand your desire to help Arnold. You did pretty well, so we'll forget what happened. Have you anything to say?'

Looking back over the events of the day, Simon could think of nothing. He shook his head. Bereaved and very tired, he only wanted sleep.

8

A new general came to displace Auchinleck. The displacement was discussed in Cairo but no one could say why one general had gone and the other had taken over the command. Harriet, walking in Suleiman Pasha, saw Auchinleck on the opposite pavement. It was, she learnt later, the very day on which he was leaving Egypt for good. She stopped to watch him. He was a very tall man with a grave, handsome face and a broad brow: the ideal of those leaders, those demi-gods, whom she had seen as ordering the lives of common men, yet he, too, owed obedience and had been sent away. Though she had not met him and would probably never see him again, she felt a profound sadness as she watched him disappear into the indifferent crowd.

Harriet, too, had lost her import, small though it was. No one now asked her for news because she knew no more than anyone else. If, among all the rumours that spread out from civilian ignorance, she learnt of some true event, she could not act upon it or pin it to a map. She wanted to replace her job at once and put it about that she was free and looking for work, but there was little work for English women civilians in Egypt.

She asked Guy if she could take up Miss Pedler's job in the library but before anything could be decided, Miss Pedler returned. Most of the evacuees, tired of life in the Jerusalem camp, were finding their way back to Cairo though nothing had happened to change the situation from which they had fled. The very fact that nothing had happened was satisfactory enough. An invader who was so long in coming, might not come at all.

Even Pinkrose had returned. The Pringles, going into Groppi's to meet Aidan Pratt, saw Pinkrose sitting in front of a plate of cakes. It was mid-day, the sun burnt through the canvas of the umbrella, but Pinkrose was muffled like a Bedouin and perhaps for the same reason. He hoped his hat, scarf and woollen suit would protect him against the heat. His hat pulled down to his eyes, his scarf up to his nostrils, he was intent on four cakes, creamed, candied, decorated with fruit and sweets, the richest that Groppi could provide. His problem was which to eat first.

When Guy and Harriet stopped beside him, he did not lift his head but put out a hand as though warding them off. He slid his eyes up at the intruders and said, 'Ah, Pringle, it's you!' Having accepted the invitation to lecture, he had to accord Guy some slight civility.

Guy said, 'You know I've been appointed Director here?'

'Yes, yes, I gathered that. Um, um, I gathered that.'

'I feel I have you to thank for the appointment. It was, I believe, the result of your cable to Bevington.'

'Oh, was it!' It was clear from Pinkrose's tone that this was not the result he had intended. A gleam of satirical contempt for Guy's simplicity came into his stone-grey eyes but he had nothing to lose by accepting gratitude, so nodded and said, 'Is that so?'

'There are some letters for Gracey in the office. I would forward them if I knew where he was. I was wondering if you could let me have his present address?'

'Present address? Present address?' Pinkrose, eager to be at the cakes, was losing patience with this conversation. 'I really can't say. I heard . . . indeed, I was *told*, the Director in Jerusalem told me, that Gracey is trying to get himself shipped down to the Cape. How and when I cannot say. I fear I cannot help you, Pringle. No, no, I cannot help you.' He twitched all over in his desire to shake off the Pringles, then he remembered that Harriet had once been a source of information and he raised his head slightly to ask her, 'The desert situation has settled down, eh? The Germans have outrun their strength. No bite left in them, eh? No bite. No bite.'

Harriet, never unwilling to disquiet Pinkrose, did not resist this opportunity. 'I don't know about the desert. No one is giving it much thought these days. The chief worry now is the Ukraine. The High Command expects it to collapse before the end of the month. When that happens, the enemy will come down on us like the wolf on the fold.'

Pinkrose, his grey colour becoming more grey, looked stunned, then falteringly asked, 'Haven't we got troops in Iraq?'

'A handful. What could they do against twenty panzer divisions?'

'Twenty? Did you say twenty? No one told me they were likely to come that way.'

'People here are living in a fool's paradise. They think if the desert situation's all right, they're all right. They forget we're threatened on another front.'

Pinkrose was sunken in his seat, gazing at the cakes as though they had failed him, then a laugh jerked out of him. '*Now*, I understand. Yes, yes . . . You wish to frighten me. Well, I will not be frightened. No, I will not be frightened. So you can take yourselves off. If you wish to spread alarm and despondency, you can spread it elsewhere.'

'Why should I wish to frighten you, Lord Pinkrose?'

'That is easily answered,' Pinkrose's voice was shrill with triumph. 'I was one of those whom the major invited on to his ship – *you were not*. You pushed your way on board. Yes, yes, you pushed on board. It would have been a pleasant trip – a very pleasant trip, indeed – but a crowd of you pushed on board and spoilt it all. Four people settled themselves in my cabin. *Four* of them. They made things very uncomfortable for me, and for the major's other guests. You young people think only of yourselves. So, take yourselves off . . .' Pinkrose lifted his cake fork and waved them away.

As Harriet drew breath to protest, Guy gave her a little push and they both went to a vacant table. Out of Pinkrose's hearing, Guy said, 'Why try and frighten the poor, old thing?'

'I said nothing that wasn't true. He may be a great deal more frightened before this war is over. If we're cut off here, what will happen to him or to us? Or anyone else? Who would repatriate us? Who would care if we lived or died? We'd be lost, the dregs of the wartime hierarchy: beggars, dependent on Moslem charity. And we can be thankful that the Moslems are charitable. We'll have no other friends.'

'Darling,' Guy lifted her right hand and put it to his lips. 'Little monkey's paw. The Russians won't give in so easily. The Ukraine will hold, you wait and see.'

'How do you know? What makes you so sure?'

'I am sure.' He did not explain his certainty but squeezed her fingers, conveying his confidence by the pressure and warmth of his flesh. He looked at her hand before putting it down and said, 'Thin, little hand!'

'Too thin. I keep getting these stomach upsets.'

'That won't do,' he said and quickly changed to a subject that disturbed him less. 'Who do you think came into the office this morning? Toby Lush. He came, ostensibly, to congratulate me on my appointment but they want work, the pair of them. They had a pretty dreary time in camp while Gracey and Pinkrose were living it up at the King David Hotel. They said that Gracey never bothered to contact them and when they bumped into Pinkrose, he pretended not to know them.'

'You surely won't employ them, will you?'

'Why not? What are they but poor derelicts of war? I'll find a use for them.'

Aidan Pratt, on what he called 'a brief assignment', had tried to ring Guy in Alexandria and not finding him there, had traced the Pringles to Dobson's flat. Getting Harriet on the telephone, he asked her to come with him to the Muski. He wanted to buy a gift for his mother. When she agreed, he said as an afterthought, 'I suppose Guy wouldn't come?'

Harriet had once persuaded Guy to go with her to the Muski but at the entrance to the narrow, half-lit Muski lanes, he had turned back saying that nothing would get him in there. He felt, she realised, as she had felt inside the ruined pyramid. Though she said, 'I'll ask him,' she knew Aidan would be disappointed.

Seeing him coming towards them as though half-fearing rebuff, she whispered to Guy, 'Do come with us . . .'

Guy was quite decided against the Muski. 'I couldn't possibly', and Aidan, sensing his refusal, said with humorous humility, 'Not coming? I suppose you have more important things to do?'

'I wouldn't say important. I've work to do.' Guy greeted Aidan with his usual amiability but he could not stay long. They talked for a few minutes but there was no lingering over the wine in his glass. Draining it in one long draught, he said, 'I'll see you later,' and went without arranging time or place.

'Is he always so *engagé*? I'm not likely to see him later – my train goes at six.'

Harriet said to excuse Guy, 'He's more than usually busy at the moment, getting the Institute back on its feet.'

Aidan gave a baffled laugh and agreed that they set out for the Muski straight away. They found a gharry waiting outside Groppi's and took it to Esbekiya Gardens. Aidan, Harriet realised, had recovered from the first pain of his friend's death and she found him easier company. Moving through the afternoon heat as through a tangible fume that smelt of sand and the old gharry horse, she tried to compensate for Guy's absence. She told him what she knew about the places they passed. The Esbekiya, she said, still had the sunken look of a lake bed and in the old days, when the Nile rose, it used to be filled with water. Now the square was a turn-around for the tramcars but a few of the old houses remained with trees dipping over the garden wall as though to reach the water that was no longer there. Napoleon had lodged in the mansion that had been turned into Shepherd's Hotel. She thought there was still a hint of the oriental, pre-Napoleonic richness about the square but it had become a centre for raffish life and raffish medicine. On the seedy terrace houses that had displaced most of the mansions, there were advertisements for doctors who cured 'all the diseases of love' and promised to the impotent 'horse-like vigour'. Gigantic wooden teeth, bloody at the roots, were hung out as a sign that cheap dentists were at work.

Aidan, his dark and sombre eyes turning from side to side, asked, 'Why has it become so run-down?'

Harriet pointed to the small, dry garden in the centre and told him that the assassin of General Kléber had been impaled there, taking three days to die. 'After that, who would want to live here?'

The Muski ran from the top of the square and Harriet said they should pay off the gharry because now it would be more fun to walk. Alerted by the word 'fun', Aidan jumped down to the road as though making an effort to enjoy himself.

Asked what he thought of buying, he was unsure: 'Jewellery, or a piece of silverware or perhaps a length of silk.'

The Muski offered such things in plenty and Harriet, who knew the shops, thought Aidan would quickly find what he wanted. There she was wrong.

The lanes were quiet under the heat. The shopkeepers lay indolently in the shade at the back of their open-fronted shops, sleeping or passing amber beads through their hands. Most of them ignored the visitors, knowing who came to buy and who came merely from curiosity, and Harriet saw they had little or no faith in Aidan's intentions. She began to feel they were right.

He fingered the bales of silk and rayons and put them contemptuously aside. They did not compare, he said, with the Damascus silks. Harriet took him into a small, glazed-in shop where scent was sold. The scent could be put into plain bottles or phials of Venetian glass decorated with gold. He agreed the phials were pretty but the scents – rose, musk, jasmin or sandalwood – were too sweet for Aidan's taste. Then Harriet thought she knew the very place to interest him: it was a large shop without windows, like a great tent. Here, in the half-light, the shelves and floors were packed with old silver and plate, engraved glass, Victorian ornaments, Indian toys, Burmese temple birds, Staffordshire dogs, horses, swans and human figures. Harriet particularly liked some iron trays painted with flowers and buildings and fanciful scenes that could be set on legs to serve as coffee tables, but Aidan shook his head. He turned over some rugs and said, 'Not the best of their kind.' In the middle of the shop there was a glass case filled with antique jewellery made of pink gold and rose diamonds. Harriet, who could not afford to buy them herself, handled the elaborate brooches, rings and pendants, and admired the large diamonds that looked more valuable than they were. 'I'm sure your mother would like these.'

'Much too showy for her.'

They set out again. Passing a window that displayed a broken Grecian head and some small Egyptian tomb finds, he stopped. 'There might be something in here.'

'Those things are terribly expensive.'

'I'll just have a look.'

Harriet stayed outside, feeling he was by nature secretive and more likely to make up his mind if left alone. When he was slow in returning, she wandered to the end of the lane where the bazaar opened out into an ordinary shopping street. Between lane and street there was an Arab café with three wooden tables and benches set out on the road. The proprietor, in a grimy galabiah, sat with one leg under him and his back to the house wall. Harriet asked if she might sit down while awaiting a friend. He did not ask her what she would drink but waved her to a bench, mumbling the conventional courtesy that everything in his house was hers.

Weary from her long walk in the heat, Harriet sat down gladly and watched the street beginning to fill with the early evening shoppers. Somewhere nearby there was a dry goods shop and the whole area was filled with a scent of pulse and spices, the scent of every back street in Egypt. A loud-speaker, fastened to the wall above her head, was telling one of the endless sagas of the Arab world. She heard the name Akbar and knew it was about the great hero whose father was a king and whose mother was Sudanese.

Being blacker than his fellows, he felt he must do courageous deeds to prove himself, but being also lazy, he often lay in his tent and could be roused only by the gentle persuasions of his mistress who was the most perfect of womankind.

There was a mosque among the shops, its minaret intricately carved and rising ochre-coloured against the deep cerulean of the sky. She could not tell whether it was made of sandstone or merely encrusted with sand. When she first arrived, she had meant to visit all the main mosques of Cairo but soon found that here it was easier to make plans than to carry them out. If one waited till tomorrow, or the next day, or next week, it might be less hot and one's body might be more willing to exert itself.

As Aidan came towards her, smiling his success, she said, 'So you've found something!'

He did not show her what it was but, sitting down, suggested they take mint tea. He did not speak while they drank it but, putting his cup down, he hesitantly asked, 'Tell me about Guy. Can he possibly be as artless and warm-hearted as he seems. He must have his *terra incognita* – his complexes, hang-ups, impediments? What should one call them? Megrims?'

Realising he wanted nothing more than to talk about Guy, she said, 'He's probably more simple than you think. I'll tell you something that happened in Bucharest just after we were married. I was about to step on a bus when Guy pulled me aside so that another woman – a woman of my own age – could step on in front of me. I was thunderstruck. And what annoyed me most was the simpering amusement of the woman when she saw Guy hold me back. I was furious and he was bewildered by me. He explained, as though to a child, that one had to be courteous to other people. I said, "What you did was damned discourteous to me," and he said, "But you're part of me – I don't have to be courteous to you".'

Aidan seemed at a loss as he imbibed this story but eventually said, 'Yet, because of Guy's intrinsic goodness, you were able to overlook what happened?'

'I didn't overlook it. I'm still angry when I think about it.'

'But he did not mean to offend you. Such intrinsic simplicity has its admirable side.'

'Yes, if you're not married to it.'

'I understand.' Aidan smiled as though the story had brought them into sympathy and putting his hand into his side pocket, he took out a small green box. He pushed it towards her and said, 'See what I bought.' She opened the box and found inside, packed in cotton wool, a cat, less than two inches high, made of iron, sitting upright on a block of cornelian. Harriet realised why Aidan had taken so long to find what he wanted. The gift he sought must be unique, and he had found the one thing she would, if she had the money, have chosen herself. She replaced the lid and pushed the box back again. He held it and looked at her, then put the box before her. 'Keep it for me.'

'But isn't it for your mother?'

'Yes. I will tell her I have it but I can't risk the posts. You must look after it till I can take it home.'

'I'd rather not. It's much too valuable to have around.'

'Please. I can't hold on to things. If I keep it, I'll put it down somewhere and forget it. I've lost the sense that anything's worth keeping.'

'You've *lost* the sense? You weren't born without it – you lost it?'

'Yes, but at the time that was the least loss. I lost much more – everything I had, in fact, including the sense that anything left had value.'

'What happened?'

'Oh,' he stared down at the table and made the gesture he had made when he spoke of the death of his friend. 'It's not easy to talk about . . . I may tell you another time.'

'Have you told Guy?'

'Not yet. When we went for our walk, he did most of the talking.'

'Had it anything to do with the war?'

'Yes, everything.' He paused then said in a bitter half-whisper, 'The war has destroyed my life.'

'It hasn't done any of us much good.'

'I'm not so sure of that. There's a chap in our unit – he used to be a bus driver and now he's a major. He feels he's found his feet at last. He's enjoying every minute of the war. But for me, it was a disaster. My career had just started when war broke out. When it's over – if it ever is over – I'll be verging on middle-age. Just another not so young actor looking for work. In fact, a displaced person.'

'We're all displaced persons these days. Guy and I have accumulated more memories of loss and flight in two years than we could in a whole lifetime of peace. And, as you say, it's not over yet. But we're seeing the world. We might as well try and enjoy it.'

'Yes, but there are some memories that are beyond human bearing, except that we have to bear them.'

'You won't tell me?'

'Not now. Not now. I have to catch that train.'

They walked till they found a gharry. Harriet asked to be put down in the Esbekiya where she could find a tram-car to Kasr el Aini. The green box was still in her hand and unwilling to keep in temporary custody an object she so much coveted, she asked him to take it back.

'No. One day I'll ask you for it.'

'Very well.' He wished to imply that their friendship would continue and she said, 'I'll keep it safe for you.'

'Did you know that the line into Syria is open? If you and Guy could come to Beirut, I'd meet you with a car and we could drive to Damascus, visiting Baalbec on the way. There are some impressive sights up there. And the Damascus bazaars are more mysterious than the Cairo ones.'

Speaking, his face came alive with enticement intended, she felt, for Guy – and that was the trouble. Guy did not want to see impressive sights. He would rather pass his spare time, if he had any, talking and drinking in a basement bar.

'Guy may come . . .'

'If he doesn't, you come without him.'

She smiled and said, 'One day, perhaps I will.'

9

There was no work for Harriet in Cairo, not even voluntary work. In Athens the English women had organised a canteen for troops but in Cairo the ladies of the Red Cross jealously kept a hold on paramilitary work and the provision of comforts for the men. Outsiders were expected to remain outside.

Finding nothing to do, she wondered if she could take over the house-keeping at the flat. She did not think that Edwina would willingly give it up but found her glad to be rid of it.

'Darling, how sweet of you. It would be divine – and save me *so* much effort. I often don't know how to get everything done.'

Harriet, when the accounts were handed to her, found that Edwina had merely muddled through them and the servants had bought where they pleased. Edwina said, 'If you have trouble with Hassan, I'm always here to help,' but Harriet though she could manage Hassan. There would be a new regime and Edwina would be left free for her main occupation, her social life.

Edwina's promise of friendship was frequently repeated but it developed no further. She would have a few words with Harriet while awaiting a telephone call or the arrival of the evening's young man, but the talk was always brief and interrupted. Harriet who had been anticipating the pleasant, gossipy intimacy that can exist between women living in proximity, now knew that Edwina would never have time for it. Her afternoon break, between one o'clock and five, was spent at the Gezira swimming-pool. More often than not she was out for dinner and at breakfast time she came to the table exhausted by the effort of getting herself out of bed. Sitting opposite Harriet, hair over one eye, she would blink the other eye and grin in rueful acknowledgement of her frail condition. Sometimes the activities of the previous night prostrated her altogether. Dobson would say, 'Poor Edwina has another migraine,' but however badly she might feel in the morning, she would be up and dressed, her languors forgotten, by the time her evening escort arrived. They would go off with a great deal of laughter and Harriet could imagine that laughter served as conversation for most of the time. Edwina had once told her that she only wanted a good time, and the lost and deprived young men who came on leave – a leave that might be the last they would ever have – had nothing else to give her.

One day, when Edwina had pleaded a migraine for the third time in a fortnight, Harriet asked Dobson, 'How do the girls she works with feel? Don't they mind her being absent from the office?'

Dobson, who regarded everything Edwina did with amused tolerance, said, 'Not really. To tell you the truth, she can get away with anything. She's rather special, isn't she?'

Harriet agreed, being herself spellbound by Edwina's special quality. She was only regretful that that quality was squandered among so many futureless encounters. She said one evening while they were together on the balcony, 'Don't you get bored, going out so often?'

'Well, yes, but what else is there for me? You're lucky. You have that nice husband. You've something to stay in for.'

Harriet supposed she was lucky even though, staying in, she spent most of her evenings alone. She said, 'We're young at the wrong time.' The war, with all its demands, took precedence over their youth and when it was over they, like Aidan Pratt, would be young no longer.

Then, a week or two later, a change came over Edwina. She started taking supper at home. When the telephone rang and some eager young man begged for her company, she could be heard sweetly excusing herself, pleading her usual headache before returning with a sigh to the sitting-room. Harriet, realising she had been expecting a different caller, concluded that someone of importance had entered Edwina's life.

Percy Gibbon eyed her as though her change of habit brought him both terror and hope, but Edwina was unaware of him. She was abstracted as though all her senses were intent on something remote from anything about her. After supper she would go to her room or sit, saying nothing, on the balcony. Now there was no wink or grin of complicity for Harriet but when they both took their coffee out into the scented air, she occasionally gave Harriet a wan smile and seemed about to confide in her. But there were no confidences. One evening, when Guy had gone to work in the spare room and Dobson had returned to the Embassy, and the two girls sat on the swaying, sinking wickerwork sofa, Harriet tried to distract Edwina with a story about Hassan.

'You know Hassan's been stealing the gin from Dobbie's decanter and filling it with water! I spoke to him about it and he swore that it was the afreets. Well, I thought I could catch him. I emptied the gin out and put in arak which becomes cloudy when you add water. Next day the decanter disappeared. When I spoke to Hassan, he said the afreets had broken it.'

'Oh, dear!' Edwina put her head back and laughed, but it was not a real laugh, rather a distracted and almost soundless effort to show appreciation while her mind was elsewhere.

Percy Gibbon, who had been moving restlessly about in the sitting-room, came out as though decided on a course of action, and spoke aggressively to Edwina, 'I suppose you're going out later?'

Edwina answered with gentle indifference, 'I may.'

Percy gave a disgusted snort and rushing to the front door, left the flat. Harriet said, 'I believe he wanted to ask you out.'

'Poor Percy,' Edwina said, as though Percy were a little dog accidently trodden upon. Harriet thought: Yes, poor Percy. Poor ugly creature. How changed he might be if he could only change his looks!

The telephone started ringing, Edwina listened till she could bear it no more and cried in anguish, 'Why doesn't Hassan answer it?' She leapt up, went to the hall and came back to say the call was for Guy. When she sat down again, she had a wet glint about her eyes.

'Who were you expecting?' Harriet asked.

'Oh, no one in particular.' Edwina, bemused, said, 'It's getting late,' then throwing back her head, she broke into an Irish song: 'My love came to me, he came from the south . . .' Her voice was light but clear and melodious. When she reached the line: 'His breast to my bosom, his mouth to my mouth,' she caught her breath and came to a stop, fearful of breaking down.

Guy, returning from the telephone, had paused to listen and as the song died, he came on to the balcony, praising her singing as one who knew what singing should be. He had heard she could sing but did not know she had a voice of that quality. He said, 'It's a lovely voice. A moving,

163

beautiful voice. If I get up a troops' entertainment, you will sing for them, won't you?'

Edwina, disturbed by her own song, could only nod her agreement.

Guy was about to enlarge on his plans for the concert but as he spoke, the telephone rang again and Edwina, whispering an excuse, ran to it. This time the call was for her.

Harriet said, 'Are you serious about this entertainment? Haven't you enough to do?'

Guy said, 'I never have enough to do,' and returned to his work-table.

Next day Harriet met Edwina's new friend and realised he was, indeed, a man apart from her everyday admirers. He was older than most of them, being in the late twenties, and his manner suggested a man of substance.

When he called for Edwina, she was still in her room. Instead of waiting in the background, nervous, expectant and barely noticed, he threw himself on to the living-room sofa and talked as though putting the company – this being Dobson and Harriet – at its ease. Dobson maintained his insouciance in the face of this affability but once or twice, losing his hold on himself, he sounded surprisingly deferential.

When introducing the new arrival to Harriet, he had said, 'You know Peter, don't you?' so it was evident that if she did not, she ought to know him. Peter, fixing his very dark eyes on Harriet, seemed satisfied by what he saw.

He was short, square built, ruddy and black haired, with a broad saddle nose and a firm mouth. He had the look of a farmer, and not a young farmer. In spite of his youth, he was as bulky as a man of fifty. Gripping Harriet's hand, he sank back in the sofa, pulling her down beside him. He had been talking when she came in and he went on talking, at the same time putting an arm round Harriet's waist and every now and then giving her a squeeze. All young attractive women, she realised, were his women, and he had no doubt at all of his right to them, or his attraction for them.

With her eyes on a level with his shoulder, Harriet could see that he was already a half-colonel, and he was complaining of this fact. 'I've been three months at GHQ and I've risen faster than I did in three years in the blue. Not from merit, mind you. Far from it. I'm a fighting man. I'm no good dealing with all that bumf. No, I'm pushed up so Sniffer Metcalf can be pushed up further. To promote himself, he has to widen the base of his pyramid. If he can fit in another major, we all go up a step. You may think that our most important aim and object is to shove Rommel back to Cyrenaica? Not a bit of it. The only thing that occupies our department is the one burning question: Can Sniffers graft his way up to Major General before some busybody at the top sniffs out Sniffers.'

Peter's laughter was loud and long and he was squeezing Harriet with his head on her shoulder when Edwina entered, subdued and virginal in a long dress of white slipper satin. Her toilette indicated a very grand dinner ahead.

'Ah, there you are, then!' Peter, jovially paternal, still holding on to Harriet, looked Edwina up and down then, releasing Harriet and jerking himself forward, he pointed at Dobson. 'And I'll tell you something else . . .'

This new subject, whatever it was, was stopped by Edwina who gave a scream and said, 'Oh Lord, m'heel!' and taking off one of her white shoes, she examined the high, narrow heel.

'Anything wrong?' Peter asked.

'Well, no . . .' Trying to put the shoe on again, she dropped a pair of long, kid gloves. She let them lie until Peter, getting his heavy body out of the sofa, retrieved them. As though the shoe were beyond her, she handed it to him and balanced, one hand on his arm, while he fitted it on to her foot.

Harriet, used to seeing Edwina in control of her escorts, disliked seeing her as she now was: flustered, silly and on edge. Her skin, its golden colour enhanced by the white satin, had an underflush of pink and she looked away from Peter, afraid to meet the emphatic stare of his black eyes. His manners were casual yet, Harriet felt, whatever he did was right because he did it. Then, as Edwina fidgeted with her bag and scarf, he gave her a slap on the rump that was more heavy than playful. Her scream this time was a scream of pain and Peter said, 'Sorry, old thing,' and led her away.

'Who is that fellow?' Harriet asked, resenting Edwina's abasement.

'Don't you know? He's Peter Lisdoonvarna.'

'What an odd surname!'

Dobson laughed at her ignorance. 'My dear girl, he's Lord Lisdoonvarna but, as you must have heard, titles are *de trop* for the duration so he's just plain Peter Lisdoonvarna.'

'I see,' said Harriet, who did see. Edwina had found her desideratum and the chance of such a marriage had quite overthrown her. 'It's remarkable to be a lieutenant-colonel at his age. I suppose he was promoted because of his title?'

'Certainly not,' Dobson was shocked by the supposition. 'While he was a field officer, he never rose above lieutenant. He was moved to base – very much against his will, I may say – and you heard what he told us: rapid promotion followed. That sort of thing goes on at GHQ. He laughs at it but I gather he's pretty disgusted. Some relative must have pulled strings to get him away from the front line.'

'I didn't know that could be done.'

'It can't be in theory, but I imagine a bit of fixing does go on. It's not unreasonable in his case. He's an only son and there are no male relatives. If he were killed, the title would die out.'

Thinking of Edwina's song, Harriet said, 'I suppose he's Irish?'

'Anglo-Irish. The best sort of fighting man. The best in the world, I'd say. A terrible waste, putting him into an office. But, then, it would be a terrible waste if he didn't survive.'

'Edwina seems very attracted. Do you think she stands a chance with him?'

Dobson did not question what Harriet meant, but said, 'Who knows? There have been less likely marriages, and these are not ordinary times. She might land him, but I only hope she keeps her head.'

The rich owner of the next door garden sent Dobson a basket of mangoes which he placed on the breakfast table.

Harriet, spooning the pulp out of the rosy mango shell, said, 'Gorgeous, gorgeous, and perhaps from our own tree.'

Reminded by this, Dobson told the Pringles they would have to give up the spare room because he had a friend coming to stay.

Guy said, 'Oh, not the spare room. Let's give up that damned tree. I hate the sight of it staring at me through the window.'

'You can say that,' said Harriet, 'when you're in the very act of eating mangoes?'

Dobson, smiling slyly, said, 'Still, Guy may be right. His could be an instinctive dislike. People here call the mango "The Danger Tree". You know that in England someone dies every year from eating duck eggs? – Well, in countries where a lot of mangoes are eaten, someone dies from mango poisoning every year.'

Edwina, who had been putting out her hand for another mango, withdrew it, saying, 'Dobbie, how could you! What a horrid joke!'

'It's not a joke. The stems are poisonous and sometimes the poison seeps into the fruit. It doesn't happen often but people *are* killed by it.'

Harriet joined with Edwina's indignation. 'You're an awful liar, Dobbie. If it were true, you would have told us straightaway.'

'Ha!' Dobson smiled. 'Had I told you straightaway, you would have said, "The greedy fellow wants to keep his mangoes for himself".'

Percy Gibbon gave his usual angry grunt and left the table. Guy, helping himself to another mango, said to Harriet, 'You see, I was right. The tree's a bad tree. We must give it up.'

Harriet knew she would have to give it up. Guy seldom asked anything for himself so when he did, he must have his way. She did not speak and he added persuasively, 'You don't really mind giving it up, do you?'

'No, I don't mind. Not really.' Harriet asked Dobson when they would have to move.

'Soon, I'm afraid. I don't know exactly when she's arriving but, of course, the place will have to be scrubbed out.'

The room had not been scrubbed out for Guy and Harriet who had taken it dust and all. Speaking of the friend who would soon arrive – a female friend, it seemed – Dobson had betrayed the same deference that had been induced in him by Peter Lisdoonvarna. Dobson's friends belonged to a higher social order than Dobson's lodgers and Harriet, who was not likley to know her, did not ask the newcomer's name.

Peter Lisdoonvarna returned three days later. This time Edwina, ready dressed, was waiting for him but Peter was in no hurry to take her away. Settling down in the sofa, he gave Dobson more military gossip and was enjoying himself so much that Edwina's gaze became strained in an effort to appear interested. When at last he shuffled out of the sofa, Edwina was up before him but they were not yet on their way. Peter stood in the middle of the room then, without warning or explanation, went to the dining-table and thumped his fist down on it. He shouted, 'Glory to the bleeding lamb,' then, marching round the table, repeatedly banging it, his voice growing louder and louder, he bawled, 'Glory to the bleeding lamb, I love the sound of Jesus' name. His spirit puts me all in a flame, glory to the bleeding lamb.'

As this went on and on, Harriet laughed to console Edwina but Edwina did not laugh: she looked hurt and amazed. At last, coming to a stop from sheer exhaustion, he said, 'I'll tell you about that,' and threw himself back on to the sofa. 'We've got this sect in the village at home. I forget what they call themselves – the holy somethings or other. Not Rollers, no, not Rollers. Well, that's what they do, the whole lot of them, men and women, children, too: they march in a circle round and round the room, all yelling out, "Glory to the bleeding lamb," etc. They go on till they're drunk with it,' and unable to control his exuberance, he rose and returned to the table, hitting it and starting the chant again. Edwina sank into a chair but this time a few rounds were enough and, pulling her to her feet, he took her off, leaving the air still tingling with his voice.

'How can Edwina stand it?'

Dobson shook his head. 'I agree, he's a boisterous fellow, but he's young. He'll grow out of it.'

Peter's appearances were irregular. He would call for Edwina three nights running then be out of sight for a week. Edwina stayed in, listening and yearning for the telephone to ring. Harriet, concerned for her, said after one of his absences, 'Don't worry. He'll ring tomorrow.'

'Who?' Edwina looked startled.

'Why, Peter, of course.'

Edwina, apparently unaware that anyone could read her obsession, gazed in wonder at Harriet's percipience, then, free at last to speak, her emotion overwhelmed her and she cried, 'Oh, Harriet, I do long for him.'

'I know. I can see you're attracted by him.'

'It's more than attraction. I . . . I adore him. I know he's not very good looking but he's fascinating.'

'Yes, with all that energy and confidence, he's compelling – but you must admit, Edwina, you're a bit dazzled by the title.'

Edwina made a wry face, laughing at herself, but said, 'Any girl would be dazzled, wouldn't she? I mean – surely you would be?'

'I don't know. I've never been offered such a thing. But Edwina, between ourselves, do you think he is likely to share his title with you?'

Edwina shrugged and sighed, her face abject. 'I can't say. He's never serious. When someone's joking all the time, how do you pin them down?'

'And you have tried to pin him down?'

Edwina had to agree and Harriet asked her, 'Does he tease you?'

'He does, rather.'

'I'm afraid it's a form of sadism. He's too sure of you and some men don't want to be sure. They're excited by uncertainty. If you could hide your feelings, pretend that all the jollity bores you, show an interest in someone else – it might sober him up.'

Edwina fervently agreed. 'You're right. Yes, I'm sure you're right.'

'Let him be the anxious one.'

Edwina said, 'Yes,' but she still drooped in her desire for one person, and one person only.

'Next time, when he rings, don't jump at his invitation. Say you have another engagement.'

'I'll do that.' Resolved, Edwina looked at Harriet with glowing admiration. 'Harriet, how clever you are!'

'Not clever, just growing old.'

Harriet felt a flattering sense of achievement but when next the telephone rang, Edwina ran to it and, lifting the receiver, said, 'Peter, oh, Peter!' Listening to her rapturous voice, Harriet knew that in future she might as well keep her advice to herself.

Dobson expected his guest to arrive on Sunday. On Saturday evening when Harriet was moving their things into the small, spare room, the low sun, richly golden, spiked in between the mango leaves. The ceiling, baked all day, exuded heat. Smothered and dizzy, Harriet could not imagine that Dobson's guest would tolerate for long the monastic simplicity of this room or the heat that was condensed here during the day, but if she did choose to stay, then the room would be her room, the tree her tree, and Harriet might never come in here again. She looked back at the tree that looked in at her and said, 'Goodbye, mango tree.' She dropped down to the bed, putting off the arduous business of moving clothes, and was half-asleep when she was startled by uproar outside the door.

Looking out, she found Percy Gibbon, naked, in an evident state of sexual excitement and beside himself with rage, beating his hands on Edwina's door and shouting, 'Open up, open up.'

'What on earth are you doing?'

'She's in there with that bally lord.'

'What if she is? It's none of your business.'

Percy, his face distorted with indignation, pointed to the baize door that was held ajar by Hassan and Aziz who clutched at each other in mirth. Percy's condition, which had been farce, became scandal as soon as Harriet appeared, and Hassan put up a long 'Uh, uh, uh!' of shocked enjoyment.

'What do you think they think of it?' Percy asked.

'What do you think they think of you? Look at yourself. Can't you see they're laughing at you?'

Percy observed himself and his anger crumbled at the sight. He began to whimper, 'It's her fault. It's all her fault.'

'Go back to your room.'

Harriet spoke imperiously and when he obeyed, she turned on the safragis, ordering them away with such scorn, they fled together. She decided to put a stop to their insolence. She knew that they saw the inmates of the flat as immoral and ridiculous, and they were contemptuous of a way of life they could not understand. Recently she had realised that the safragis supposed Dobson's tenants lived off Dobson's charity. A Moslem household was always full of dependants and hangers-on and Edwina, Percy and the Pringles were despised for their supposed penury. Dobson, she suspected, was aware of this and did nothing to discourage it. He ruled that no money should be paid to him in front of the servants but Guy, who could never remember such trivial proscriptions, had recently thrown a bundle of bank notes across the table while Hassan was in the room. 'Our share of the housekeeping,' said Guy and Dobson whipped the notes out of sight, but Hassan had seen them and his eyes rolled in astonishment.

Hassan now knew that the lodgers paid their way. He had seen money change hands and to him money was power. Harriet, wife of the man who had paid the money, had taken on stature and she decided that in future Hassan and Aziz would keep their contempt to themselves.

It was Wednesday when the guest eventually turned up. She came at tea-time when Harriet was setting out for the midsummer reception at the Anglo-Egyptian Union. Guy had agreed to go with her but, as usual,

170

some engagement detained him and he telephoned to say he would come later. The reception was a tea party merging into an early evening wine party. He said, 'It'll go on all night, I'll get there as soon as I can.'

Descending into the small front garden, where poinsettias grew like weeds, Harriet saw two gharries at the kerb. One, it seemed, had been hired to take an excess of luggage and Hassan, Aziz and the boab from the lower flat had been called out to unload it. The cases, mostly of pigskin or crocodile, were elegant and their owner, a tall woman in a suit of pink tussore, looked as elegant as the cases. She was paying off the drivers and her voice had a disturbing effect on Harriet who would have kept out of sight had there been any point in doing so. Knowing they had to meet sooner or later, she let the gate click and the woman turned.

'Hello. I'm Angela Hooper. Do you live here?'

'Yes. Can I help you with your things?'

Angela Hooper said, 'We've met before, haven't we?' Apparently recalling nothing more distressing than some past social occasion, she held out her hand. 'How nice to see you again. I knew if I came to Dobbie's, I'd find congenial company.'

Neither Dobson nor Edwina were at home so Harriet went back to the flat and showed Angela to her room. 'I'm afraid it's very hot about this time of day.'

'Oh, I'm conditioned to heat. I don't mind what the place is like. I just want to be among friends.'

Harriet showed her the bathroom then went to the sitting-room. Feeling it would be discourteous to leave a newcomer alone in the flat, she waited while the cases were brought up and stacked along the corridor.

Angela Hooper, when she joined Harriet, was in no way discomposed by her unfamiliar surroundings, but gazing at Harriet, her eyes brilliant with vivacious enquiry, she said, 'You were going out, weren't you? Anywhere exciting?'

'Not very. In fact, rather dull. There's a reception at the Anglo-Egyptian Union. They serve wine later but the chief entertainment is the tea party because the Egyptian guests, who come early and go early, are more likely to be there. I don't suppose you would care for it?'

'Why not? I'm ready for anything. Let's see if we can stop the gharries.' She ran to the balcony and shouted down to the gharry drivers who had lingered in hope of a fare back to the centre of town. Catching Harriet's arm, she said, 'Come on. I've had the most boring journey. Let's go out and see life.'

It was now too late for the tea party but, as Guy had said, the drinking would go on all night. On Bulaq bridge the gharry steps were boarded by two small boys who had made necklaces by stringing jasmin florets on to cotton. Clinging to the gharry with dirty hands and feet, their galabiahs blown by the river wind, they shouted, 'Buy, buy, buy,' and swung the necklaces like censers in front of the women. Their arms were hung with necklaces and the scent overpowered even the smell of the gharry. Angela bargained with the boys who were glad of any reward for their day's work. Taking the money, they sprang down, leaving a heap of jasmin in her lap. Twilight was gathering and Angela, looking up into the glowing turquoise of the sky, said, 'Oh, what fun to be back in Cairo!'

So she was back in Cairo! But where, Harriet wondered, had she come from? And why had she taken one of Dobson's small rooms when she had her own splendid house in the Fayoum?

She said, 'I've been out here a long time. I love Egypt. I don't really want to leave.'

'Are you leaving?'

'I don't know. I've been thinking about it. There's talk of sending some of the English women and children home by sea. That would mean round the Cape. It could be an interesting trip, or it could be the most excruciating bore. So . . . to tell you the truth, I'm rather *bouleversé*. I don't know what to do.'

The Egyptian guests had left the Union and the English had settled down to an evening that would be like every other evening except that the com⁄mittee had provided a carafe of wine for each table.

The lights had come on in the club house. Inside, men could be seen moving round the snooker table while outside people were sitting beneath the darkening foliage of the trees. The club house lights shone out on to the grass and the beds of bamboo and the plants that climbed up between the windows. Jasmin scented the air.

Harriet and Angela found a vacant table at the edge of the lawn and as soon as they sat down a safragi brought over a carafe and four glasses. Angela picked up the carafe, which held little more than a pint of red Latrun wine, and laughed at the man. 'This is expected to go far, isn't it?' Looking round to disseminate her laughter, she said, 'And that's all the party fare? Dear me! Let's have something more festive,' and ordered a bottle of whisky.

Those sitting nearby were displeased by her ebullience until they realised who she was, then they gave her smiling attention. She was known to be a rich woman and the rich did not come often to the Union. And she was not only rich but had been the centre of the extraordinary story of the Hooper boy's death. Clifford, two tables away, rose to get a better view of her and Harriet feared he might come over to join them. He thought better of it but when he sat down again, he bent towards his companions and talked eagerly, probably describing, all over again, his visit to the Fayoum house.

The Union shared its lawn with the Egyptian Officers' Club but the lawn went far beyond both clubs, stretching eastwards into a belt of heavy, ancient trees. Behind the trees some players were performing an Arabic version of *Romeo and Juliet* and voices, though remote, reverberated on the night air. There was a frenzied shout of 'Julietta' and, in response, a flat, sonorous and solemn 'Nam.'

'Oh dear, deathless passion!' Angela was shaken with laughter and Harriet, observing her, reflected, as others were certainly reflecting, on the dead boy. Angela knew she had met Harriet somewhere but did she realise where and when? If so, what was the nature of her cheerfulness? Was it defensive, or hysterical, or had she already recovered from that tragic afternoon?

The moon was rising from behind the trees. It was only a sliver of moon, no bigger than a nail paring, but so brilliant that it cast an ashen light over the grass. The Officers' Club had its own light, green like verdigris, which fell from the awning and shone on the men who sat, still and contemplative, like wax figures. Most of them were growing stout but a few, still in early youth, looked lean and virile. One of these, who sat alone, was very hand⁄ some and his figure was enhanced by a uniform and riding boots of immaculate cut.

'I must say,' said Angela, 'I rather fancy him. Do you think we could get him over here.'

Harriet thought it unlikely. The officers had never been known to cross the dividing width of lawn and no one had ever thought of inviting them to do so. Though they were dressed like the cavalry officers of most Euro⁄ pean countries, they wore the fez and that set them apart. They were Orientals. They were Moslems. Though they were polite to each other if they happened to meet, the English and Egyptians could not converse together for long. Angela, however, was in no way inhibited by the lack of common ground. She kept her eyes on the young officer, trying to will him to respond, but he remained impassive, looking in another direction, apparently at nothing at all.

Harriet said, 'I think they're waiting to see the last of us.'

'They may not have to wait long.'

'You think we're finished here? Is that why you're thinking of leaving?'

'No.' Angela forgot the officer and, looking at Harriet, her merriment died. 'You think I've forgotten where and when we met?'

'I was hoping you didn't remember.'

'I remember it all, and in exact detail. I remember everyone who was in that room. I remember that fellow over there. What is he called?'

'Clifford.'

'And a British officer?'

'Simon Boulderstone.'

'I brought in my boy and the room was full of people. He was a beautiful boy, wasn't he? His body was untouched – there was only that wound in his head. A piece of metal had gone into the brain and killed him. He was almost perfect, a small, perfect body, yet he was dead. We couldn't believe it, but next day, of course . . . We had to bury him.'

Wishing this would end, Harriet said, 'We were upset and wondered if there was something we could do, but all we could do was go away. We knew we ought not to be there.'

'I went away, too, not long after. I couldn't stay in that house. I didn't know what to do with myself. Bertie agreed that I needed a change so I went to Cyprus. I didn't tell him, but even before I went, I'd decided never to go back. Everything ended that afternoon: child, marriage, that ridiculous life of dinner parties, gaming parties, shooting parties. It was never my life. I'd been an art student in Paris so I'd known a quite different sort of world. Do you know the English here go duck shooting on Lake Mariotis and kill the birds in thousands. Quite literally, thousands. And when they've killed them, they don't know what to do with them. The whole set-up made me sick. I tried to escape by painting but I stopped painting after that happened. I didn't do anything. I just moped and wouldn't go out. I knew people were talking. Even Bertie thought it was better for me to go.'

'But what about him? He must have suffered terribly . . .'

'Yes, but he is much older than I am. He's an old man while I'm young enough to marry again.'

'You are getting a divorce?'

'I've asked for one. Bertie will have to divorce me. It would be cruel to refuse.'

Looking into Angela's face with its delicate features and mild expression, Harriet wondered where cruelty began and ended in this painful story. And Angela could marry again. Her fine sallow skin had aged only slightly round the eyes. She might be in the mid-thirties, young enough to replace the lost child and let the new one take on the identity of the dead. For her there could be some sort of restitution but for the elderly father the loss would be with him till the end of his days.

Harriet was silent and Angela said, 'You think me ruthless, don't you? But what could I do? I blamed myself for what happened. At times I felt I'd be better dead. If I'd stayed, I might have killed myself. And Bertie was part of the trouble. He did not accuse me. In fact, he was kindness itself, but I felt his very kindness was a reproach. Do you understand?'

'I understand how you felt – but abandoning your husband, leaving him to bear it alone! Wasn't that rather hard?'

'No, because there was nothing to leave. The marriage had been over a long time. Only the boy kept us together. It is a mistake to marry an older man however charming he is. It can't last.'

While Angela was talking, Castlebar came from the club house. He glanced towards Harriet, noted her companion and crossed to them. Stopping a few feet from the table, he stood there till Angela turned to look at him.

Instantly reverting to gaiety, she laughed at the sight of him as he swayed about, a sleepy smile on his face. 'Who's this?' she asked Harriet.

'Bill Castlebar: one of my husband's time-wasting cronies. Describes himself as a poet.'

Angela gave a high yelp of laughter and Castlebar, become alert and expectant, crossed to them and asked about Guy, 'Is the old thing c-coming?'

'Yes, later.'

Castlebar, having excused himself with this question, turned to Angela and gave a little bow. Nervousness increased his stammer. 'M-may I join you?' He spoke to Angela, taking it for granted that he was free to join Harriet if he wished.

'By all means!' When he sat down, she pushed the whisky towards him.

175

'Oh, I s'say! Not on the house, is it? I thought not. Oh, how kind!' Castlebar's gratitude gurgled down his throat as, having filled his glass, he gulped the whisky neat. When he had drunk half the glass, he paused to set up his cigarette packet in the usual way, one cigarette half out in readiness to take the place of the one in his hand.

Harriet asked, 'Where's Jake Jackman?' because the two men were seldom apart.

'Oh, h'he's inside, phoning his stuff to Switzerland.'

'Is there any news?'

'No more than usual. He's got hold of some story.'

This was the first time Harriet had Castlebar's company without Guy or Jackman being present, and she took the opportunity to ask about Jackman's career in Spain. 'Tell me, Bill, you've known Jake for some time. Did he really fight in the International Brigade?'

'F'f'fight?' Castlebar, taken off guard, was too surprised by the question to do more than tell the truth. 'Jake's never fought anywhere. He's never held a gun in his life.'

'But he was in Spain, wasn't he?'

'Yes, but not to fight. Some left-wing paper sent him out, rather late in the day. Too late, as it turned out. The government front collapsed soon after and Jake jumped a car and made it over the frontier. A timely get-away. He didn't even wait to pick up his clothes. His wife wasn't so lucky.'

'So he has a wife?'

'He had a wife. No one knows what became of her. She was running a camp for war orphans and Jake says he couldn't persuade her to leave them.'

'I see. He didn't wait to pick up his clothes but he did wait to try and persuade his wife to go with him.'

Castlebar dropped his head, snuffling at Harriet's disbelief, and said, 'Well, wives are expendable.'

Jake Jackman coming out of the club house, looked about and seeing Castlebar with Angela Hooper, his keen eyes became keener. Moving rapidly to the table, he was about to sit down when it occurred to him that Angela's presence called for unwonted courtesy. Muttering, 'OK?' he threw himself down before receiving a reply and pulled a glass towards him. 'Mind if I help myself?'

Angela pushed the bottle over. It was half-empty. She had drunk one glass, Castlebar had taken the rest.

Harriet had no love for Jackman and she feared that Angela, used to Sporting Club circles, would find both men unacceptable, but Angela was observing them with the intent amusement of one who could afford to indulge the world. Harriet thought of a story that Guy was fond of telling. Fitzgerald was supposed to have said to Hemingway, 'The rich, they're different from us,' to which Hemingway replied, 'Yes, they've got more money.' Guy saw this as a debunking of Fitzgerald but Harriet felt that Fitzgerald showed more perception than Hemingway. A person who grew up in the security of wealth was different. It seemed to her she saw this difference in the tolerant, even admiring, amusement with which Angela watched the men lowering her whisky.

Castlebar said to Jackman, 'Get your stuff away all right?'

'Yep.' Jackman, pulling at his nose, sitting on the edge of his chair, looked directly at Angela. 'Quite a story. The Vatican's come out in the open at last. The Pope's given Hitler his blessing. Said the victims of Nazism asked for all they got. I knew this would happen as soon as Russia came into the war.'

Harriet said, 'It's over a year since Russia came into the war.'

'These things take time to leak through.'

'I can't believe it.'

'You can't believe it? That's how the crooks get away with it. People are too simple-minded to credit what's going on. I can tell you this: the whole bloody dogfight is financed by the Vatican.'

Angela laughed. 'Both sides?'

'Yep, both sides.'

Harriet asked, 'Where did you hear this?'

'I've got m'sources. If you knew the financial shenanigans that went on before the war between Krupps, Chamberlain, the Vatican and a certain British bank, nothing would surprise you.'

'Which British bank?' Angela spoke as one with a knowledge of international finance and Jackman, sniffing and looking uneasily about, brought out the name of a bank which was new to Harriet. Angela made no comment and Jackman, having silenced the women, went on to describe the prewar relationship between Allied and Axis arms manufacturers and banks, describing a corruption so complex that Harriet and Angela were lost in its machinations.

Castlebar, who had heard all this many times before, sat with eyelids down, his chin sinking into his gullet as though about to fall asleep.

Growing bored with Jackman's rigmarole, Harriet looked towards the gate, feeling it was time for Guy to arrive and divert them. Jackman came to a stop at last and Castlebar's loose, violet-coloured lips gradually trembled into speech. 'B-b-bad news from all quarters these days. My wife's pulling strings, thinks she can get back here.'

Castlebar's wife had gone on holiday to England and been trapped there by the outbreak of war. Harriet, surprised that any ordinary civilian might get passage to Egypt, asked, 'How could you wangle that?'

'Me wangle it? You don't think I want her back?'

'Then, how could *she* wangle it?'

'If you knew my wife, you wouldn't ask. The shortest known distance in the world is the distance between my wife and what she wants.'

Angela's amused gaze focussed on Castlebar as he spoke. He looked at her and their eyes held each other in serious regard for a long moment, then Angela laughed and said in a teasing tone, 'So you don't want your wife here! I wonder, is there some special reason? Another lady, perhaps?'

Castlebar tittered and taking up the poised cigarette, lit it from the butt of its predecessor and propped up the one that would succeed it. He started to speak but was hindered by a fit of coughing and Harriet said, 'He has a whole library of other ladies.'

Angela raised her brows, uncertain what was meant, then suddenly screamed with laughter. 'I know, you buy those dreadful little books they sell in Clot Bey and the Esbekiya!'

Grinning, Castlebar put his hand into the breast pocket of his limp, grimy linen jacket and pulled out the corner of a limp and grimy booklet. Before he could put it back again, Angela snatched it and began to look through it. He made a half-hearted attempt to retrieve it but left it with her, looking rather proud of his sensational possession.

Angela, pushing her chair back, keeping the book out of reach, read the title: '*The Golden Member* – what have we here? The life story of some wealthy member of parliament? Hm, hm, hm . . .' She turned the grey, coarse-textured pages, piecing the story together. 'Dear me! The author claims that his was so be-u-u-u-tiful that his female admirers had a model of it made in pure gold and organised a ceremony in which several virgins deflowered themselves on this object. How interesting!' Angela surveyed Castlebar, pretending wide-eyed innocence. 'Do you think it is all true?'

Jackman clicked his tongue, as bored by Castlebar's sexual fantasies as Castlebar was by Jackman's politics. Between them they had finished off the whisky and the wine and Jackman, interrupting Castlebar's play with Angela, shouted to a safragi, 'Encore garaffo.'

The safragi, taking up the challenge, replied, 'Mafeesh garaffo.'

Jackman argued and the safragi, wandering happily over to him, made a gesture of finality. 'Garaffo all finish. Not any more.'

Jackman, not reflecting the good humour of this refusal, shouted, 'You heard me, you gyppo bastard. Encore garaffo.'

'What for you say "gyppo bastard"?' the safragi asked with dignity. 'Gyppo very good man, You go away. Party finish.'

'And a bloody awful party it was!'

Angela was talking behind her hand to Castlebar while he, enfeebled by laughter, tried to push *The Golden Member* back into his pocket. A taxi came through the gate and Harriet looked longingly towards it, but it was an empty taxi, come to take people away. She noticed how few remained. The party was indeed over. The safragi returned with the bill for the whisky. Jackman seemed too preoccupied to notice it but Castlebar made a vague move towards it. Angela, as was expected, lifted it up, saying, 'My treat.'

That settled, Jackman became more cheerful. 'Let's go on somewhere,' he said then, as a finale to the Union party, he slapped his knee and began to sing to the tune of the Egyptian national anthem:

> King Farouk, King Farouk,
> Hang your bollocks on a hook . . .

His voice was pitched high and he was directing it, with venomous intent, towards the Egyptian officers who still sat in reposeful silence under the green light.

> Oh, Farida's feeling gay
> When Farouk has got his pay,
> But she's not so fucking happy
> When she's in the family way . . .

As the verses went on, the officers seemed to awaken. One rose and went towards a table where three sat together and the four heads were bent in consultation.

Castlebar said, apprehensively, 'We'd better get out of here,' but Jackman, drunk and defiant, sang louder, then his voice trailed weakly away. The officer who had risen, a large man, was crossing the lawn towards the

English group. A sick expression came over Jackman's face but the officer was friendly. When he reached the table he bowed, smiled at them all and began to speak in Arabic. Angela, the only one who understood him, was disconcerted by what she heard. 'He says the officers wish to thank us for the homage paid to their king.'

'Is he being ironical?' Harriet asked.

'I don't think so. He says he regrets that none of them can speak English.'

The officer had more to say and Angela translated. 'He says they have felt for some time that the Union should have a piano. They have decided to present you with one.'

The officer, thanking Angela for her help, kissed her hand, then kissed Harriet's hand and bowing to Jackman and Castlebar, departed across the grass.

Castlebar, feeling the incident called for a speedy departure, said, 'Oh, come on,' but Harriet begged them to wait saying, 'Guy always turns up at the last minute.' But the club house was dark and the safragis were waiting to lock the gates. They had to go. Angela suggested they all go and see the belly-dancing at the Extase but Harriet, with no heart now for the Extase or anywhere else, asked to be dropped off in Garden City.

'Oh, no, you don't,' Angela said forcefully. 'You're not leaving me alone with these two. Anyway, it's my first evening back in Cairo, so let's enjoy ourselves. And you men, be sports – let me be host.'

This appeal to male chivalry stirred Castlebar who mumbled, 'Can't let you ...' but as Angela insisted he agreed without further protest. Angela would be permitted to act as host.

Harriet said, 'Guy must be home by now. I really ought to go back.'

'Wouldn't bank on it,' said Jackman. 'He's probably out on the loose. You stick around with us. I bet we find him somewhere.'

The Extase, one of the largest open-air night clubs, was in a garden beside the Nile. It was always crowded. Angela's party had to wait in a queue composed chiefly of officers and their girls. As the safragi set up make-shift tables in any vacant corner they could find, the queue dwindled steadily. Moving towards the club centre, Harriet, made unreasonably expectant by Jackson's bet that they would find Guy, looked over the tables. This was the last place in Cairo she would be likely to find Guy yet, not finding him, the whole crowded, noisy, busy garden was pervaded for her by a desolating emptiness.

On the stage a man in flannels and striped blazer was imitating the sound of a car changing gear uphill. His imitation was exact and the audience, that would have objected to the sound of a real car, gave him enthusiastic applause.

The Extase served only champagne and some of the officers were hilariously drunk. The arc lights that lit the stage added to the summer heat. The audience seemed a compacted, sweating, shouting, restless, amorous mass of men and girls who, like Edwina, only wanted a good time. Harriet wondered how long she would have to stay.

A safragi led Angela's party to the furthest corner of the auditorium and there Harriet saw Guy. He was with Edwina. Harriet stood, cold with shock, and stared at them while Angela said, 'Come on, Harriet, sit down.' Harriet remained where she was, transfixed, and Angela caught hold of her arm.

'My dear, is anything the matter? You look as though you'd seen a ghost.'

Harriet sat down but had to look round again to be sure that Guy was Guy and not an apparition of the mind. She could not bear what she saw but it remained with her. Guy was leaning towards Edwina and her hand, which rested on the table, was covered by his hand. 'I had too much faith in him,' Harriet thought. She was determined not to look at them again but then it came to her: Perhaps it's not Edwina! In spite of herself, she turned her head and saw Edwina's hair falling as it always fell, over Edwina's right eye. And that was that.

Angela said, 'Don't you feel well?'

'No, not very. I get these stomach upsets.'

'We'll go as soon as Calabri's done her dance.'

The dancer, Fawzi Calabri, was in no hurry to appear. As star of the cabaret, her act came last and she delayed it until the audience was in a frenzy of anticipation. She was announced and Harriet had to move her chair in order to see the stage. Doing so, she saw the table at which Guy and Edwina had been sitting. They were no longer there. The chairs were empty. The sight of them agitated her. She wanted to run off in search of Guy but could only stay and watch.

Calabri, a plump, moon-faced beauty with flesh powdered to an inhuman whiteness, had come on to the stage. She advanced to the centre and stood there, arms lifted, hands above her head, clad in diamonds and a few gauzy, sparkling whirlabouts, until the uproar died down. Then the diamonds began to throw off sparks of light, the gauze lifted and her abdomen moved. The movement began gently, a slight roll and swell that worked itself gradually into a strong muscular rotation so it seemed the structure of the stomach was going round in circles. The music increased with the pace while Calabri stared at her own belly as though it were an unattached object which she swirled like a lasso. Music and movement reached a convulsive pitch then began to slow until there was silence and the dancer was still.

Amid the commotion that followed, Harriet whispered to Angela that she would leave by herself.

'No, we're all going.'

A taxi was waiting outside the club. Harriet was driven to Garden City but Angela made no move to get out with her.

'I feel I must see my poet safely home,' Angela laughed at Castlebar who smiled complacently and put his arm round her.

Jackman, pulling his nose and sniffing in gloomy disgust, said, 'You can drop me at Munira while you're about it.'

Harriet could scarcely give thought to the fact, astonishing at some less anxious time, that Angela could be attracted by Castlebar. She only wanted an explanation from Guy and was relieved to find he was in the flat. Sitting up in bed, a book in his hand, he mildly enquired, 'Where have you been? It's after midnight.'

'Where have *you* been? I waited for you till the Union closed.'

'I'm sorry, darling, but Edwina begged me to take her to the Extase.'

'You went to the Extase, of all places? – when you'd promised to join me at the Union!'

'Don't be cross. You'll understand when I tell you what happened. I was going to the Union but I came back to have a shower and change, and I found Edwina in a terrible state. She had been waiting for Peter Lisdoon-varna for over an hour. When she realised he did not mean to turn up, she collapsed. I found her lying on the sofa, crying her eyes out. So what could I do? I had to help her. She thought he had gone to the Extase . . . And, I may say, it was all your fault.'

'How could it be my fault?.

'You advised her to put up a show of indifference and go out with someone else. She did this and went with the new boy-friend to the Extase.

The first thing she saw there was Peter enjoying himself hugely with another girl – some "Levantine floosie", according to Edwina. She was convinced that Peter was at the Extase again with the same floosie and she was beside herself with jealousy. The only thing that would satisfy her was to go to the Extase and see for herself. I was really afraid she would do something desperate. I felt I had to go with her.'

'Supposing Peter had been there, what would she have done?'

'Well, I'm thankful to say he wasn't. But you can see I had to comfort her a bit . . .'

'You were comforting her more than a bit. I saw you. You were holding her hand.'

Guy was jolted, but not for long. 'I felt sorry for the poor kid.'

'She's not a kid. She's the same age as I am. I went alone to the Union. She could have gone to the Extase by herself.'

'Be reasonable, darling. The Extase and the Union are very different places. And you're a married woman, you have status. She's just a frightened kid.'

'Frightened of what?'

'Losing out, I suppose. She's set her heart on this fellow, Lisdoonvarna, God knows why. Come on, darling, don't look so black. Little monkey's paws, come to bed . . .' He tried to take her hand but Harriet, remembering Guy's hold on Edwina's hand, moved away. He tried to coax her to return to him but she remained on the other side of the room, and looked at the window where there was no tree to befriend her.

The sense of chill and distance between them so bewildered Guy that he started to get out of bed. She said angrily, 'Leave me alone.' and he remained where he was, watching her as though by watching he could divine what was wrong with her. He found it difficult to accept that his own behaviour could be at fault. And if it were, he did not see how it could be changed. It was, as it always had been, rational, so, if she were troubled, then some agency beyond them – sickness, the summer heat, the distance from England – must be affecting her. For his part, he was reasonable, charitable, honest, hard-working, as generous as his means allowed, and he had been tolerant when she picked up with some young officer in Greece. What more could be expected of him? Yet, seeing her afresh, he realised how fragile she had become. She was thin by nature but now her loss of weight made her look ill. Worse than that, he felt about her the malaise of a deep-seated discontent. That she was unhappy concerned him, yet what could he do about it? He had more than enough to do as it was, and he tried to appeal to her good sense. 'Darling, don't be so grumpy!'

She turned on him. 'I *am* grumpy, and with reason. I'm sick of your solicitude for others – it's just showing off. You don't show off to me. I'm part of you, as you say, so I can put up with anything. You don't come to the Union, as you promised, and where do I find you? I couldn't believe my eyes. It was . . . it was incredible.'

'The girl needed help.'

'Everyone needs help. Except me, of course. I can go round alone. I can look after myself. Here I'm usually more ill than well, but that doesn't worry you, does it?'

'It does worry me. This place doesn't agree with you. You're too thin, you look peaky. I've noticed it. I've been thinking about it,' Guy said, thinking about it for the first time. 'You know, darling, there's a plan to send some of the women and children home. Why don't you apply for a passage.'

'Me? Go back without you?' she was dumbfounded and, sinking down on to a chair, she stared at him in disbelief. 'You want me to leave you?'

Made uneasy by her expression, he looked away from her. 'Of course I don't, but you said yourself that you're usually more ill than well. And you're nervous.'

'I'm no more nervous than anyone else. It's a nervous time.'

'That's true. No one knows what will happen when the Germans get their reinforcements. That could be any day. You said yourself, they could arrive almost without warning. If we ended up in a prison camp, I really don't think you'd survive.'

'At least we'd be together.'

'We wouldn't be together. We'd be in different camps. We might even be in different countries. If you were in England, at least I'd know where you were. And you would have war work – that would take your mind of things. You'd be happier, and your health would pick up there. All those bugs just die in a northern climate. Now, darling, be sensible. Think about it.'

'I don't intend to think about it.' She went to the chest of drawers that served as dressing-table and put cleansing cream on her face. 'We came here together. When we leave, we'll leave together.'

She was dilatory in preparing for bed, feeling pained and suspicious. He had never before suggested that she return to England to face life alone; why suggest it now? It came to her, with dismay, that he wished to clear the way for a possible pursuit of Edwina. Was it possible? Everything was possible. If the affair with Peter broke up, as it very well might, Guy would be at hand, again the comforter and perhaps, in the end, more than comforter. She had seen many marriages fail in this place, and men whose wives were sent out of harm's way, were quick to find consolation.

When she got into bed, Guy put his arms round her, imagining he could conciliate her with physical love, but her response was cool. The fact he could think of their separation, even for her own good, was not so easily forgotten.

In spite of her resolution, the thought of England had come into her mind and she recalled the vision of England that had overwhelmed her once in a Cairo street. It returned in her memory, a scene of ploughed fields and elm trees with a wind smelling of the earth; she thought if she were there, she would be well again. Here she was not only unwell, but at risk from all the diseases known to mankind. She remembered how she had danced at the Turf Club with an officer who was feverish and complained of a headache, and who went away to be sick.

Next day they heard he had gone down with smallpox and everyone who had been at the party, had to be revaccinated and kept under surveillance for a fortnight.

She whispered to herself, 'That was a narrow escape.'

Guy, half-asleep, asked, 'What was? What are you thinking about?'

'I'm thinking about England,' she said.

10

Trench was replaced by a man called Fielding. Fielding, a little older than Simon, had a plain, pleasant face and hair bleached like Trench's hair. He and Simon, being concomitants, should have been friends but Simon was becoming wary of friendship. His instinct was to avoid any relationship that could again inflict on him the desolation of loss. The only person whose company he sought was Ridley. Ridley had known Arnold and Trench and he let Simon talk about them so, for short periods, memory could overcome their nonexistence.

Not much was happening at that time. The Column went on sorties carrying out small shelling raids, but there was no more close action. Even the main positions were quiet so it seemed the fight itself had sunk beneath the load of August heat.

Ridley still brought gossip and news, but there was not much of it. In the middle of the month, when Auchinleck lost his command, the officers asked each other why this had happened. Ridley, who had once seen the deposed general standing, very tall, up through a hole in a station-wagon, spoke of him regretfully as though, like Arnold and Trench, he had gone down among the dead. 'He was a big chap, big in every way, they say. He slept on the ground, just like the rest of us. No side about him, they say. A real soldier.'

'What about the new chap?'

'Don't know. Could be a good bloke but we all felt the Auk was one of us.'

Later in the month, the Column, on patrol in a lonely region near the Depression, came upon three skeletons, two together and a third lying some distance from them. The sand here was a very dark red and the skeletons, white and clean, were conspicuous on the red ground. The nomad Arabs had stripped them of everything: not only clothing but identity discs, papers, even letters and photographs, for these things could be sold to German agents to authenticate the disguises of undercover men.

The staff car stopped and Hardy and Martin got out to look them over. Simon, following from curiosity, was startled when Martin said that the skeletons were of men recently dead. Had they lain there long the sand would have blown over them. They might have been the crew of a Boston that had come down in an unfrequented part of the desert and managed, in spite of injuries, to crawl this far before giving up. He touched the bones with his toe and said: 'The kites have picked them clean.'

Simon, shocked that flesh could be so quickly dispersed, remembered his friends, dead and buried, and stood in thought until Hardy called to him, 'Get a move on, Boulderstone.'

Simon turned to him with an expression of suffering that prompted Hardy to put a hand on the young man's shoulder and say with humorous sympathy, 'You won't bring them to life by staring at them.'

That evening there was no mention of the Middle East in the radio news. 'A dead calm, eh?' Martin said. 'Wonder how long it'll last?' When he went to fetch his whisky bottle, Hardy spoke to Simon. 'I remember you mentioning your brother, Boulderstone. I couldn't let you take leave at that time but I understood how you felt. Have you any idea where he is?'

'Yes, sir. Ridley says there's a Boulderstone with the New Zealanders, near the Ridge.'

'Right. I'll give you a few days and you can take the staff car and look him up.'

When Simon began to express his gratitude, Hardy enlarged his concession. 'I don't see why you shouldn't take a week as there's nothing doing. But check up on his position. You could waste a lot of time scouting round the different camps.'

As soon as he could get away, Simon went to tell Ridley of his good fortune but Ridley merely grumbled, 'What's he think he's doing, giving blokes leave at this time?'

'Why? Is anything about to happen?'

'Chaps down the line think so. Then there's old Rommel. He's not moving forward but he's not exactly dropping back, neither. If his reinforce-ments arrive, he'd be through us like a dose of salts.'

'That's not likely to happen in one week.'

'How do you know. I got a feeling it could happen any day. If it hots up, it'll hot up sudden like.'

Simon begged Ridley to keep his premonitions to himself, saying, 'This may be my only chance to see my brother,' and Ridley relented enough to admit that his 'feeling' could be 'just a twitch'. It occured to Simon that Ridley's annoyance might come from envy of Simon's luck, or perhaps simply an unwillingness to have Simon out of his sight. Whatever it was, he began to take an interest in the vacation, saying, 'If you got a week, you could nip back to Alex. Or Cairo, even. Which'd you rather – Cairo or Alex?'

Simon did not know. He was enticed by the thought of the seaside town, but he knew people in Cairo. Had he been granted leave during his first days in the desert, he would have wanted only one thing: to return to Garden City. Now, though he sometimes thought of Edwina, she had lost substance in his mind and her beauty was like the beauty of a statue. It related to a desire he had ceased to feel.

Here in the desert, either from lack of stimulus or some quality in the air, the men were not much troubled by sex. The need to survive was their chief preoccupation – and they did survive. In spite of the heat of the day, the cold of night, the flies, the mosquitoes, the sand-flies, the stench of death that came on the wind, the sand blowing into the body's interstices and gritting in everything one ate, the human animal not only survived but flourished. Simon felt well and vigorous and he thought of women, if he thought of them at all, with a benign indifference. He belonged now to a world of men: a contained, self-sufficient world where life was organised from dawn till sunset. It had so complete a hold on him, he could see only one flaw in it: his friends died young.

The staff car, assigned to him for twenty-four hours, would take him first to the Ridge where he hoped to track down Hugo, then to the coast road where he could stop a military vehicle and get a lift into the Delta. His new driver and batman, a young red-haired, freckled squaddie called Hugman, had little contact with Simon. He did not expect Simon to speak to him and Simon did not wish to speak. He was wary of Hugman, as he was of Fielding, and sat in the back seat of the car, holding himself aloof. Hugman very likely thought him one of those 'spit and polish' officers that he despised, but Hugman could think what he liked. Simon was risking no more emotional attachments, no more emotional upsets. To excuse his silence, he sprawled in the corner of the car, propping his head against the side and keeping his eyes shut. They had started out early. Simon, anxious to be off before Hardy could change his mind, almost ran from Ridley who came towards him with a look of doom. 'There, what did I say, sir? The gen is that the jerries are preparing a push on Alam Halfa.'

'Christ!' Simon threw himself into the car and ordered Hugman to move with all speed. They were out of sight of the Column before he remembered he had not reported his departure to Hardy.

As the sun rose, he did not need to simulate sleep but sank into a half-doze which brought him images of the civilised world he was soon to re-enter. He no longer could, nor did he need to, exclude women from his dreams. Now that he was due for a week of normal life, he could afford to indulge his senses a little. He remembered not only Edwina but the dark-haired girl who raced him up the pyramid, and even poor forgotten Anne returned to him become, with his change of circumstances, more real than Arnold. His attention reverted to Edwina. She was the supreme beauty although he had been too dazzled to know whether she was beautiful or not. Another face edged into his mind, a woman older than the others, with a dismayed expression that puzzled him. He could not immediately recall the dead boy in the Fayoum house, but when he did he dismissed both woman and boy as intruders on his reverie. Wasn't it enough that he had lost his friends?

When he opened his eyes, the Ridge was in sight. They were driving through a rear maintenance and supply area where petrol dumps, food dumps, canteen trucks, concentrations of jeeps and ambulances, a medical unit and a repair depot were all planted in sand and filmed with sand that covered the green and fawn camouflage patches. It was a skeleton town with netted wire instead of house-walls and sand tracks instead of streets. The noon sun glared overhead and men, given an hour's respite, lay with faces hidden, bivouacked in any shade they could find. Unwilling to disturb them, Simon told Hugman to drive until he found he Camp Comman-dant's truck. Both men were drenched with sweat and when Simon left the car, the wind plastered the wet stuff of his shirt and shorts to his limbs. It was a hot wind yet he shivered in the heat.

The Commandant, fetched from his mid-day meal in the officers' mess, had no welcome for Simon. 'How the hell did you get leave at a time like this?'

Simon, more wily than he used to be, said, 'Only a few days, sir.'

'A few days!' The Commandant blew out his cheeks in comment on Hardy's folly, but the folly was no business of his. He advised Simon to find the New Zealand division HQ. 'About a mile down the road. Can't miss it. You'll see the white fern leaf on a board.'

The car, driven out of the maintenance area into open desert, rocked in the rutted track, throwing up sand clouds that forced the two men to close the windows and stifle in enclosed heat.

The board appeared, the fern leaf scarcely visible beneath its coating of sand, and beyond, on either side of the track, guns and trucks, dug into pits, were protected by sand-bags and camouflage nets. Simon realised they were very near the front line.

At the Operations truck, a New Zealand major, a tall, thin, grave faced man, listened with lowered head as Simon explained that he was looking for a Captain Boulderstone. The major, jerking his head up, smiled on him. 'You think he's your brother, do you? Well, son, I think maybe he is. You're as like as two peas. But I don't know where he's got to – someone will have to look around for him. If you have a snack in the mess, we'll let you know as soon as we find him. OK?'

'OK, and thank you, sir.'

The mess was a fifteen hundred-weight truck from which an awning stretched to cover a few fold-up tables and chairs. Simon seated himself in shade that had the colour and smell of stewed tea. The truck itself served as a cook-house and Simon said to the man inside, 'Lot of flies about here.'

'Yes, they been a right plague this month. Our CO said something got to be done about them, but he didn't say what. I sprays DDT around and the damn things laugh at it.'

The flies were lethargic with the heat. Simon, having eaten his bully-beef sandwich and drunk his tea, had nothing better to do than watch them sinking down on to the plastic table-tops. He remembered what Harriet Pringle had said about the plagues coming to Egypt and staying there. The flies had been the third plague, 'a grievous swarm', and here they still were, crawling before him so slowly they seemed to be pulling themselves through treacle. The first excitement of arrival had left him and he could not under-stand why Hugo was so long in coming. Boredom and irritation came over him and seeing a fly swat on the truck counter, he borrowed it in order to attack the flies.

A dozen or so crawled on his table and no matter how many he killed, the numbers never grew less. When the swat hit the table, the surviving flies would lift themselves slowly and drift a little before sinking down again. He pushed the dead flies off the table and they dropped to the tarpaulin which covered the ground. When he looked down to count his bag of flies, he found they had all disappeared. He killed one more and watched to see what became of it. It had scarcely touched the floor when a procession of ants veered purposefully to it, surrounded it and, manoeuvring the large body between them, bore it away.

Simon laughed out loud. The ants did not pause to ask where the manna came from, they simply took it. The sky rained food and Simon, godlike, could send down an endless supply of it. He looked forward to telling Hugo about the flies and ants. He killed till teatime and the flies were as numerous as ever, then, all in a moment, the killing disgusted him. He had tea then, still waiting, he thought of the German youth he had killed on the hill. Away from the heat of battle, that killing, too, disgusted him, and he would have sworn, had the situation permitted, never to kill again.

The mess filled with officers but none of them was Hugo. About five o'clock a corporal came to tell him that Captain Boulderstone had gone out with a patrol to bring in wounded.

'Has there been a scrap, then?'

The corporal did not look directly at Simon as he said, 'There was a bit of a scrap at the Mreir Depression two days ago. Last night we heard shelling. Could be, sir, the patrol's holed up there.'

'You mean, he's been gone some time?'

The man gave Simon a quick, uneasy glance before letting him know that the patrol had left camp the previous morning. Hugo had, in fact, been away so long, his batman had gone out in the evening to look for him.

A sense of disaster came down on Simon and he got to his feet. 'They should be coming back soon. I'll go and meet them.'

'With respect, sir, you'd do better to stay. The wind's rising and there could be a storm brewing.'

Simon refused to wait. He wanted to move, as though by moving he could hasten Hugo's return to the camp. He had sent Hugman to the canteen and decided to let him stay there. The corporal told him that there was a gap in the mine fields where the track ran through the forward positions into no-man's-land and continued on to the enemy positions at El Mreir and Miteiriya. As Simon went to the car, the corporal followed him.

'You're not going alone, sir?'

'Yes.'

The car, its steering wheel almost too hot to handle, stood beside the Operations truck. The corporal said, 'Like me to come with you, sir? Only take a tick to get permission.'

'Thank you, no. I'll be all right.'

Even a tick was too long to wait while he had hope of meeting Hugo. The sand was lifting along the banks between the gun pits. Small sand devils were whirling across the track, breaking up, dropping and regathering with every change in the wind. The sky was growing dark and before he could reach the forward position, his view was blotted out. He had driven into the storm and there was nothing to do but pull to the side, stop and stare into the sand fog, watching for the batman's truck to come through it. Nothing came. He got out of the car and tried to walk down the track but the wind was furious, driving the searing particles of sand into his eyes and skin, forcing him back to shut himself in the car. He was trapped and would remain trapped until the storm blew itself out.

At sunset the sand-clogged air turned crimson. When the colour died, there was an immediate darkness and in darkness he would have to remain. He could see nothing. He could hear nothing but the roar of the wind. He opened the car door an inch expecting a light to switch on but the sand blew in and there was no light. He switched on the headlamps that showed him a wall of sand. Realising that no one was likely to see them, he switched them off to save the battery. Then, aware there was nothing more to be done, he subsided into blackness that was like nonexistence. The luminous hands of his watch showed that it was nearly nine o'clock. He climbed over to the back seat and put his head down and slept.

He awoke to silence and the pellucid silver of first light. He was nearer the perimeter than he realised. Before him was a flat expanse of desert where the light was rolling out like a wave across the sand. Two tanks stood in the middle distance and imagining they had stopped for a morning brew-up, he decided to cross to them and ask if they had seen anything of the patrol or the batman's truck. It was too far to walk so he went by car, following the track till he was level with the tanks, then walking across the mardam. A man was standing in one of the turrets, motionless, as though unaware of

Simon's approach. Simon stopped at a few yards' distance to observe the figure, then saw it was not a man. It was a man-shaped cinder that faced him with white and perfect teeth set in a charred black skull. He could make out the eye-sockets and the triangle that had once supported a nose then, returning at a run, he swung the car round and drove back between the batteries, so stunned that for a little while his own private anxiety was forgotten.

The major was waiting for him at the Operations truck, his long grave face more grave as though to warn Simon that Hugo had been found. He had been alive, but not for long. All the major could do was try and soften the news by speaking highly of Hugo, telling Simon that Hugo had been a favourite with everyone, officers and men. His batman, Peters, was so attached to him, he was willing to risk his own life to find him. And he was alive when Peters came on him, but both legs had been shot away. The sand around him was soaked with blood. He didn't stand a chance.

'And the rest of the patrol? Couldn't they have done something?'

'All dead. Young Boulderstone just had to lie there with his life-blood running out till someone found him.'

The major sent for Peters so Simon could be told all that remained to be told. Peters was a thin youth who choked on his words. 'When I found him, he said, quite cheerfully, "Hello, Peters old chap, I knew you'd come".' Tears filled Peters' eyes and Simon felt surprise that this stranger could weep while he himself felt nothing.

Peters, regaining himself, explained that the patrol had been returning to the camp at sunset when it was attacked by German mortars. The ambulance moving against the red of the sky must have been an irresistible target. 'They knew what it was, the bastards. And they went on firing till they'd got the lot.'

Peters, having found Hugo, could not move him because movement would increase the haemorrhage. He intended to return to the camp for help but the storm blew up, so he had to spend the night with the wounded man.

'He told you what happened?'

'He did, sir. His speech was quite clear, right to the end. About two a.m., he said, "I think I'm going, Peters. Just as well. A chap's not much use with two wooden pins." I said, "You hold on, sir. They can do wonders these days with pins", and he laughed. He didn't speak again.'

'Thank you, Peters.'

Peters had brought in the body. The burial party had already set out. There was nothing for Simon to see and he felt: Thank God for that. Knowing that his presence was an embarrassment in the camp, he held out his hand to the major and said he would be on his way. Hugman, who had been waiting for him, eyed him with furtive sympathy and muttered, 'Sorry to hear what happened, sir.'

Simon nodded, 'Rotten luck', then there was silence between them until they reached the coast road and he said, 'Don't wait, Hugman. The car's due back. You might tell Ridley what happened. He'll understand.'

A truck appeared on the road before Hugman was out of sight. The squaddie beside the driver offered Simon his seat but Simon refused and said he would ride in the rear. The back flap was let down for him. He threw his kit aboard, jumped after it, and the truck went on again.

Simon, sitting with his back to the cabin, looked out over the desert that had become as familiar to him as his childhood streets. He was reconciled to its neutral colour, its gritty wind, the endless stretches of arid stone and sand, but now a darkness hung over it all. He felt death as though he and Hugo had been one flesh and he was possessed by the certainty that if he returned here, he, too, would be killed.

'Both of us. They would lose both of us.'

He thought of his mother going into the greenhouse to read the wire, imagining perhaps that one of her sons was coming home on leave. He found a pad in his rucksack and began to write.

'Dear Mum and Dad, By the time you get this you will have heard about Hugo. I was there in the NZ camp when he didn't come in. His batman found him, legs blown off . . .' Simon stopped, not knowing if he should tell them that, and started on another page.

'Dear Mum and Dad, By the time you get this, you'll know that Hugo is . . .' but he could not write the word 'dead' and what else could he say?

Hugo was dead. The reality of Hugo's death came down on him and his unfeeling calm collapsed. He gulped and put his hands over his face. Tears ran through his fingers. There was no one to see him and the men in front would not hear his sobs above the engine noise. He gave himself up to grief. He wept for Hugo – but Hugo was safely out of it. He wept for his parents who must live with their sorrow, perhaps for years.

In the end, having stupefied himself with weeping, he lay on the floor of the truck and slept. He was wakened by passing traffic and, sitting up, he read what he had written and knew that neither letter would do.

There was nothing to be said. He tore the pages into fragments and threw them to the desert wind.

OLIVIA MANNING

Olivia Manning spent much of her childhood in North Ireland and subsequently lived in Rumania, Greece, Egypt, Cyprus, Transjordan and Palestine during the years of the second world war. She is the author of a number of novels and three volumes of short stories. She currently lives in London.